When Sidney Lak  Brontë's novel *The Tenant of Wildfell Hall* had been stolen, he firmly believed he would never see it again, much less hold it in his hands. But there it was. In the hands of an appraiser at the *National Arts And Crafts Show*. Could it be the same three-volume first edition of the book? He had to find out.

Assembling his experienced team of investigators, they begin searching for the appraiser, who is believed to be from Savannah, Georgia, in the hope of being led to the young man who claimed to be the owner of the book. But before they get fully underway, Tillie James, his Gullah companion, and confidant drops out of the group as a ninety-year-old Gullah woman is threatened with losing her home at a delinquent tax sale. The woman had been deceptively tricked by a real estate attorney into not paying the tax claiming he had a way around it.

Could there be a connection between rare book thefts and attempts to steal land from Gullah residents of the Pirate Islands?

Sidney and his associates decide to pursue both the tax fraud deception and the possible Brontë book forgery at the same time and keep running into coincidences. But are they?

The Lowcountry of South Carolina takes center stage as Sidney Lake and Tillie James pursue the answers to questions not everyone wants asked.

Acknowledgments

The initial plot for *Deception* grew out of the extensive research I undertook as a graduate student at Drew University in Madison, New Jersey. It was there I became fascinated with the Brontë family while studying Victorian literature. The novels of the three sisters taught and entertained me but their life story hooked me as it has so many others. Bits and pieces of Brontë material can be found in collections all over the world and I began to wonder how the personal letters and artifacts escaped from Haworth. The deceptive practices of the literary scoundrel, Thomas J. Wise, led me down an interesting trail.

The Brontë Society of Haworth, Yorkshire, England, where I have been a member for more than thirty years, and the Brontë Parsonage Museum were invaluable resources for me. Over the years I have managed to acquire every copy of the *Brontë Society Transactions* from the late 1920s to the current editions.

In crafting the novel my first and last reviewer, critic, and editor has been, as always, my wife, partner, and best friend, Carol Kent Holland. Her keen eye and sense of reading rhythm has been indispensable. And then there are the members of The Silver Quill Writers, the critique group I formed eight years ago, who reviewed and analyzed every chapter and rewrite I produced: Peter Stype, Elizabeth Brown, Cindi Freeman, and Cynthia Fridgeon.

Deception enticed Susan Humphreys of Black Opal Books to become a fan of Sidney Lake. Even today she still encourages me to have Sidney's knee repaired and is anxiously awaiting the next volume in the series.

Finally, the stars of the Sidney Lake stories are the people of the Lowcountry of South Carolina. The Gullah, first and foremost. They are the heart and soul of coastal South Carolina. The people, the land, the water, the farms, the churches, the shrimp boats, the Marine Corps Recruit Depot at Parris Island, they are not just backdrop they are what makes the region unique.

Books by Tim Holland

What the Mirror Doesn't See

Sidney Lake Lowcountry Mystery Series
The Rising Tide
The Murder of Amos Dunn
Deception

Deception

A Sidney Lake, Lowcountry Mystery

By Tim Holland

A Black Opal Books Publication

Black Opal Books

BECAUSE SOME STORIES JUST HAVE TO BE TOLD

GENRE: Mystery

This is a work of fiction. Names, places, characters and incidents are either the product of the author's imagination or are used fictitiously, and any resemblance to any actual persons, living or dead, businesses, organizations, events or locales is entirely coincidental. All trademarks, service marks, registered trademarks, and registered service marks are the property of their respective owners and are used herein for identification purposes only. The publisher does not have any control over or assume any responsibility for author or third-party websites or their contents.

Dedication

Tim, Mike. This one's for you.

ONE

Howard Springwood found his garage door open as he pulled into his driveway. At first, he hesitated, but then he began to second guess his caution. It wouldn't be the first time the automatic door started to close only to reverse itself as it encountered an obstacle in its path. It had happened before. He knew it started to close when he drove off this morning but he didn't stay around to see if it finished its cycle. Besides, if someone tried to break into his home they wouldn't leave the garage door wide open, would they?

Springwood sat in his car at the curb across from his home and looked around him. He waved to a neighbor walking down the street with her dog. Coming home from work, another neighbor up ahead turned into his driveway, slowing his car as his garage door opened, Howard continued to wait. A minute passed. He waved to another person on the street. Was he being too cautious? Everything certainly seemed normal. He looked up and down the street, checked his rearview mirror, waited another thirty seconds, and then drove into the garage.

He got out of the car taking his brown leather lawyer's briefcase with him, which had been sitting in the passenger's seat, carefully closed the car door behind him, and walked up to the inside door to his home. Seeing the red light on the security system was still showing "ARMED," he entered the security code and paid close attention to the way he pressed the "ENTER" button to shut off the alarm system. As soon as the system light turned green, he pressed the garage door button and watched the door close to make sure it went all the way down.

He would never do it again.

The bullet entered the back of his head and blew away the front of his skull. He saw no one and had no idea why someone took his life. The killer, his assignment completed, stepped over Springwood's body, and pushed open the door from the garage to the house with a gloved hand. Entering the laundry room, he went through it to the kitchen. Stopped. Waiting a moment before he continued, he cautiously looked around and then walked over to the patio doors at the back of the room. Stopped again, looked around, opened one of the patio doors, stepped outside, closed the door behind him, and left.

TWO

When the phone rang, it startled Sidney Lake. He had been reading quietly in his library at 111 Howard Street and dozed off. That was happening more of late. His life had become too predictable. Retirement had finally caught up with him.

Sidney Lake, the former English professor of Victorian literature, didn't know what to do with himself. His plan had been to do research and writing, but much of that came to an end when he finished his latest project: a meticulously researched analysis of the exploits of Thomas J. Wise, one of the great literary forgers of all time. The book was now with his publisher and out of his control—for the time being. He foolishly believed he would be content with working with his roses and the local garden society. Travelling had also been high on the agenda but the recent injury to his knee placed that activity on the side for now. The phone continued to ring annoyingly on the small table next to his chair. He reached for it unsuccessfully and fumbled the handset of the landline as he tried to clear his head. His cell phone was nowhere to be seen, but no one ever called him on it anyway, as he made it clear he disliked the intrusiveness of the technology. Mickey, his Labrador retriever, paid no attention to it and never moved from her preferred position next to him.

He finally got hold of it and mumbled almost incoherently, "Hello?"

"Did you see it?" a woman's voice asked rather excitedly on the other end.

"Did I see what? Who is this?" Sidney struggled to straighten up in his chair as he continued to fumble with his phone. His injured right leg stayed in place on the hassock in front of his chair and inhibited his movement. The problem with his leg had become his favorite excuse for his immobility, notwithstanding his failure to lose any of the 230 pounds he carried around on his five-foot eight-inch frame.

"It's Hattie, of course. Did you see it?" Hattie Ryan asked again.

"See what? I have no idea what you're talking about."

"The *National Arts and Crafts Show*. You're watching it, aren't you? You always do."

Sidney finally got into a more relaxed position, if you could call it that, as he huffed and puffed his response, "No...unfortunately, I'm...not. I'm afraid...I missed it this evening."

"Oh, no. You missed it. The books were on it."

"What books?"

"Well, actually it's one book in three volumes. The Brontë book you've been hoping to find again."

Now wide awake, Sidney sat up straight, "You're not serious. But...you are. Aren't you? This is Hattie, isn't it? It's not a joke?"

"No, Sidney, it's not a joke. Someone had the books at the *Crafts Show* to find out if they were worth anything." The phone at Sidney's end was silent. "Sidney are you still there?"

"Yes, I'm here." The tone was level now, the initial excitement gone. His mind raced. *This can't be true. The book out in the open. Ridiculous.*

"Good. I thought you fainted, or something."

"I don't faint."

"Well, I almost did. I spilled my drink."

"I hope it wasn't a good one. Wine or sherry?" Fully awake now, he became his old self: assertive, in control.

"Naturally it was a good one. I wouldn't drink anything else. Sherry," Hattie said with a huff.

One of the main attributes of Hattie Ryan that Sidney liked was her no-nonsense approach to just about everything. He couldn't bully her, as he used to do with his students and former colleagues—although she had been a member of his English Literature Department at Morgan College—she would not permit herself to be bullied, by anyone. He liked that. It's also why Sidney liked and admired Tillie James, his housekeeper— although she was more friend and confidant than employee. More than once Tillie had chastised him as an older sister would a younger, arrogant brother. They were an interesting threesome and quite formidable when they got together on a project.

Sidney relaxed slightly. At least the initial tension and shock were gone. "You're positive it's the same Anne Brontë volumes?"

"I can't say that. I wasn't there. But the man who looked at them seemed impressed." Hattie also calmed down and now spoke in a normal tone.

"What did he say about them?"

"He said they were the real thing. Right look and feel. Right publisher. The only thing he questioned were the notations inside. Seemed to be by Anne Brontë, but he had no way of verifying it."

"Hah! Yes. I thought that too when I first saw them. The best person's handwriting to forge is someone who left few examples with which to make a comparison. Wise was good at that. But unless we can get some

experts to look at it we'll never know." Sidney stopped
and checked the time on the large bookcase clock across
the room. "The show's still on."

"Yes. I immediately started recording when I saw the
books."

"Good. Keep doing it. Record what you can.
Especially the credits. We'll get the book dealer's name.
I'm sure they'll show the program again at a different
time of day and then we'll get everything. I have a
program guide in the living room."

"It's probably streamable also."

"Well, I wouldn't know about that technical stuff.
That's your department. I want the name of the book
dealer who appraised it. Where was the show from this
week?"

"Charlotte."

"Ah, let's hope he's local, so we don't have to chase
after someone well out of the area."

The two friends spoke for another five minutes before
ending the call. Sidney Lake, wide awake now and
bursting with energy, couldn't tone down the excitement
he felt. After finishing with Hattie Ryan, he had to speak
with someone and decided on Ray Morton, a close friend,
and retired policeman who served as his intermediary
when dealing with Morgan's police chief.

"Hello, Sidney. What's keeping you up this late?"

"What time is it?" Sidney Lake, startled by the
unexpected question, reached for the location of his
pocket watch but he was not wearing his usually ever-
present jacket. He again had to look at the clock across
the room.

"Just past nine," Ray answered.

"I'm so sorry." He was clearly embarrassed. Sidney's

eagerness to communicate the news he had just learned caused him to break one of his cardinal rules—never telephone anyone after nine in the evening. "I had no idea. I didn't disturb you did I?"

"No, not at all." Ray, hearing the eager tone in Sidney's voice, continued with, "What has you all excited?"

"The three volumes."

"The *Loss of Eden Trilogy* you loaned me?"

"No, no. Not the John Masters books. The ones that were stolen."

"Stolen?"

"The Brontë books. Remember, back when George Reed was murdered?"

"Oh, yes. But that was some time ago. What about them?" Ray sat erect in the chair. The three-volume set of Anne Brontë's *The Tenant of Wildfell Hall* had been stolen from the back seat of a police car during the Reed murder investigation and continued to be a black mark against the Morgan police department. The volumes were believed to be Anne Brontë's own author's copies in which she had made personal notations. There had also been a personal note from Anne to Ellen Nussey, Charlotte Brontë's best friend.

"They were on television tonight."

"What!" Ray moved to the edge of his chair and shook the table next to him with the sudden movement.

"I just received a call from Doctor Ryan who said that she saw them on the *National Arts and Crafts Show* this evening."

"No way!"

"That's what she said."

"And they're definitely the same books?"

"That needs to be verified. We can't say for sure. Someone would have to look at the volumes themselves, which is why I suggested Doctor Ryan make a copy of the program for me."

"Where are you?"

"At home but I have to be at Clemson tomorrow and Wednesday."

"Clemson? Getting some tips for your roses?"

"No. I'm participating in an Elderhostel program. Giving a series of lectures on Victorian gardens in literature. It fits in with the tours of the South Carolina Botanical Garden, which are the main features of the program."

"How long will you be away?"

"Just the two days."

"Well, I hope you can stay involved. If it wasn't for you, we wouldn't have known about the books in the first place. Should I be doing anything?"

"Not at the moment, no, I don't think so. I'll have Hattie give you a call."

"Okay." He paused momentarily. "Say, Sidney, Hattie Ryan didn't happen to say what those folks on the Crafts *Show* thought the books were worth did she? You know we never did get a chance to have them appraised before they were stolen."

"Hattie said an appraiser at a book dealer's booth put a price of thirty-five thousand on the books by themselves as a rare first edition but could probably double that, at least, if the writing inside could be confirmed as Anne Brontë's. However, verification will probably be tough to do given the very few examples of her writing that exist."

"Really?"

"The accompanying annotations would have to be certified as authentic. Also, there was no mention of the note addressed to Ellen Nussey which had been with the original volumes. Everything would have to be confirmed as being in the handwriting of Anne Brontë. Virtually all of Anne Brontë's records were destroyed by her sister Charlotte, as a way of protecting her from any further criticism. *The Tenant of Wildfell Hall* was pretty much vilified by the critics for its subject matter. Imagine someone in the 1840s producing a female character that would stand up to her husband and run away with their son to protect him from the male-dominated macho, blood sport culture of the early Victorian age. Outrageous, they said. Ban the book, they said. Don't let your wives and daughters read it, they said. Today, that would make it an immediate bestseller, but in the 1840s it was a killer. Charlotte even said she thought Anne was misguided to write it and wanted to protect her reputation. It has often been wondered what else Anne wrote that went up in flames in the Brontë Parsonage's fireplace."

"Now you've even got me interested. I thought she was supposed to be the meek, retiring, unworldly one?"

"Hah, just the opposite. But it's hard to change the image of someone after a hundred and fifty years."

"Damn, that would be something to do though. I can see why someone would want to steal them. Want to read, unfiltered, anything she wrote that expressed an opinion."

"Yes, but keep in mind there are a good many forgeries circulating about. It's always been a curiosity to me as to why the existence of these volumes was unknown. Brontë material is well cataloged and there appears to be no knowledge of this particular original author's edition of *The Tenant of Wildfell Hall*. But then, collectors are unusual people. Some are simply motivated by the desire to have an object once held by a famous person, regardless of value, while others are more interested in what is known as bragging rights, and don't have a true understanding of what they possess."

"Yeah, well somebody knew about it.."

"True. Well, I just wanted to keep you abreast of what Hattie and I are up to as I wouldn't be surprised to be needing your help as we look into all of this."

"Thanks Sidney. You know I'll do whatever I can. I'll wait to hear from Hattie."

THREE

The following morning, frustrated by not being able to get more information about the participants in the *National Arts and Crafts Show* program that aired on Monday, Sidney limped back and forth across his office and complained to his primary sounding board, Mrs. Micawber, Mickey, his Labrador retriever. "I understand the problem, the show was filmed over a month ago and they haven't been able to reach the people involved yet. But it's frustrating. Yes, very frustrating, Mickey, it's been what, almost two years since the books went missing? Isn't anyone interested in the theft of rare books? Now," he stopped and looked directly at Mickey, who immediately raised her head waiting for the next comment, "if it was a painting by Pissarro or someone, there would be all sorts of interest." Mickey was used to the routine. A long time ago she learned to simply be quiet and listen. When Sidney talked to her, she knew he didn't expect an answer. Sidney never did. He was thinking, working something out. Just needed to talk. So Mickey stayed put and kept an eye on him.

Turning back and continuing to walk in the direction he had been going he continued, "What I find interesting is that Hattie said the man who owned the books didn't know anything about them. Didn't even know Acton Bell was Anne Brontë's pen name. Said he picked them up at an antique and craft fair near Walterboro. They looked old, so he thought they might have some value. He bought the three volumes for twenty-five dollars. Can you imagine Mickey? A first edition of the original three-volume-set of *The Tenant of Wildfell Hall* by Acton Bell for twenty-five dollars. Anne Brontë, Mickey, and he didn't know. And the man who sold him the books at the craft fair didn't know either. Or..." Sidney stopped pacing. "What if he did know?" He now addressed Mickey directly again, "Yes. Hmmm...What if he did know? What if he's the one who stole them in the first place, but didn't know what he had? No, that doesn't make sense." Sidney paused, placed his right hand around his chin, and shook his head almost imperceptibly from side to side. Thinking. Wondering. He quickly dropped his hand and looked across the room, "Mickey, if he knew their value he wouldn't be trying to sell them for twenty-five dollars. So where did he get them? Mickey, I think we have a trip to Walterboro in our future."

"Walterboro. Why you want to go to Walterboro?" Tillie had managed to slip into the front hallway unseen as Sidney talked with Mickey.

"Oh, Tillie. Didn't see you come in," he said taken aback at getting a response to a question he'd asked Mickey.

"Kinda figured that. Both of you so involved with talkin' to one another I coulda driven a truck through here. What's goin' on?"

"Oh, that's right. You probably don't know." Sidney smiled. Could it be he knew something that Tillie didn't? That might be a first. Tillie not knowing of something of interest to Sidney that occurred in Morgan, South Carolina. With her Gullah housekeeper network connections all through the Lowcountry and beyond, could it be that something got by her? But then, technically, it happened in Charlotte, North Carolina, even if it was broadcast around the world. Sidney might be a step ahead of her for a change.

"What you smilin' about? Oh...I know. You think I don't know about those books on the *National Arts and Crafts Show*? Yeah, that's it, isn't it?" She had a big smile on her face.

"How in the world..." Sidney stood in front of her, completely deflated.

Mickey, tail wagging from side to side, got up and walked over to Tillie.

"Saw it. Love that show. Never miss it. Besides, I cleaned for Miss Hattie this morning an we had a long chat about it. Yeah, I know you know about it too. Figured you'd be frettin'. But whatcha goin' to do about it? Old police business, right?"

Sidney looked long and hard at his friend and housekeeper. He kept silent for a moment. Thoughts raced through his head as he reflected on her last sentence. "Exactly. You're right on the problem, as usual." He moved toward her. "You're right, it's just that, 'old police business,' and not very important either."

"Why not important? Those books are worth a lot of money. I heard the man say they was worth more than thirty-thousand dollars."

"But that's the point. The books that were on the show could be worth thirty-thousand dollars—or maybe even more—but are they stolen property? Are they the same exact ones? We don't have any way of knowing. It's not like a painting where there's only one original. With books, all first editions are original and we don't know how many first editions there are and how many are still in existence. The stolen books were never logged in as evidence and never appraised, so no real value was ever given to them."

Tillie nodded her head slowly, "Yeah, as I said, old police business. I'll bet the Morgan police would like those books to stay in hiding. Claim nobody could prove they were worth anything."

"Now you have it. The fact that evidence was taken from the back of a Morgan police car is embarrassing, but if the evidence didn't have any meaning or value—or no one could prove they did—Chief Hornig doesn't have a problem."

"Let sleeping dogs lie," Tillie said with a smile, which quickly turned to a frown. "But we ain't gonna do that are we? We gonna get ourselves in trouble again, ain't we?"

"No. no. I've been thinking a good deal about this. We're going to forget all about the police side. We'll leave that all up to Chief Hornig. The police don't have to be involved. We're going to find out all we can about the books that were at the *National Arts and Crafts Show.* Who brought them to the show? Where did he get them? Where did *that* person get them? And most important, where are they now, and are they the real books?"

"Professor, you always make it sound so simple an logical an all, an then sompthin' seems to go wrong. I don't know, I sure hope you're right this time.

FOUR

On Wednesday, the morning program and luncheon at Clemson went off as expected. Sidney Lake loved it all—the center of attention, surrounded by lovers of English literature hanging on his every word. But the books never left his thoughts. Clemson sat between Charlotte to his east and Walterboro to his south. He knew he would need more help than usual on the puzzle at hand. Never spry, the damage to his right knee slowed him down even more. His retired-policeman friend, Ray Morton, would be able to help and, of course, Tillie and Hattie, but he would need an expert on rare books this time—someone who knew about 150-year-old bindings, paper, and ink. But that kind of expertise didn't exist at Morgan College. There were plenty of resources around. Morgan sat within easy reach of Savannah, Charlotte, Charleston, Columbia, and the Raleigh-Durham area. The ultimate resource would be The Brontë Society in Haworth, Yorkshire, England. As a member, he already had good contacts there. So, if he could just sit at home with Tillie doing the local legwork, and Hattie and Ray doing the regional, he could keep his own leg out of trouble and focus on gathering and analyzing information.

Among other talents, Sidney Lake had the ability to coerce others into doing his bidding. Although having a reputation for being a curmudgeon, people were ready and willing to assist him when he came out of character and turned on the charm. His close friends knew how it worked, the dinner invitation, the flattery he would give to the person—coming from someone not known for pleasantries—and the praising of the person's area of expertise. What made it work was Sidney's sincerity. While he could be abrasive and somewhat challenged in the tact area, he was neither mean-spirited nor intentionally mean in any way. His associates knew his problem derived from his desire to always be truthful and honest, which can be a dangerous attribute. Admittedly, he didn't suffer fools lightly and if he found out you didn't have the level of knowledge and understanding your reputation required, you would be taken to task for it very quickly.

Sidney Lake needed an expert, and he would do whatever was necessary to get the right one.

The interesting part about an Elderhostel program—like many life-long learning programs—is that there's often as much knowledge about a subject in the audience, as there is at the lectern. The program at Clemson proved to be no different. During the question-and-answer period at the end of his presentation, Sidney maneuvered the topic of bookbinding and Victorian age printing into the conversation by referring to flowers pressed into Victorian novels. From there they digressed to writing instruments.

A participant in the class happened to be a retired pharmacist and recounted having worked for a local pharmacy in Aiken, SC in the 1940s where the owner made his own ink based on a formula dating to the 1830s in England. "It was apparently very common back then for the local chemist to make the ink used by the townspeople. Those that would usually buy from him would be the local gentry, the clergy, and educational people, mostly governesses and schoolmasters."

All sorts of bells and whistles went off in Sidney's head when he heard the terms clergy and governess in the same sentence. Authenticating the handwriting of Anne Brontë might be an easier process than he thought. A forensic examination of the ink used to write the note to Ellen Nussey would be a simple task in the twenty-first century. What someone might have passed off as valid in the twentieth century might not so easily stand up today.

That evening Sidney had dinner with the director of the Elderhostel program and two other presenters. Sidney managed to get the conversation around to document fraud and forgery and asked if anyone had viewed the *National Arts and Crafts Show* on Monday evening. Everyone had.

"Oh, the books. Yes, that was fascinating," the Elderhostel director said. "I was captivated by it. *Jane Eyre* is an all-time favorite of mine," she went on. "I don't think I've read *The Tenant of Wildfell Hall* by Anne Brontë, but I did see a PBS presentation of it on *Masterpiece Theatre* some years ago. The appraiser seemed to be very enthusiastic about the books. He did say the books were certainly original but couldn't validate the handwriting inside. I suppose this is one of those occasions where having someone write in a rare book makes it even more valuable than less, as long as the writing can be confirmed as the authors and not a subsequent owner."

Sidney responded with, "Yes, it all depends on who made the notations. That's the key. You wouldn't happen to remember who the appraiser was?"

She sat back in her chair. "You know I can see his face right in front of me." The director bit her lower lip, closed her eyes, and tilted her head back trying to draw the name out. "It was a funny name. Not humorous. Not John or Bill or something. Just unusual. She squeezed her eyes firmly and grimaced, tying with all her might to recall the name. Finally she blurted it out. "Burke. Yes, that was his first name, Burke. That's why it struck me." She looked at Sidney with a big smile on her face and grabbed his arm and squeezed it. "Burke Mansfield. Yes, that's it, Burke Mansfield." She gave another big smile to her dinner companions. "How about that? How did I ever remember that? I even remember where he was from. Savannah, Georgia. Don't remember the name of the company though."

After dinner, Sidney stopped at the hotel's cocktail lounge, found a quiet, out-of-the-way corner, and made himself comfortable with a glass of port and his leather-bound notebook. It had been an interesting week and it was only Wednesday. He needed to think but he found hotel rooms claustrophobic. He also wanted a soft comfortable chair. Mickey stayed upstairs. He thought about bringing her down but didn't want to be relegated to the patio or some other uncomfortable location.

The nice part about a summer Elderhostel program at a college proved to be the accommodations—the students stayed in the empty college dormitory so they could experience the student lifestyle they often romanticized, while the instructors got the hotel. A perfect arrangement.

Taking a sip of the port, Sidney leaned back in his chair and began to think about...the book. It had been on his mind for years. Ever since he had the short opportunity to hold its three volumes in his hands, he longed to find it again. He had held other rare books over the years, some even by Hardy and Dickens. But this was different. This was Anne Brontë, the often maligned youngest of the Brontë sisters. Pictured by her sister Charlotte as a gentle, quiet soul, Charlotte set an image of her that many modern Brontë scholars had taken issue with—and Sidney Lake was among them. He wanted to get his hands on the book and see Anne's candid comments about it. He wanted to read and analyze the accompanying letter to Ellen Nussey. A brief look at the letter indicated the book was Anne's author's copy of *The Tenant of Wildfell Hall* and she was lending it to Miss Nussey, a close friend to the sisters who was unable to obtain a copy of her own to read, as sales had skyrocketed. Sidney also wanted to explore the relationship between Ellen Nussey and Anne Brontë, as Ellen has always been considered one of Charlotte's closest friends.

Sidney sat, sipped, and pondered. Having spent so much time researching and writing about Thomas J. Wise, the scholar, and bibliophile who went down the literary forgery route for fame and profit, he found himself looking at every rare book and document with a newly critical eye. It was not only the Brontës Wise pursued with his literary memorabilia misappropriations and forgeries but also the likes of Shelley, Browning, and their contemporaries.

Wise was not alone at the beginning of the Twentieth Century. There were plenty of opportunities for fraud at the time. Europe was being overrun with newly minted American industrialists and their families. Tons of money to spend. They were buying up Europe. Anything that looked old and had culture and history written all over it became a target. Everything from literature to art to buildings to noble titles could be bought for the right price. Rarely did the rich Americans have a knowledge base of their own to guide them, so they employed an army of experts to lead them to the undiscovered riches they sought as trophies to validate the newly acquired worldliness they could brag about. Opportunities were everywhere for both the uneducated Americans to spend and the unscrupulous guides ready to direct them to bargains, both genuine and fake. Charlotte Brontë's good friend Ellen Nussey, as well as Nicholas Bell, Charlotte's husband, were both duped by Wise into loaning much of Charlotte's memorabilia to the British Museum only to later learn some of it was sold to American collectors.

Taking another sip of port, Sidney chuckled to himself thinking of the report of the American industrialist who paid a fortune for what he believed to be the ultimate prize. In Paris, he purchased an *authorized* letter written by Mary Magdalene explaining her relationship to Jesus. Upon returning home with his treasure, it was explained to him there was no evidence to support the assertion Mary Magdalene could write and the letter, rather than being written in an ancient form of Hebrew, was written in modern French.

Could the mysterious copy of *The Tenant of Wildfell Hall* be a similar example of an American collector acquiring something deemed to be authentic, sold for a large sum of money, and yet have forged notations inside? Was this another case of a wealthy businessman with degrees a plenty but no education? Sidney knew the possibilities, but the remote chance the handwriting inside might be Anne Brontë's drove him to keep looking and researching. The rare book expert's validation at the *National Arts and Crafts Show* encouraged him, but he had to know for sure. He had to track down Burke Mansfield of Savannah, Georgia.

Back in his hotel room, he continued to explore the

matter with his trusted confidant. "So why someone would steal a rare, valuable, three-volume Victorian novel and then agree to be on television to find out what it was worth?" Sidney Lake rhetorically asked the question of Mickey. The black Lab made no movement from her position. Nicely curled up on the sofa next to Sidney, she just redirected her eyes from time to time to look at him.

"I suppose we could have a case of the bank robber who writes the hold-up note on the back of a deposit slip containing his name, address, and account number. But no, I don't think so. People don't steal books unless they know they have some value." He directed his comment to Mickey, peering over his glasses as he did. "That's monetary value not intellectual. The idea of stealing a book for its intellectual value, well, in this day and age, I think it's safe to eliminate that theory."

Sidney moved from the sofa to the desk nearby. His final lecture would not be until 10:00 a.m. so he decided to use the time to draft the article Jim Cunningham of the Morgan Times asked him to write about the murder of George Reed. With the second anniversary of the event due in a few weeks, Cunningham planned a retrospective spread for the coming weekend. Morgan, not being a hotbed of crime like some of the faster-growing places in the country, the local population needed to be reminded that violent crime was possible, even though not a daily or even weekly event.

Sidney continued to interrupt his writing with long pauses interspaced with comments to Mickey, the way he usually worked out ideas. Every time he began to recreate the earlier events his thoughts kept bringing him back to the present and the call from Hattie on Monday evening about the *National Arts and Crafts Show*. The more he kept thinking about the missing book the more unanswered questions it raised.

He lifted himself from the chair, not always an easy task with his injured leg and excessive weight to contend with. Sidney was determined to get his weight down and had succeeded somewhat, having lost ten pounds over the past year, and only putting back five. Hattie's forcing him to diet helped a good deal. Exercise for the professor was certainly out of the question. He walked across the room and headed for the coffee maker near the door of the two-room suite. The set-up worked well for him and Mickey, which was why he chose not to stay with the participants in the program and opted for the accommodations Elderhostel offered to provide for instructors. Alone, aloof, in control of his own environment, yes, that was Sidney Lake.

FIVE

Ray Morton took another sip of coffee and continued multitasking: reading an op-ed in the newspaper beside him while giving Hattie an update on his meeting with the Morgan police chief. After Ray's seven a.m. appointment with Chief Hornig, the City Hall Café was the best place for them to meet. Breakfast was his favorite meal and any excuse for bacon, eggs, grits, shrimp gravy, and biscuits at the Hall, was a good excuse. "I don't know, Hattie, I mentioned it to the chief and he hasn't heard anything about those books since they were lifted from one of his cars. I think he'd like to forget the whole thing and I don't blame him."

"Is that usual, not hearing anything for all this time?" Hattie inquired. She was working on orange juice, wheat toast, and tea—English breakfast.

Recently, Hattie in her usual straightforward way had made a significant objection to the tea the Café's owner provided, as it was the generic brand the food service truck carried.

"How can you serve that poor excuse for tea?" she complained.

"Hey, tea is tea."

"No, it isn't. Especially as you said you want to upscale the café a bit to attract more tourists. You should serve real British tea."

"Aw come on Ms. Ryan, people drink coffee here."

He gave in, as everyone usually did with Hattie once she set her mind to something.

Ray continued to tell her of his meeting with the Morgan police chief. "Stolen art objects are a bit different from cars and electronics. Art disappears. The market is limited, and sales are mostly to private collectors. You usually don't find stolen stuff in reputable places, which is why this *National Arts and Crafts Show* thing is kinda strange. It's all in the NCIC anyway and can be checked. Technology sure has changed things." The grits and biscuits were almost gone.

"NCIC? What's that?"

"Oh, sorry. Yeah, you wouldn't know. National Crime Information Center. It's an FBI database. Every piece of stolen property gets entered into it. Hornig's people probably put those books in right away. If anyone thinks they've got something that looks funny, they can check. Police tend to dump into it just about everything they find at a crime scene. You never know what might pop up."

"You mean the FBI is investigating the books?"

"No, no. It's strictly a local deal." The eggs were gone. "Feds defer to locals unless it's obvious something has gone interstate or a federal crime is involved. If that TV program was from Charleston, it's still a local matter. Where was the show from?"

"Charlotte."

"North Carolina. Well, if it turns out they can be identified as the same books, the feds could get involved." Ray finished off the last piece of bacon.

Hattie watched with a sense of wonder at the speed at which the food on Ray's plate disappeared and said, "I suppose there isn't much we can do, although I promised Sidney I would call the local PBS station this morning and see what I had to do to get an official tape of the program."

She continued to bring Ray Morton up to date on Sidney Lake's whereabouts and his thinking about the missing three-volume book.

As she spoke, she thought about how much things had changed and how a stable world could so easily unravel. She could see the article on Iran that Ray was peeking at from time to time—much saber rattling from the new administration in Washington—but there was local change as well. Change that evolved rather than unraveled. She now headed the English Literature Department at Morgan College—Sidney Lake's position before he retired—and while they had always been friends, their relationship had grown over the past two years. Her daughter had graduated from Georgetown and now worked for JP Morgan Chase in New York. There was a new pastor at the Catholic Church, the old one having been transferred rather suddenly and the subject of much gossip. She continued as an active member of St. Luke's Episcopal Church, her refuge after her divorce. Reverend Prentice at Bay View Presbyterian had a new assistant, a young man with a wife and two small children. Morgan's new mayor, Steele Wilcox, was a continuing source of controversy. Yes, much had changed, as it should, but much had stayed the same.

That's why I'm still here, thought Hattie, as she read a wire service story about automobile commuting, gas prices, and an expanding crime rate. Over the years, she had received offers from other, larger universities located in major metropolitan areas and had rejected them. Morgan was home now and, as long as the college was willing to put up with her, this was where she would stay.

Hattie continued to read the newspaper that Ray Morton left behind. For a retiree who didn't play golf, he had more things to do than most of the currently employed. Ray left a few minutes earlier as he had to be at the County Courthouse in Beaufort, where the solicitor had asked him to be available to testify as an expert witness about procedures between the city and sheriff's departments. Her own schedule was a bit more flexible and she didn't have to be anywhere today, especially with Sidney out of town. Her tentative plan was to spend time at her office working on a series of lectures on the life and poetry of Percy B. Shelley, which she agreed to do for the adult, continuing education program.

As she continued to read through the article about the crime rate and the wide variety of excuses for it, her briefcase made a humming noise. She had turned it off her phone while they spoke earlier.

Seeing the call was from her daughter, Hattie gathered up her belongings, neatly folded Ray's newspaper, so that someone else could read it if they wished and left a tip. Ray picked up the tab for breakfast. Hattie viewed her extra gratuity as a table rental fee and thank you for the second cup of tea.

She knew the call to be an unusual one. Claire was so busy at work that calling Hattie at any time other than in the evening signaled a need to tell her something important. Just outside the back door, she stopped at one of the round, wooden picnic tables, complete with an umbrella, and checked her voicemail.

"Mom, Claire. Just had to call. You know that thing about the books, you know, the ones that were stolen and you mentioned seeing them on the *National Arts and Crafts Show* last night, well, I have a friend who taped the whole show. Call me when you get a chance. Love."

Hattie sat down at the table and immediately returned Claire's call.

಄಄಄

Ray stepped out onto the plaza area outside the Beaufort County building and, holding his breath, headed for a shady spot out of the way. The front entrance to most public buildings had become smoking zones. A former smoker himself, he still had some sympathy for people who were trying to quit, but the more gauntlets he had to make his way through, the more tempered that sympathy became.

He dialed Hattie Ryan's number. "Hattie, Ray, can you relay some information to Sidney for me? I don't have a local number for him at Clemson and he never remembers to plugin that phone of his."

"Yes, I know. How can I help?"

"He's writing a piece about Reed's murder for Cunningham. Anniversary of the event or something and he couldn't remember the full name of the lawyer in Charlotte who worked up that inventory list. It was Springwood, Howard Springwood."

"Yes, I remember. Sidney said he was the lawyer for Brewster's uncle, the original owner of the books."

"Yeah, so if you could just pass it on to him I'd appreciate it."

"Certainly. You wouldn't happen to have a phone number for Mr. Springwood, would you? You know how thorough Sidney is, he might want to call him."

"Can't help you there. General Brewster probably knows though. Understand Springwood bought a place on Crow Island not too long ago, you know, that fancy place north of Morgan. Could be in the phone book. Although I think most of those folks tend to be a little shy when it comes to bein' in the public eye. Which is why they have all those armed guards around the place. If you'd like, I'll see if I can find a number for him."

"No that's all right. If Sidney wants to contact him he can ask. It's never easy to anticipate what Sidney does or doesn't want."

"You have that right."

"How did you know he had a place on Crow Island?"

Silence.

"Ray, are you still there?"

"Still here. Just tryin' to figure out how to answer you without causing trouble."

"Trouble?"

"Hattie, just keep this to yourself and don't tell Sidney or he'll be all over me with questions. One of the guys in the sheriff's department I spent the morning with said there was some rumor Springwood was involved with stolen goods. The feds apparently had him under loose surveillance, you know, that person of interest terminology they use today."

"How did you find all this out?"

"Two of the sheriff's guys were in Charlotte at a seminar at UNC and they were discussing the new Art Theft Division the FBI put together. Discussed some things in class and his name came up. Cops are always in school anymore. Rules and regulations always changing."

"Is he still under investigation?"

"Don't know. They didn't have anything on him at the time. Can't really say if the case was ever wrapped up. I can find out though. Might be interesting."

"You also mentioned stolen property, could that mean rare books?"

Ray paused. "I see where you're coming from. Yeah, it could. Don't know the specifics of what they thought Springwood was involved with but, yeah, it's an interesting idea. He could have been the one that sold the books to Brewster's uncle."

"That could also explain why there doesn't seem to be a record of their existence in any bibliography that Sidney could find. Then, o there's always the possibility they weren't real."

"Weren't real?"

"Literary forgeries. Fakes. You may recall Sidney making reference to T. J. Wise."

"Wise? Oh, yeah. The turn of the century guy. Fleeced some little old ladies and family members of writers and poets in England. Yeah, I remember now. What was it that Sidney called him?"

"A scholar and a scoundrel."

"That's it. Leave it to Sidney. Who uses words like scoundrel anymore?"

"Personally, I think it's most descriptive and appropriate." She was also thinking about reminding him that poets are also writers but decided to let it go. Unlike Sidney, who had a problem with letting anything go by without correction, Hattie took a more practical approach; preferring to save her challenges for more meaningful infractions of speech and etiquette. Sidney, on the other hand, viewed everything as a learning experience—for others.

"Okay. You literary types sure make life interesting," he said with a laugh.

Ray Morton had learned to enjoy both Sidney and Hattie. His somewhat gruff, straight-forward, down-to-earth approach, while appearing to be at odds with the professor's, was quite compatible. All three did not suffer fools well, it was just the approach and response that differed. Ray's use of the English language made effective use of three, four, and five-letter words while

Lake and Ryan accomplished the same effect with the longer variety. All three managed to make themselves clearly understood to their constituencies.

Ray continued, "My experience has told me that a creep and a crook is still a creep and a crook no matter how smart he may be."

"True."

"Anyway, I have to get back inside. Just relay the info back to Sidney—without the last part."

"Agreed. Oh, by the way, I've managed to find someone who taped the *Crafts Show* last night, and as soon as I have the names of the people I'll pass them on to you."

"Good. I'll be back in town this afternoon and mention it to the chief. As long as he still has jurisdiction he gets first crack at taking action if he wants to. Got to go, Hattie."

SIX

Finding Burke Mansfield proved to be more challenging than Sidney Lake first thought. Yes, they did have a copy of Monday's *National Arts and Crafts Show* that Hattie's daughter, Claire, provided but the name "Burke Mansfield" only identified him as "A rare book dealer, Savannah, GA," without further explanation or the name of the company with which he was affiliated. Just to be certain, Sidney checked again with the director of the Elderhostel program, but no, she had no further information to provide.

Upon returning to Morgan, Sidney got together with Tillie and Hattie and went to work. They scoured the Savannah phone book—but no Burke Mansfield. They checked the listing of antique and rare book dealers—nothing with either the name Burke or Mansfield could be found anywhere. They tried just initials. Tillie called people she knew. Hattie tried every variation of the name possible—nothing matched. Off and on for three days they searched, telephoned, tried everything they could think of, and still had nothing to show for their efforts. They were thoroughly frustrated. A week had passed since the program aired and they still had nothing. They planned to watch the program that evening to see if Mansfield showed up, as well as obtain the names of other rare book experts.

In speaking with the local PBS station in Charlotte, North Carolina where last week's program originated from, all they could tell them was that he was a regional import for the show and not a regular. Even though Mansfield had been listed as being from Rare Books of Savannah, it didn't mean his business was located in Savannah itself, but could be in the general region and used the city of Savannah as an identifier.

They expanded their search to the Savannah suburbs and even into Jasper County, South Carolina. The local PBS station also offered to find out what they could for them.

When Sidney heard Ray had mentioned the National Crime Information Center's database of stolen property, he questioned why Burke Mansfield and other experts on the show didn't spot the stolen Anne Brontë novel right away. As the experts always mentioned talking among themselves before they determined the value of an item, wouldn't they also check the NCIC database to make sure it wasn't stolen? Sidney asked Ray to check with Police Chief Pete Hornig, his old boss and learned the book hadn't been entered into the database, as they had no proof of its authenticity or an estimated value. Another dead end.

The plan for the evening's watch of the program would be to get the names of any rare book dealers and call them to see if they knew a Burke Mansfield. As they discussed their plan, Hattie looked as though a light went off in her head. She blurted out, "Antiquarian Booksellers Association of America."

"What?" Sidney said.

"The Antiquarian Booksellers Association of America. When I was doing searches online, every rare book dealer's website always indicated they were members of the Antiquarian Booksellers Association of America. I'll bet every reputable rare book dealer in the country belongs to it."

"Do you have an address and phone number?"

"No, but I can have it for you in a minute," Hattie said opening her ever-present laptop.

When Sidney and Hattie shifted positions at the dining room table and moved the chairs together, Tillie looked at her watch and said, "Professor, I got to get over to the Oak Street Community Center by two o'clock. I'll come back when I'm finished."

Hattie asked, "No trouble is there?"

"No, I just promised to support Ester Averille. They got her place listed for a tax sale an' we all plan to be there to speak up for her."

"How much taxes does she owe?"

"Not much. Couple a hundred. She's in her nineties now. Spent her life cleanin' houses and cookin' for people. Lives alone in her place over on the Pirate Islands near Carson Point. She don't have no money an' everybody knows it. Don't even have a bank account. County knows it too, but they have to put the place up for tax sale for no-tax payment. It's the law. Happens a lot around the Lowcountry County asks for payment an' she pays what she can an they agree to waive the rest if she promises to come up with it, if nobody bids on her land. Accountant from the n-double-a-c-p gave a talk to the county people an' showed them it was cheaper to waive the amount she couldn't pay than ship her off to the county home. Makes sense. She has some family nearby but most have moved away. Once she passes, the place will go to somebody an' the taxman will get paid, but long as she's livin, she'll get to stay there, if she's able. She was born there and plans to die there. She got that right."

Hattie listened carefully and said, "Very interesting,

Tillie, I'd like to hear more about that when you come back."

While Hattie and Tillie chatted, Sidney kept looking over Hattie's laptop and the web pages for the ABAA. He made notes on a few items and when Hattie came back he asked her to print out a few pages for him. He could have done it himself but Hattie forbid him to touch her computer when she wasn't with him. When it came to technology, the one person you didn't want around your electronic devices was Sidney Lake. The devices panicked when he got close. They froze, lost their memories, erased files, got viruses, and wouldn't respond to any commands. She had been through it many times before. She made sure to keep up with as much modern technology as she could, although she would be the first to admit her skills were no match for those of her students. Sidney, on the other hand, had problems making sense of his smartphone. He used his computer to search for information, but he never trusted what he found. He would page down to the end of the article first and check the author's notes and bibliography to review the source material. If he approved of it, he would read the article and then head to the library to do his own research.

"Sidney, this is interesting."

"What is?"

"The website for the Antiquarian Booksellers. The ABAA. Down at the bottom here. It says there is an International League of Antiquarian Booksellers Stolen Books Database."

"Really? Can we search it?"

Hattie quickly moved around the website. "I don't think so. I wouldn't be surprised if you have to be a member to do that...or the police."

Sidney leaned over to get a better look at the screen. "I

think you're right. Look, it says that rare book dealers all know one another and keep track of one another's inventories. Quick, do a search on *The Tenant of Wildfell Hall.*"

Hattie found a search window and entered the title followed by "first edition." They waited no more than a few seconds when a picture of three bound volumes appeared on the screen with the following below them:

First edition NOTE: Price $37,500

by Brontë, Anne; Bell, Acton

London: T. C. Newby, 1848 "A Portrait of Debauchery That is Remarkable"

One of the First Modern Feminist Novels

No. 1 on Sadleir's list of "Comparative Scarcities"

First edition, first issue, of Anne Brontë's second novel, with all the flaws noted by Smith.

Hattie read further down the page, "Look, it says '...this book is the rarest of any Brontë title in first edition, in any state whatsoever.' It goes on the say '...and is virtually unobtainable in any original publisher's binding, in any condition.' Sidney, that three- volume edition you held in your hands a few years ago must be worth a fortune. The picture they're showing for thirty-seven thousand is one that was rebound in nineteen hundred. Wow."

Sidney sat there looking at the screen and said nothing for a full five seconds. "Hattie, we've got to find Burke Mansfield."

SEVEN

The search for Burke Mansfield continued throughout the afternoon without further success. Hattie continued to explore the internet under a variety of subject headings. Sidney sat next to her at the dining room table and kept interrupting when she came across a topic that interested him. The interruptions didn't always relate to the object of their search, but something unrelated that caught his interest. Sidney always had a dozen projects going on at once. But he never truly left one project for another, just reordered their priority based on what popped into his head at the moment. Hattie was more straight-line focused. Eventually they both became absorbed in reading about rare book thefts. Never in their wildest dreams did they ever think there could be so many. Sidney kept telling Hattie to print this one and then that one.

"Hattie, you have to print that article on Stephen Carrie Blumberg. They say he stole more than twenty-four thousand volumes of rare books and manuscripts from three hundred twenty-seven libraries and museums across North America. He did it for sixteen years. Looks like they finally put him away in nineteen ninety-one. I've never heard of him, have you?"

"No."

"And he's listed as the number one book thief in America. We've spent our whole lives analyzing and teaching about literary masters from two and three hundred years ago, marveling over original manuscripts, books, and bindings, and not having a clue this was going on. Fascinating."

"Oh, look, Sidney. Here's a new word for you. Haven't seen it on *Jeopardy* yet: bibliokleptomania: the 'gentle madness' of book theft. Although, from what I've seen so far, I'm not so sure it's so gentle. And look," Hattie continued, excitedly, "when they arrested Blumberg at his place in Iowa—a three-story mansion—everything was there, all the books and manuscripts. He never sold any of them, he just kept them for himself."

Sidney thought for a moment and then said, "All the books they know about were there. I'm beginning to see the problem. There's an awful lot of material scholars have written off as lost forever or believe might exist but can't confirm it. Book collectors can be a strange bunch. Only they know what they have. They can be so secretive that even their heirs had no idea what lurked in the bookshelves. With a painting it's easy, two or three paintings that look completely different hanging on a wall and catching your eye versus a thousand books sitting in bookshelves that would occupy the same wall space as the paintings but all look alike."

Hattie turned to Sidney with a look suggesting the proverbial light bulb just went on in her head. "That's why all these people show up at the *Crafts Show* with some old, dusty books that belonged to a grandparent. They have no idea of what he or she had."

"Exactly. The real value is what made it important in the first place—what the author wrote. Heaven forbid they should read the book."

"Let's not be unkind, now," Hattie admonished. "Remember, you can't tell a book by its cover and that goes for people too. One does not need a university education to be an educated person. You and I both know that. And yes, we've met a good many people who have attended very fine schools and claim to have high IQ's who are as dumb as the nearest light post." Having said her piece, she went back to the matter at hand. "I wonder if that's what we're facing with the Brontë book. Just saw it as an old book when cleaning up the estate of a relative and had no idea what they had."

"Could be. But no, I don't think so. Not in this case." Sidney sat back in his chair. "Although...I wonder...if the person at the *Crafts Show* really didn't know what he had and that Acton Bell was the pen name of Anne Brontë...Hmmmm. Could it have been stolen along with other material with more recognizable names? Should we expand our search to include recent art and book burglaries in the Charlotte area three to six months ago?"

The front door opened with an angry thrust and Tillie marched in. Sidney knew something had gone wrong. She not only didn't call out to Sidney and Hattie but also blew past Mickey without any form of acknowledgment. Tillie mumbled to herself as she went down the hallway to the kitchen. They heard her purse hit the table and a few not very well-chosen words blistered the air. Words not usually uttered by her.

Sidney and Hattie both knew the pattern and remained quiet. When Tillie was ready she would let them know what happened. Even Mickey kept her distance and lay down, facing in Tillie's direction, halfway between Sidney's chair and the entrance to the kitchen.

It seemed obvious something went wrong at the tax sale but neither Sidney nor Hattie had any intention of asking her. The three friends had been through a lot together over the years and, while they were all very private people, there were very few secrets among them.

They trusted each other and kept one another's confidences, but never probed into private areas without an invitation. Opening doors to their inner joys and demons was a voluntary process. They were not opposed to sharing, but it would be at their own time and choosing. So Sidney, Hattie, and Mickey went on about what they were doing, confident in their belief that if Tillie wanted them to know what bothered her, she would tell them.

They didn't have long to wait.

As Sidney and Hattie continued reviewing cases of rare-book theft and Mickey kept one ear aimed toward the kitchen, Tillie paced back and forth alternating muttering aloud and under her breath. The pattern continued until she stopped, and all noise ceased. After a few moments, she peeked into the dining room. Mickey got up and walked toward her.

"Sorry," she said. "They stole Ester's home." Tillie reached down and patted Mickey's head. She had herself under control but maintained a fierce, angry look. "She's got to get out. No place for a ninety-year-old lady to go. There's mean, mean people in this world."

Hattie got up from her chair and said, "Oh, Tillie, how could they do that? I thought it was agreed that no one would bid on the property?"

"That's how they told us it would work. We were all there for her—friends, neighbors, family. But it didn't make no difference."

Sidney chimed in as Hattie made her way to Tillie and told her to sit down with them. "I thought it was all arranged with the tax people and the town?" Sidney asked.

Tillie sat and Hattie pulled up a chair next to her.

"It was, Professor. That's what they told us, but it's a

word agreement. Nothin' writtin' down about it. The tax people said no payment was made and the tax had to be paid before the auction. They can't enforce the law with some people an' not others." She paused and said, "That seems to be okay with the police though." A frustrated breath of air escaped her. "Ain't there anything you can do?"

Sidney sat back in his chair. "Well, I don't know," he said defensively. "I'm not an attorney and I don't have any expertise in tax law. Tell me what happened."

"Shoulda known sompthin' was up. Fancy-pants lawyer from outta town showed up. A couple of 'um. Most times nobody cares about people's tax problems. Lawyers only show up for the companies with tax problems. Business stuff always come before people stuff. Lots of money involved so the vultures come out. Don't understand. Ester only owed five hundred and seventy-five dollars. It's a two-room wooden place. Had a dirt floor until last year. Folks got together an' fixed it up for her. New roof too. Was told not to do too much or the taxes would go up. We just wanted to make it livable so she could get one of those no-pay mortgage things they got now. Good Neighbors did the work."

"Oh, I know them," Hattie said, "Saint Luke's is part of that group."

Sidney looked puzzled.

"It's a community group, Sidney. A mixture of Black and White churches in town along with the service clubs. They go around and fix up houses like Ester Averille's. They try to take care of the elderly who can't do things for themselves anymore so they can stay in their homes. I even did yard work on a place on the west side once. You must have heard about them at Rotary. I know Ray Morton works with the group all the time. In fact, what about asking Ray to find out what happened this afternoon?"

"Yes, I could do that." Sidney turned back to Tillie. "Tell me more about what happened."

"They took her home."

"I know that, but how? What happened?"

Tillie took a deep breath. "Found out a big plan was put together by the new lawyer up the street."

"Colvin?"

"No, that new one. The young one from Charlotte. Don't remember his name. Don't *want* to know it now...'sept to throw mud at. He said it'd solve her tax problem. Was putting together a plan with some banker so she could keep the house till she passed. Miss Ester's been in trouble before with tax stuff an' last time we took a collection to help. Shoulda done the same this time."

"Wait Tillie," Hattie interrupted, "are we talking about a reverse mortgage?"

"Yeah, that's what they called it. Said since the place had a new floor and roof, she could get the reverse thing. Her place sits on a nice spot. Don't think the land is too big. Can't always tell where the property line is with these old places. Lot of open land around there though. Lots of places like it over there. Morgan River's about a football field away. Anyway, the bank man saw her an' said he'd get everything set up, but it'd take some time. Said he'd explain everything to the tax sale people who was supposed to say the place wasn't up for tax sale anymore since there was a new mortgage on the property. The cash from it would pay the taxes for the next ten years."

Sidney said, "I've heard about those loans, they advertise them on television a lot."

"Yeah, that's them."

"Sounds like a good deal. Where did everything go wrong?" Sidney now had all his antennae up.

"Bank man didn't show. Taxman said he didn't know anything about a mortgage so they had to sell. Couldn't stop the sale if someone wanted to buy. It was the law. He couldn't change it."

Sidney became quiet and had an angry set to his mouth. He rubbed his chin and looked at the ceiling. He said softly, "What did the new lawyer from Charlotte say?"

"Wasn't there. 'Nother lawyer. Someone said he was from Washington."

"I'll bet someone was all set to buy."

"You got that right. Offered two thousand dollars for Miss Ester's two-room shack. Cash. That real estate guy, Casey, made an offer too."

"Casey Yarbrough?"

"That's him. First guy outbid 'um. Paid seven thousand for Miss Ester's place." Taxman jumped at it."

"Whoa," Hattie looked shocked. "Sidney, there's something wrong here."

"I'll say. Do you know the name of the lawyer who bought Miss Ester's place?"

"The weasel. Said he was representin' someone else. Some company. Nothin but a bunch of letters: 'C A B' or sompthin."

"What about the bank that was mentioned? Was it local?"

"Never heard of it but someone said it wasn't a bank. Just a guy who said he had bank connections."

Hattie leaned forward, "I'll bet he was a mortgage broker. Probably connected to a real estate company. They're pretty common these days."

"Coulda been. Who knows, he coulda been workin'

for Mr. Yarborough." Tillie looked frustrated. She shook her head and continued. "What chance we got with all these vultures hangin' around."

Sidney asked, "Did Miss Ester say the broker person was connected to a real estate company, as Hattie suggested?"

"No, she said he had some weird name with lots of capital letters in it and the word 'sunshine.' She kinda trusted him 'cause he was Black an spoke some Gullah. Shoulda known better, but it all sounded like it would be a big help Miss Ester. I mean she's ninety years an' more old. She ain't got long to go. Why couldn't they just wait? Nobody wanted that old place but Miss Ester."

Sidney did some thinking again before he spoke. "That may be the point. Somebody did want Miss Ester's place. They wanted it a lot. Tillie, do you know if anyone who lives near Ester Averille sold their property recently?"

Tillie looked astonished. She sat back in her chair and then raised her right arm straight out with the finger pointed at Sidney. "You know, now that you mentioned it some folks have sold. Somebody even asked Miss Ester if she'd sell. She said no. Wasn't ever gonna move."

Hattie looked at Sidney and said, "Are you thinking the same thing I am?"

"Oh, yes. It's starting again."

Sidney referred to an age-old problem for the Gullah people on the sea-islands off the coast of South Carolina. After the Civil War ended and all the plantations were abandoned, the former slaves stayed and kept working the land. Eventually, they were given the rights and ownership of what they worked. As long as the Gullah stayed out on the islands nobody seemed to care. They became self-sufficient. They bartered amongst themselves for what they needed and left the islands only when necessary. The rules they lived by came from the culture they brought with them from West Africa and the Bible they adopted. There were no bridges and no paved roads. Fishing, hunting, and local gardens sustained them. When one generation died off the children took over. Some of the children stayed on while others moved north in search of more opportunities. Land transfers were never recorded. There were no wills, trusts, or deeds.

Summers were hot and the mosquitoes and no-see-ums vicious. Nobody wanted the land but the people who lived on it. The White population moved inland away from the coast and set up their farms and plantations and summer houses. A string of fishing villages cropped up along the Georgia and Carolina coast. Canneries processing shrimp, oysters, and crab dotted the land and provided work for more of the Gullah population. Then came air-conditioning, and tourism and seaside resorts. All those sea islands with their sandy beaches, deep water coves and inlets became a developer's dream come true.

The problem—who owned all that land and could they prove it? The land grab was underway.

Over the years the problem came and went like the tide. When the economy was good, the courts were filled with land ownership challenges and when things got bad, nobody cared.

Ester Averille lived on the Morgan River, which was an estuary that weaved in and around a whole series of islands off the coast called the Pirate Islands. Her island had a causeway to it that the US government built during the Second World War. Other islands received the same treatment as there was fear of German U-boats using them as safe harbors, just as the pirates of the eighteenth century did. The Pirate Islands were well named. Thirty

years ago a local business group acquired some of the
island waterfronts, established a small resort, and named
it Blackbeard's Treasure. After some years of success it
fell on hard times and went into bankruptcy during the
recession of the early 1990s. Coastal Rivers County
records of the last few years would reveal that someone
had become interested in the Pirate Islands once again.

EIGHT

Hattie had been working at Sidney's dining room for over two hours when Tillie came back with the news about Ester Averille and the tax sale. Her concentration broken, she gave a big smile to Mickey, when the black Lab came into the room carrying her lead in her mouth and went over to Tillie with an obvious quest for a walk. Hattie said, "I think Mickey's got the right idea. Okay if I come along?"

Tillie turned, looked at Mickey, and couldn't resist a laugh. "Yeah, let's go," she said to Hattie, "Think we all need a break."

"Sidney, want to come along?" Hattie tossed the question knowing full well he would refuse. Once engaged in something he rarely interrupted his focus, which is why Mickey made her request to Tillie.

"No, no. I need to call Ray Morton. He needs to know about this tax sale problem right away."

"That's fine. We're only going around the block anyway."

As the three females in Sidney's life got themselves together for a walk, Sidney decided to call Ray from the landline in his office—for him, cell phones were still only for emergencies. He pushed his chair back from the table, grabbed his now ever-present cane and walked from the dining room to his office in the front of the house.

Settled in with his leg in a comfortable position, Sidney sat at his desk and stared blankly across the room.

Faced with two completely different tasks, which should be his first priority, pursue finding Burke Mansfield or solving Ester Averille's housing difficulties? As the Burke Mansfield hunt would normally be first on his list, since it involved an area of primary personal interest for him, Tillie's and Ester Averille's problem dealt with people, which made it more important than finding a book—regardless of its literary or monetary value. Sidney Lake had a very simple approach to life in that people and all living things take precedence over non-living ones. Regardless of what the Supreme Court had decided about corporations having the same rights as people. He knew the danger of that decision for the future and that it was wrong. He believed the living always came first. Tillie and Ester would be his first priority.

Sidney called Ray Morton and explained what happened at the tax sale.

"Aw shit, Sidney, not again. I thought we had all this stuff under control."

"What do you mean?"

"Leaving the poor people alone. Right around when the Great Recession was sneaking up on us, the developers promised to go easy on tax sales of old people on the islands. Corporations and house flippers were fair game. A lot of them are sleaze bags anyway, but leave the little old ladies, and the poor people alone. Was there a recognizable name on the bid?"

"No, just a lot of letters followed by LLC."

"Okay, let me check into it. I'll find out who it is. I must admit the reverse mortgage is a new wrinkle. Haven't run into that before. It's got a ring to it that might be beneficial, but I can't see it working for Ester. Can't see any bank willing to make a loan that small."

Ray remembered the lengths to which some

developers would go to get their hands on island beach front property. They would track down out-of-state long-lost relatives of the current residents of the property. Show how through inheritance law they still owned a percentage of the land. The current residents who believed they owned the property would then be approached by a developer who claimed to have enough signatures representing fifty-one percent of ownership to permit them to go to court and grab it away if they didn't agree to sell. A number of law firms in and around the Lowcountry now specialized in helping—pro bono—people fighting the land grab.

Ray said, "I'm going to have a chat with the county solicitor and see if I can get him to take a look at this. Tell Tillie and Ester to hold on. This isn't over yet no matter what the tax people say."

Over the years, Hattie and Tillie had become good friends. Yes, she was her housekeeper but their relationship expanded well beyond employer and employee. While Sidney was ten years her junior and Hattie twenty, Tillie looked upon Sidney as an older sister might a younger brother in need of care. With a twenty-year age gap, she thought of Hattie as a niece. The three of them had developed a family-like bond. Tillie, now closing in on her mid-seventies, had eased off on the number of her housekeeping customers and just kept the old relationships—with a heavy focus on people who worked at Morgan College.

Mickey didn't need a leash, but Tillie always attached it. Rules were rules and Tillie lived by the standard of if you expect others to obey the law, you have to do the same. If the laws need to be changed, then you worked to change them. You didn't go around them and you didn't break them just because no one will see you do it. Tillie knew God saw it all. Well, she would temper her view by claiming it didn't have to be God as, God's got a lot of territory to cover, but she believed His agents were everywhere. All those billions and billions of angels all over the universe. She believed they knew what you were doing and tried to help. But if you tried to beat the system and didn't listen to them, they would eventually get even. The day would come when you wanted something and they would make sure you received it but it would come with a lot of unexpected consequences.

Hattie had a different point of view. While honesty and truthfulness were comparable to Tillie's approach to the world, she had serious problems with laws that were unjust or established to control the population for the political benefit of the lawmakers. Raised a Roman Catholic and educated by nuns and priests from grade school through college, she began to see a great divide between blind faith and reason, where the former often trumped the latter and the bible could be deceptively used to justify the most heinous of acts.

Although divorced, Hattie still saw herself as a Catholic, only no longer a Roman one. The Episcopal Church became her new religious home. Her husband went through the same schooling as Hattie did but came away with a different view. They met when she was in graduate school working toward her master's while he attended the neighboring law school. Once married, they headed for Washington, D.C. where he took a position with a law firm that specialized in lobbying for the financial industry, while she went on to obtain her doctorate in English Literature.

Hattie and her husband grew apart as he became more and more involved with promoting financial deregulation while she could see the evils that the deregulation would bring to the average family. She focused on people. He focused on profit and the legitimizing of deceptive practices. The marriage lasted eight years.

Harriet Ryan never remarried. She believed in the marriage bond and of swearing something before God. Her husband could always find an argument to get around whatever rules stood in front of him.

The two women were comfortable in their own skins. They knew who they were. They both believed in the Golden Rule of "...do unto others..." a rule that existed long before it ever appeared in the bible. The first rule of a civilized society. They enjoyed each other's company. If there was one departure place for them, it expressed itself in Tillie being the realist and Hattie the idealist.

Now, when Tillie would come to clean for Hattie it played out as a social gathering. They would talk about family and friends. Problems with children, relatives, and grandchildren were always a topic and, naturally, Sidney Lake.

"How much pain do you think he's in?" Tillie asked, as she stopped at the corner and let Mickey sniff at a lamp post.

"A lot. He won't admit it. That knee is in bad shape."

"I hear the doctors want to do another operation. That would make three."

Mickey moved on around the corner pulling Tillie with her as she headed for a nearby tree. They both followed.

"He won't talk about it." Hattie slipped her arm into Tillie's as they strolled along the sidewalk. "Stubborn."

"Yeah, that's him all right. Got that bulldog in him. Mostly it's a good thing but could hurt him this time."

Hattie stopped. "Do you think there might be some

way we could work on him together?"

Mickey tried to keep going but Tillie stopped her and looked at Hattie. "You mean like sneaky. We collude—sure do hate that word—an get him to do sompthin' he don't wanna do?"

If Hattie had glasses on she'd be looking over them at this point. "Tillie, I don't think God Almighty could get Sidney Lake to do something he didn't want to do."

"Hah, you got that right."

Hattie already had her left arm hooked into Tillie's right, now she reached over with her right and tapped Tillie on her arm, and started them walking again. "No, Tillie, what we're going to do is get Sidney to think getting his knee fixed is a good idea after all."

"Yeah, that's what I said...sneaky stuff. Sounds like you been taken lessons from that ex-husband of yours."

Hattie stopped, looked at Tillie, and began to laugh. She gave her friend a light shove and they started walking again.

Tillie began to giggle and Mickey wagged her tail enthusiastically. If they had been fifty years younger they would have skipped the rest of the way down the street.

Having successfully put Ray Morton back on the trail of the people trying to defraud Ester Averille of her home, Sidney's concentration again drifted to how to find Burke Mansfield the elusive rare book dealer. Searching for someone online in the twenty-first century can be an easy task to complete, if you have the skills to do it. Sidney certainly didn't have them and Hattie, while computer literate by most standards, couldn't compete with most teenagers when it came to the internet. Literary research? Yes. But weaving in and out to find the whereabouts of anyone other than Keats, Shelley, and

Byron, well, her skills were just not up to the task. Put Sidney in a university library and he could find just about anything, plus he had lots of experts on hand to help him find any link possible to complete his search. He trusted what he found in libraries, as the information could easily be cross-checked and verified, not like the suspect information found on-line. Although online, with public and private libraries now being linked to the internet, their digitized card catalogs were becoming vulnerable to hacking and general mischief.

One of the reasons the missing first edition of *The Tenant of Wildfell Hall* so interested Sidney had to do with the research he had done on Thomas J. Wise. Literary forgery seemed to be rampant in the late nineteenth and early twentieth centuries. Wise wasn't alone in selling bogus material to collectors, but he stood out because of his standing in the academic world of the time. He carried a résumé that included the presidency of The Shelley Society and The Brontë Society as well as a long list of memberships in similar organizations. He had also published a variety of books related to the Victorian era and earlier literary figures.

As a noted bibliographer, Wise sought out and recorded everything that an author wrote as well as everything anyone wrote about the author. He carefully cataloged the information with every bit of documentation he could uncover. Scholars doing research on Shelley, Browning, the Lake Poets or the Brontë sisters routinely used a bibliography produced by T. J. Wise or someone with similar literary standing to research, verify, and analyze the works of the author under study. Bibliographies created by respected scholars were in great demand and Wise made the conscious decision to take advantage of the trust he had earned to enhance his own pocketbook.

In performing the research they had completed in the search for Burke Mansfield, Sidney and Hattie discovered a whole new world they were not aware of—the theft by noted scholars and museum and library directors of rare books and manuscripts. It wasn't just master thieves like Stephen Carrie Blumberg, there was Anders Burius, the former head of the National Library of Sweden's manuscript department, who stole more than fifty books from his own department. In 2012 the famous Girolamini Library in Naples, Italy confirmed that its director, Marino Massimo de Caro had "misappropriated" 1,500 rare books and was arrested along with four accomplices. Most recently, in 2018, the Carnegie Library in Pittsburg reported 314 rare books, folios, maps, and other items missing from the rare materials room. The list of items included at least ten books printed before 1500.

What made Wise of interest to Sidney was not only the theft of literary material such as letters and unpublished writings of famous literary figures, but also the actual creation of literary material attributable to them. He occasionally listed a poem or letter in one of his bibliographies of an author and then created the document himself and sold it to a collector with the bibliography being the validation of the document.

At the time that Wise was believed to be producing his forgeries, the forensic capabilities of today's investigators did not exist. As a result, questionable material is still out there in private collections and unscrupulous dealers and private parties are still passing them off as originals. The holders, for tax and other reasons, kept their special literary treasures hidden away and exhibited them only on rare occasions to massage their own egos.

Sidney believed that Anne Brontë's novel could be a

legitimate first edition but her own notations about it—in the margins—could have been forged to enhance its value. The reason it was being kept under wraps would be that someone knew it to be a forgery and didn't want it exposed.

From the beginning, Sidney suspected there could be something unsavory about the provenance of the unknown edition of *The Tenant of Wildfell Hall*. When it was stolen from Lawrence Brewster, the general had no idea he had it. Had no idea of its potential value. The other question Sidney explored at the time dealt with whether the general's uncle, from whom the book was inherited, knew about the book and its significance. And then there appeared the unanswered questions about the lawyer who administered the estate. What did he know about the book and its history?

Sidney gave his head a shake and spoke out loud to himself, "Got to stay focused on one thing at a time. Keep it straight. Ester Averille first, the book second." He picked up the phone on his desk and called Tillie to tell her what Ray had said. It turned out that while Ray and he were engrossed in conversation on the phone from Sidney's office in the front of the house, Tillie and Hattie had come back into Sidney's kitchen and Tillie had put the kettle on for tea.

When Tillie saw that Sidney was calling her from his office she gave a laugh and whispered aside to Hattie, "He's callin' me from the front room."

Hattie went to make a comment and Tillie waved her off as she answered the call. "Professor Lake? That you?"

"Why, yes."

"Oh, good. Thought maybe somebody stole your phone. We're in the kitchen."

"Who's kitchen?"

"Yours."

"Mine?"

"Yessir. Just down the hall. Want us to come over?"

Hattie suppressed a laugh.

Sidney stammered. "Oh...I'm sorry. Didn't hear you come in."

"That's okay. We'll be right there."

Tillie ended the call and said to Hattie, "Not the first time he's done that. Usin' the landline. Been trying to get him to use his cell phone more."

"Well I think he should. Ever since he and Mickey almost got themselves killed by that madman and he used it to call nine-one-one, it's supposed to be by his side."

"Yeah, well, I suppose you're right. Just that sometimes he's using that gimpy leg of his to stay put an have folks come to him."

Hattie laughed, "Ha! I don't think there's anything new about that."

Once reaching the office, Tillie went in first and said, "Professor can I get you some tea? Me and Miss Hattie was just gonna have some."

"Oh, yes, that would be fine."

As she turned to go back to the kitchen she stopped and said over her shoulder, "Oh, by the way, you know that fella we been lookin for, Burke sompthin' or other, there's a note about him in the *Island Packet*. Just spotted it when I was at the tax sale. Was readin' the paper while we waited."

"Burke Mansfield?" Sidney and Hattie asked in unison.

"Yeah, that's him. Said he just joined that Sackville-Bedford outfit."

"The big auction place?" Sidney said.

"Yeah, that's the one."

NINE

Ray Morton may have retired from the Morgan Police Department, but he never left policing. He defined himself by his chosen career. Ray didn't have or need a hobby. His work was his hobby. After forty years of wearing a uniform—first, a dark brown one for the US Marine Corps, then the light brown one of the Coastal Rivers County Sheriff's Office, and finally a dark suit for the Morgan City Police Department—the idea of lounging around in a golf shirt and shorts never occurred to him. In fact, nothing other than police work ever occurred to him. Marie, his wife of thirty years gave up her attempts to re-direct his focus. She came to grips with the simple fact she married a policaholic and developed her own world as a grade-school teacher.

Ray entered the Marine Corp straight from high school and became a Gunnery Sargent in his seventh year. He received his BA from the St. Leo University's facility on the naval base in North Charleston, South Carolina, and met Marie at a social event at the Marine Corps Air Station in Beaufort, South Carolina. They've been at each other's side ever since. Policing came into his life when he received a temporary assignment with the Naval Criminal Investigative Service in Quantico, Virginia, and later spent part of his career as an Intelligence Specialist.

When on vacation with Ray, Marie learned how to orchestrate their time so she and Ray would both enjoy themselves. For Marie it was art galleries and museums.

For Ray it was local police departments. He never went anywhere without stopping into the local police headquarters and introducing himself. He exchanged cards with detectives, police chiefs, and county sheriffs. Ray and Marie were often invited to local events at the homes of law enforcement officers during their vacations. Marie kept track and made sure that for each such event, Ray would accompany her to a local gallery reception or special museum exhibit. On one recent cruise to the Caribbean, Ray spent his time with the captain reviewing security measures of the cruise line in general and the ship in particular. Compensation for Marie were the dinners at the Captain's Table and special on-board events.

It worked.

Ray established an LLC for himself but never used it as a vehicle for pursuing consulting assignments. However, he did use it when people came looking to him for professional advice or expertise. Solicitors and local law enforcement in South Carolina often looked to him to testify about police work and procedures and, at times, asked him to do some work for them on the side. He occasionally taught a course at the local community college on police procedures, which included the sometimes politically charged but required interaction among various law enforcement entities such as the FBI, ATF, and DEA. Members of Interpol as well as the Justice Department, Homeland Security, the US Marshalls Service, and Secret Service also had business cards in his Rolodex.

He had connections everywhere and he knew how to use them.

When Sidney asked Ray to find out the full story of how Ester Averille lost her home at the tax sale, he knew exactly where to find the information he needed.

It took one simple phone call to the county solicitor to start the process. Within a half hour he received the answer he knew he would get.

"Ray, the tax people have put a hold on the sale. I explained your complaint on behalf of Miss Averille. I'm not happy about what happened. Damn, I thought we had this stuff under control."

"Me too."

"The tax office is just downstairs, I want to check on the purchaser. Name didn't ring a bell, but those developers change LLCs the way Imelda Marcos used to change shoes." He paused. "Did I just say that? Ray, I'm getting' old...like you."

"Hey, I didn't say it. I know what you meant, but I didn't say it." Ray did his best, unsuccessfully, to stifle a laugh.

The solicitor joined in the laughter. "Okay, smart ass. Tell you what you're gonna do. You're commin' over here right now an' we're gonna sit ourselves down with the video of that tax sale an' see how many of these people we can identify. Figure out who they're workin for."

"You got a deal. Be right over."

∾ᴔ∾

Tillie's casual mentioning of seeing Burke Mansfield's name in the *Island Packet* generated an immediate need to find a copy of the newspaper. Neither Sidney nor Hattie subscribed to it and the website wouldn't let them search earlier editions without a subscription. Hattie agreed to go over to the Morgan Regional Library on Courthouse Street where copies of local newspapers were maintained.

While Hattie headed for the library, Sidney received a call from Ray relaying the information about the sale of Ester's home being halted. He also learned that the solicitor's office would be investigating a possible fraud action against the people who promised Ester access to a reverse mortgage.

"Does that mean that Mrs. Averille is in the clear?" Sidney waived to Tillie to come to the phone. He put it on speaker.

"Not entirely. There's still a tax lien on the property. Have Tillie get it paid. Hell, I'll give her the money if she needs it."

"Thanks, Ray, but I believe Tillie and her friends have that under control. The money to pay the tax was raised right in the room during the bidding, but the tax people wouldn't take it once the public bidding began. Against regulations. Tillie's still holding the funds."

"Good. Tell her to get over to the tax office right away."

"She's here now. I'll send her right out."

Tillie turned and went to the utility closet under the hall stairs where she kept her purse. "I heard you. I'm goin'."

With the call ended and Tillie off on her errand, the house was empty, except for Mickey. Sidney sat behind his desk and began to sort out some of what just happened. The situation with Ester Averille and her house seemed to be under control, but it raised a lot of questions. Was someone making a run at the Pirate Islands for development purposes? Had other residents of the islands lost control of their land in ways other than the tax sale route? After the first attempt at resort development failed, the county designated the land as being too low and environmentally sensitive for commercial development, but never put any restrictions on it. The erosion on the north side of the islands had been encroaching rapidly and many old buildings along the shore had already been lost to the ongoing battering of both summer and winter storms. The islands had recently been proposed as a candidate for "National Monument" status, as a way of preserving their historic place in the Lowcountry Existing landowners would be grandfathered but new development would be prohibited without obtaining official exemption status. Sidney Lake mulled all of this over. A natural skeptic when it came to the motivations of the small business-dominated state legislature, he knew there had to be something going on behind the scenes. Could Ester Averille's land be a key to something else? It didn't seem to be very large, but it did sit on a high spot and if combined with neighboring properties might be very valuable.

Sidney sat back in his chair, looked up at the ceiling, and rocked. "Hmmmmm...yes, this might be a great project for me...and Ray too." He then looked at Mickey sleeping quietly next to his desk. "Ray and I don't have a lot on our plates at the moment. There is the Brontë book of course, but I can manage that with Hattie. Tillie and Ray between them know everything about the islands. You and I can manage both projects, can't we, Mickey?"

The professor became almost cheerful, as he realized he could have two projects to keep him going for the summer: the Pirate Islands and the mystery of the Brontë novel. He envisioned endless amounts of time being spent on both. Sidney looked down at Mickey who continued to doze by the desk, unimpressed. "I think this is going to be a very good summer, Mickey. Yes, a very good summer."

Tillie, Hattie, and Ray had the same thought independently of one another. *He's doing it again. He's sitting at home and here I am running around town doing errands for him.* However, none of them thought it was a bad thing. They were all doing exactly what they loved: Tillie helping a neighbor in need, Ray rummaging around the legal system, and Hattie pursuing a literary mystery. What could be a better activity for sleepy hot summer afternoons in the Lowcountry of South Carolina?

Ray joined the solicitor and the tax department official involved in the tax sale, as they peered at a large monitor affixed to the far wall of the conference room. The room was rectangular with six chairs on each side of a large wooden table, which had seen better days. Scratches and stains were clearly visible giving evidence to its having been used actively over the years. It was an heirloom piece from the old county offices that were demolished to make way for the new city hall and county complex. It functioned as the primary meeting venue for tax disputes, with the tax administrators lined up on one side and corporate lawyers—and sometimes individual taxpayers—on the other.

The solicitor introduced the tax official to Ray. They exchanged cards and Ray now had a new contact to add to his Rolodex. Papers were spread about on the table and the three men focused their attention on the large monitor that displayed the video of the recent tax sale.

The papers contained a listing of all the properties that had been up for sale. They totaled 157. The amounts due ranged from $50,000 down to $425 and most of the owners of the properties were LLCs. Individuals made up no more than fifteen percent and many of the names were

listed more than once. There were twenty-eight properties
with delinquent taxes in the $500 range, similar to Ester
Averille's.

Bidders for the properties were mostly attorneys
representing LLCs, who were there to purchase properties
owned by other LLCs. A number of attorneys represented
multiple companies.

"Wait. That one there. The tall fellow. The one who
just took the two properties on King Street. He's also one
of the people who bid on the Averille place," the tax
official pointed out.

"You don't seem to know him like you do some of the
others. Is he new to the auction?"

"Yes. He also bought a few of the LLC-owned
properties. A couple of them had LLCs with the word
'Pirate' in them." He picked up another piece of paper
from the table. "The Averille place and the three Pirate
properties were purchased for Jude LLC. The other
bidder for the Averille place and a property on King
Street were bid on by King Development LLC. That's
Casey Yarborough. He's local. Always looking for a
bargain. He dropped out of the Averille property once
there was another bidder."

"He's a sneaky one," said Ray. "He knows he agreed
not to bid on places like Averille's. But since someone
else bid before he did, he figured all bets were off and he
might be able to slip one in on everybody. Hate guys like
that. Nothin' we can do though."

Ray and the solicitor quietly continued looking at the
video and then Ray said, "Would you say that the
attorney bidding for Jude, LLC could be working for two
separate clients or one?"

"Wait a minute," the solicitor interrupted and put his
hand on Ray's arm. "He just nodded at someone off to his

left. Run it back a bit."

The images moved backward on the monitor. "Hold it right there." The solicitor got up from his chair and moved toward the monitor. The three men stared at the images in front of them. "Do you know this man?"

The taxman and Ray looked carefully at the person the solicitor pointed out.

The tax official spoke first, "I have no idea who he is. Don't think I've ever seen him before. It's not unusual for the attorney's client to be in the room and remain anonymous."

Ray kept looking. "You're right. There's something familiar about him. I just can't place him, but I know I've seen that face before."

"Gruber!" A voice shouted out.

Ray turned to look at the solicitor. "Gruber? Gruber?"

"Lucien Gruber. What in the world is he doing in Morgan and why a tax sale?"

ᘒᘒᘒ

Hattie Ryan completed her assignment at the library and made it back to Sidney's within a half hour. Located only two and a half blocks from Howard Street, she didn't bother to take her car as she knew she would spend more time looking for a parking space than it would take to walk the distance to The Morgan City Library.

The original building stood as a link to another era. It had its beginning as a private residence dating back to the late 1700s built partly of tabby and wood. Over the years it went through a variety of renovations, expansions, and restructurings. Like the City of Morgan, it survived the Civil War intact as much of the area came under Union control at the beginning of the war. Unlike many of the small towns and villages that were destroyed, including their historical and municipal records, Morgan City Library served as a major resource of local maps and records used by Union forces in their march into the heart of South Carolina.

The library became a part of Morgan College when the school was originally founded on the property of a small, abandoned plantation in the late 1870s. When the college expanded and added a new library building on the edge of the growing town, the original building reverted to private hands. After spending time as a small hotel, the Morgan Ladies Society and the Historical Society joined forces to make it into a library once more. In the 1950s and the beginning of desegregation, the library asserted its non-governmental status and became a private subscription library and closed access to all but White members. The 1960s saw the first cracks in library segregation practices and with newly available federal funds and grants it became part of Morgan City and expanded to three times its original size. Another complete expansion occurred when the new combined City-County complex was created on the location of the old original college campus site next to it. All barriers to access were now down and it became the home of the Coastal Rivers Regional Library Authority filled with every modern research capability and a renowned South Carolina Historical Documents Department. Although Morgan College had its own well-equipped library, the Morgan City Library became the primary resource location for local scholars focusing on South Carolina and Lowcountry history, as well as lawyers trying to trace historical documents related to land ownership.

"I found it," said Hattie as she came into Sidney's office. "Made a copy of the ad and announcement." She handed it to Sidney.

"Excellent. Now let's see what we have." He looked at the paper in front of him. "Oh, I see. He's not in Savannah anymore. *Savannah Antiques and Auction* was disbanded after the building was sold. Burke Mansfield is now on Skidaway Island working for *Sackville-Bedford and Company (Auctioneers)*. Apparently they're expanding into rare books and manuscripts, and Mansfield is heading up the new venture. *Sackville-Bedford* seems to have a rather large operation on the island."

"Well that's where all the money is," observed Tillie who stood in the doorway. "Between Skidaway and that Sea Island, Georgia place, that's kinda what you'd call the Georgia gold coast along there."

"Yes," Hattie agreed. "If you're looking for people with deep pockets to buy rare old books and expensive antiques, that's where you'll find them."

TEN

Sidney Lake's division of labor hummed along nicely. Ray, with his knowledge of the ins and outs of the city and county, focused on finding out who was behind the land acquisitions on the Pirate Islands. Tillie navigated the gossip and rumors swirling around people who had been approached to sell their properties, as well as those who had accepted a firm option from a buyer but were supposed to keep quiet about it. Sidney felt comfortable that they were on the right track, so he turned his full attention to the missing copy of *The Tenant of Wildfell Hall*.

The first attempt to contact Burke Mansfield failed. He was out of town on an appraisal assignment in Macon, Georgia. However, the office manager at Sackville-Bedford set up a tentative appointment for the following day. "I'll leave a message for Burke. He should be back from Macon later this evening. He does have an appointment scheduled for the morning, but his afternoon looks clear. I'll text him your interest in the Brontë book and the information you provided. I'm sure he'll contact you as soon as he can. He's very good that way. I know how excited he was about the book at the time."

Sidney thanked her, ended the call, and turned to Hattie. "Hope you don't mind my committing us to be on Skidaway Island tomorrow afternoon?"

"Oh, certainly not." Hattie smiled. "It's a nice drive. We can leave here around eleven, stop in Savannah, where you can take me to lunch at my favorite Irish Pub on Bull Street before heading off on the wonderful marsh-view drive on the causeway to Skidaway."

Sidney remained silent as he leaned back in his chair and looked at her over his glasses. He knew he couldn't intimidate her, but that didn't stop him from trying.

Hattie turned the tables on him before he could respond. "You know, Sidney, if you would consider obtaining a second opinion, or maybe even a third, on that right knee of yours, you wouldn't need someone to drive you everywhere." She held up her palm to him to stop him from interrupting. "Now, I don't mind doing it. Actually I'm as intrigued as you are with the Brontë book and I'm looking forward to meeting Burke Mansfield, but if I had been out of town, this opportunity might have escaped you."

Sidney leaned forward, unconsciously moving the injured leg to a more comfortable position. "I'm aware of that. However, for the time being, I would appreciate keeping the issue of my leg out of the conversation."

"Just a thought," Hattie said as she looked past him at the bookcase. This was Sidney's research station. He surrounded his desk area with reference material including two sets of encyclopedias, probably the only two sets together in a private home in the state of South Carolina. Behind his chair his desktop computer sat on a credenza. Covered with a plastic enclosure, it would only be used as a support tool in his research and not as a primary one. His place for quiet reading—and napping— was the library at the back of the house. No television and no computer. However, the kitchen resided in the next room where he did some of his best analytical thinking while cooking. If it looked as though he had gained weight it would be because he was having difficulty solving a problem.

"I appreciate your concern. And, yes, lunch is included." He smiled. "But not dinner. Not in Georgia anyway. I suppose we could get something in that diner in Bluffton on the way back. Depending on the time." He paused and gave her a serious look. "I'm dying to meet with Burke Mansfield and find out what he has to say."

"So am I."

The following morning Tillie did not have any housekeeping assignments, so she began calling all her contacts that did housekeeping on the Pirate Islands. Over the years she had a few customers there but replaced them with people downtown or on one of the closer-in islands. She sat at her kitchen table with her cell phone in hand and paper and pencil at the ready.

"Both of um?"

That made four sales so far. Although they weren't really sales. They were contracts to make a sale. At least that's what the lawyer claimed.

"An' you think there's more bein' offered big money? But only if they keep quiet."

Keeping quiet meant you didn't tell anyone. It didn't mean preventing your housekeeper from overhearing your conversation.

"An' they's all White people?...Yeah, I got it...No, don't worry...If you know who the real estate people are I can find out the rest...Really?"

There were no real estate people involved. They were attorneys acting on behalf of the buyers. Tillie's plan had been to find out who the real estate companies were so she could ask some of the cleaning people she knew to keep their ears open. Housekeepers, cleaning people, they were invisible as a rule. No one paid any attention to them, but they heard and saw everything. This was going to be harder to decipher than Tillie thought.

Within the local Gullah population, there were rumors about the same offers-to-buy having been made, but nothing could be pinned down. Also, some residents had heard from relatives living out of state that some lawyer had come by offering money for signatures. In total, Tillie came up with ten people being approached about selling their homes or land. It was all being handled the same way: attorneys acting on behalf of an unnamed buyer. A contract to make a contract, no real estate people involved.

By eleven o'clock, she had covered as much as she could and called Ray Morton. "That's the best I could do this mornin.' Gotta go to work now. I still got some folks who gonna call me back. Got everythin' writtin' down an' I'll drop it off at Professor Lake's this afternoon. Oh…that's right. The professor and Miss Hattie are in Georgia this afternoon. How 'bout I stop by and give it to Miss Marie for you, since you not gonna be home all afternoon?"

"Perfect Tillie. This is great stuff. By the way, did you take care of Ester Averille's taxes?"

"Yeah, we got all that done yesterday afternoon. Tax lady said we could do it 'cause the tax sale been stopped. Yeah, we got that taken care of. Oh, an' Miss Ester said that before the lawyer fella offered the mortgage thing another lawyer offered the same kinda deal the people I talked to this mornin' got. The deal to make a deal."

"Ah, very interesting." Ray paused for a moment and then spoke as though he was thinking out loud. "So there were at least two lawyers working the buyouts. Hmmmm. Yeah, Tillie, we really have something going on here. I'll give Marie a call and tell her you'll stop by later on."

The most enjoyable way to drive from Morgan to Savannah was to take the coastal route through Beaufort and Bluffton, but that's not the way Sidney and Hattie went. Hattie driving, they went down I-95. The stretch between the Beaufort turn-off and the one to Savannah earned the nickname 'Blood Alley' for all the deadly accidents along the route. While not the preferred way for local residents to get around, it was the fastest when going lengthy distances

Since injuring his leg last year, Sidney had not been able to drive. Had it been his left leg he could have managed, but not his right. Hattie's being forced to drive him to meet with Burke Mansfield continued to provide opportunities to work on Sidney about seeing another doctor about surgery. "It's not that I mind doing the driving, Sidney, you know I don't. I want to meet Mansfield as much as you do. It's just that I enjoyed our trips together more when we could share duties. I also have to admit I hate this road. The idea of driving it twice in one day rattles me. It's white knuckle driving all the way."

"I understand, I really do."

Two pick-up trucks zipped by in the fast lane almost bumper to bumper.

Hattie's car caught the wind they created and she gripped the steering wheel as tightly as possible. "My God! How fast were they going?"

"Look's like you're at seventy-five so they have to be in the eight-five range. Just stay in the right lane here and do your best. We only have another twenty miles or so to go to reach the Savannah turn-off."

Hattie eased off her speed and got it down to a comfortable seventy—five miles per hour below the speed limit. They rode along quietly for a few minutes and Hattie relaxed her grip on the steering wheel. "You sure I can't convince you to have that leg looked at again?" Traffic or no traffic Hattie had planned to bring up the subject. She had a captive audience. It was too good an opportunity to pass up.

Sidney looked straight ahead and said in a monotone, "No. And I don't want to discuss it. Especially on this road. Look, we'll stop in Savannah as we planned and have a nice lunch at that pub you like. It's a short drive from there to Skidaway. On our return trip, we'll go the back way across the Savannah River and Hutchinson Island, and then through Bluffton. We'll have dinner at the café on the May River. How will that do?"

Hattie gave a quick look toward Sidney and smiled. As she was about to speak an eighteen-wheeler came zipping by in the adjacent lane. Their car was pushed partially out of its lane and the right wheels hit the rumble strips. Her head snapped back to the front and her elbows locked in place to control the car. Sidney pressed against the back of the seat and grabbed the armrest.

The truck moved on while Hattie put her foot on the brake and struggled to get the car under control. She continued to slow and guided the car onto the shoulder. The left wheels growled as they went over the rumble strips and Hattie pulled the car to a stop.

"Oh, my God, that was scary."

"I'll say." Sidney released his grip on the armrest. "Are you all right?"

"Yes. My heart's going four hundred miles an hour though. My goodness. I'd give anything for a train that went from Charleston to Beaufort to Bluffton to Savannah. I'd never drive this road again." She got her breathing under control. Took a deep breath and let it out slowly.

"I agree. You know I think there used to be one." Sidney wanted to calm her so he kept talking. He was good at that, pick a subject and he could go on forever no matter what the topic. "There are still tracks and railroad beds all around. Trains used to go right into Port Royal. Used to be able to go from Charleston to Columbia by train. Didn't need a car for everything. The railroads brought the country together. Town by town. The superhighways have now isolated a lot of what the railroads joined."

Hattie listened to his voice. It droned on. It always did. She took another breath. She knew what he was doing. The iron exterior, soft to the touch. She first saw it when he cared for his dying wife, Cynthia. Hattie, calmer, turned back to Sidney.

"...and I'll bet that would make a good research paper. Corporations wouldn't like it though. They're way too political these days. They used to stay out of politics, now they drive the political conversation."

Hattie decided they'd better move on. She felt better and wanted to get their focus back on track. "Do you think Burke Mansfield knows about Thomas Wise?"

Sidney smiled and gave Hattie's hand a pat. It was still on the steering wheel, although now relaxed. "Oh, certainly." He straightened up in his seat. "Every rare book dealer worth his salt knows Wise. There are so many forgeries out there, they have to suspect everything they touch. And it's not just the forgeries, it's all the stolen books that are available. The thing with books is there are so many of them. They're also small and easy to hide on a bookshelf."

Hattie took another deep breath, checked the view with her mirrors, and started moving slowly, waiting for a break in the traffic so she could move into the right lane.

The rumble strips complained again as she moved over them and gunned the engine to get up to speed. Keeping her eyes on the road she asked another question that kept to the topic. "You know, I've always wondered about General Brewster's uncle. Where the Anne Brontë novel came from. It wasn't given any special mention by him in his records, just a routine listing in his inventory. And what about that lawyer of his? Spring... something or other."

"Springwood. Yes. Always thought there was something unusual going on there. He left town right after the Reed investigation concluded. I don't believe anyone pursued the matter. Just like Chief Hornig not putting the theft of the novel into the FBI database. Claimed they couldn't prove it had value as it had never been authenticated and appraised. No pictures of it—until now. The *National Arts and Crafts Show* took care of that. I'll bet it is on every rare book dealers' radar. That's why it's so important to talk with Mansfield. I'll bet he's done some personal research on it." Sidney stopped and thought for a moment.

Hattie noticed the silence and was tempted to give him a look but didn't. She kept her eyes glued to the road as a bright red Ford SUV blew past her.

Sidney began to speak again, "This thing with Springwood—his full name was Howard Springwood— it's very curious. I think I need to give him a call. I don't think anyone has asked him about the book. Its origins. I wonder if he knows how and from whom Brewster's uncle obtained it."

Lunch in Savannah was just what they both needed. A relaxing meal of very tasty food. Sidney couldn't resist the bangers and mashed potatoes and promised to make it at home once they got back to Morgan. Hattie devoured the fish and chips. The conversation centered on the food and the place. It gave them the respite they needed after the tension of driving I-95. They relished the relaxed setting of the pub but also the holiday atmosphere of Savanah. Charleston and Savannah were the two jewels of the southeast coast. Even if you lived in the region, you had the feeling of being someplace else, of being on vacation, of knowing you were in a special place.

The meeting with Burke Mansfield came off even better than Sidney anticipated. Here was a kindred soul. A man who not only loved books but also cherished their historical significance. His enthusiasm and sense of wonder came through as he told them about his first seeing Anne Brontë's *The Tenant of Wildfell Hall.*

"He came up to my table station and I asked how I could help him. Holding up a brown paper bag he replied, 'Got some old books here. Picked 'um up at an outdoor market a few weeks back. Hopin' y'all might tell me they's worth somethin.' He took the three volumes out of the bag. Given how he identified them, I anticipated he had three separate books for me to look at. But I noticed as he dumped them on the table in front of me, the bindings matched. Ah, a three-volume set I said to myself. Early Victorian possibly. I picked up the volume marked ONE, read the title, looked at the binding again. I must tell you my heart was already thumping. I then quickly opened it to the title page and almost passed out."

As Burke spoke he became animated reliving the experience. He and Sidney were of similar height although Burke's slimmer waistline made him look taller. He wore a three-piece suit and shirt and tie, which also seemed to add to his height. Wire-rimmed glasses and brown shoes, polished to a fine shine, completed his costume. If Hollywood put out a call for character actors to play the part of a rare book dealer for a 1930s classic movie, Burke Mansfield would be a prime contender for the job.

When describing the volumes, he kept positioning his hands to form a rectangle to show the size of each one and then the three as a unit. He moved his head up and down as he spoke with enthusiasm. First, he looked at the image created by his hands and then at Sidney. Hattie also received a look before he went back to imagining the volumes he wished he still held.

"Professor Lake, I must tell you, I was beside myself. I've seen many rare books in my day, but that three-volume first edition of *The Tenant of Wildfell Hall*—in its original binding no less—well…it took my breath away."

"Please call me Sidney."

Hattie did a double-take with Sidney's offer. She could not remember the last time she heard him make such a comment. It seemed almost out of character, as unpredictable as he could be. Familiarity? Sidney Lake? The words just didn't go together when describing him. It always took a long time for him to warm up to someone. There were many who would like to claim him for a friend but he would rarely lower the drawbridge for them.

"Well thank you, Professor…or Sidney. Yes. And please call me Burke. It's not often that one finds a seeker of rare books for other than pure collecting purposes. Do you know how I can tell?"

"I think I have an idea. The double copy? One to collect and one to study,"

Burke had a big smile on his face. "Exactly. Oh, that is quite remarkable. Do you know I have been in the homes of many avid collectors, who were proud to show me their collections, but had never studied the books they displayed? They just liked being surrounded by them. In many cases they touted their value as the only reason for acquiring them."

"Yes, yes. I'm only too familiar with such people. They do have their place though. Without them a great many literary treasures might be lost. Consider the very fact of the Anne Brontë book we are currently pursuing. Someone has had it tucked away someplace for a very long time. Are you certain the volumes were originals?"

"Oh, quite so," replied Burke as he leaned forward in his chair. "One of the first things I did when I saw the three volumes was to carefully inspect them and make as many notes as possible. I also took some pictures. Next, I called the JP Morgan Library in New York where there is one of the best collections of original Brontë material in America. The following day I contacted the Brontë Library in Haworth. They were all amazed that an original first edition existed. They confirmed that everything about the volumes was correct but would need to see them and have them tested before any verification could be made."

Hattie sat there fascinated. She was speechless. A condition that didn't affect her very often. Sidney Lake and Burke Mansfield acted as though they'd known one another all their lives. She didn't know Mansfield so she had no idea if his reaction to Sidney was common for him, the way he would react to any educated book lover. But she did know Sidney. Sidney the skeptic, who never trusted anyone or anything. He even questioned his own judgement. Getting close to him and having him trust you, well, her experience had told her many visits, encounters and meeting would be a requirement.

As Sidney had received answers to most of his questions concerning Burke Mansfield's book verification efforts, it became his turn and he explained how he had come in contact with what appeared to be the same novel. He emphasized the word *appeared* as, while they both held a first edition of the novel in their hands, they could not be sure it was the same one. Burke knew nothing of the note to Ellen Nussey and was astounded when he heard the story.

"Burke, this fellow who had the book, he claimed to have purchased it from someone at an outdoor market near Walterboro, South Carolina. Were you able to learn who the seller was?"

"I did try, Sidney, but he said he didn't know—or at least didn't remember. Although, he said he did see a white van parked behind where the man's tables were set up. He also had a double booth with two white canopies and a great deal of merchandise to sell. Oh," Burke stopped. He raised his right hand with the index finger extended and shook it in Sidney's direction. "I just remembered something else. The young man said that the van had a magnetic sign stuck to the passenger side door but didn't remember what it said."

Hattie decided to remind them she was in the room. "The non-descript white van could be a rental used to transport antiques from a local store. There are lots of antique stores and gift shops in and around Walterboro. I would think that if he had a sign he also has a business of some sort that is incorporated in some way. Wouldn't be surprised to find out he was buying as well as selling."

Sidney turned to her and said, "Yes, you're right. It reinforces my feeling we should go to that location." Turning to Burke he asked, "I imagine I would be correct in assuming you do not have the address of the young man?"

"That is correct..."

Hattie interrupted, "Yes, but the local TV station would. I believe most people attending the *National Arts and Crafts Show* need to have a ticket to get into the venue and those are mailed to the people attending."

Burke had his finger up in the air again, but this time aimed at Hattie, "Something else I just remembered. I'm sure he said something about 'getting back home smoking and telling everyone.' I don't know if that means anything. He also asked if I was interested in buying the books from him. I declined. I'm sure you know the *Crafts Show* prohibits that."

"Yes." Sidney sat quietly for a moment. Leaned back in his chair and looked at the ceiling. He focused on a small section where the chandelier attached to an iron ring over the table where they sat. "I wonder?"

Hattie broke the silence, "Sounds like some regrouping is in order. Burke?" She decided since he and Sidney were on a first name basis she assumed the same applied to her. "Have you made any effort to pursue the book yourself?"

"Only in pursuit of validating what I had seen. I did check with the Antiquarian Book Association in New York to see if they had a record in their database. I am a member. And I exchanged a number of emails with *The Brontë Society*, but I didn't pursue the young man. This was my first appearance on the show and I'd love to do it again. Quite frankly, it was responsible for the Sackville group asking me to join them. I didn't want to jeopardize that."

"I understand," said Hattie.

Sidney came alive and almost shouted, "Smoaks."

"Smoke?" Hattie looked at him strangely.

"No, S M O A K S. It's a town in South Carolina. He lives in or near Smoaks. That's why he was at the market near Walterboro. It's not that far away. Now I know where we're going to, Walterboro."

Burke was now excited and looked from Sidney to Hattie. "Oh, my. I would love to join forces with you both." He paused. "As long as you take the lead. I don't think the *Crafts Show* people would object to my tagging along for the purpose of adding my expertise to yours."

"Hmmmm," Sidney rubbed his chin. "I think that would be a big help, as long as it won't get you into trouble."

With a tentative agreement in place, the three of them began to explore possible provenance routes for the three volumes beginning with the initial transfer from Anne Brontë to Ellen Nussey.

ELEVEN

O nce the LLC form of corporate structure became available, every industry took a long look at its possibilities and the lawyers for real estate developers and builders adopted it "wholeheartedly." There were LLCs that owned LLCs, which, in turn, owned or invested in other LLCs. Trying to find out who owned what was almost impossible for the average person, and it wasn't any easier for state and federal tax authorities. The LLC being a state incorporation vehicle, came under the jurisdiction of the local Secretary of State, Corporations Commission, State Commerce Commission, or other business agencies of the state government. There was no such thing as "one-stop shopping" or investigation when it came to corporate ownership. The rules were made by the state legislatures, which in most states is composed of small business owners and lawyers, both of which were often involved with the real estate industry in some way. Keeping all of this in mind, Ray knew where to start his search about the people and LLCs involved in the tax sale: the usual suspects—real estate related companies.

His first break came with the list developed by Tillie. She managed to get copies of business cards and phone numbers left behind with some of the people she talked with, as well as numbers left on answering machines. Not one of them indicated a relationship with a local realtor or developer. The next break in narrowing down his search came from a contact in the Secretary of State's office who told him that two of the LLCs he asked about had partial ownership by a third out-of-state LLC, which also had partial ownership of four other LLCs in the state. The master LLC had its primary offices in Virginia just outside of Washington, D.C.

Ray called the company just before nine, turned up his small-town friendly southern accent, and had a nice chat with the receptionist. It turned out to be a law office specializing in lobbying for the agricultural sector and also included some hedge funds as customers. While on the phone with Ray, the receptionist was interrupted by someone who came to her desk. Rather than put him on hold, she merely held on to her handset and laid it down in front of her. He could hear her side of the conversation but only bits and pieces of what the other person was saying. "Good Morning, Ms. Zutter...Yes everyone's here but Mr. Rostov. He called earlier to say he missed the Acela, but would be on the express behind it."

"(Garbled)...start later?"

"Yes, Messers Lynch, Pazzini, and Cortez said you should meet with them there."

"Okay...(garbled)...Thank you."

She turned her attention back to Ray. "I'm sorry, Mr. Morton."

"No, no. It's fine. Ah didn't mean ta interrupt ya this mornin.' It's jus that my aunt passed away a week ago an your phone number was in her things. Poor old woman. Lived alone. Didn't have much contact with the resta the family. Ahm jus' tryin to piece together her finances. Ah think ah mighta got the number wrong. You a law firm or somethin'? Don't think my aunt would be one of your customers. You in Washington aren't ya? Yeah, ahm pretty sure ahm in the wrong place. 'Preciate y'all talking to me though."

The story of the deceased aunt was one Ray often used when talking with receptionists as a way of getting them to open up to him about the company that employed them. It usually worked but in this case, it was not what she told him outright but what he heard her say to someone else and especially the names Zutter, Lynch, Pazzini, Cortez, and Rostov.

Within seconds of getting off the phone, Ray had an internet search in progress for the name Zutter, in connection with anything having to do with real estate. Zutter Industrial Alliance, LLC jumped out at him. The company, among other things, dabbled in resort properties in Florida, The Bahamas, and the Dominican Republic.

Next he went after Rostov. Assuming a New York base, since he missed the Amtrak Acela high-speed train from New York to Washington, he combed the corporate Wall Street listings. The only Rostov he could find was Rostov Partners, LLC. He didn't see a connection to the real estate industry but had a feeling it would show up someplace.

Knowing that Sidney had been on Skidaway Island the previous day researching the Brontë book, Ray left him a message to meet him for lunch at the City Hall Café. There was no point in trying to do anything sooner, as Sidney would be early to bed after the drive and Ray knew mornings were Sidney's "Do Not Disturb" under any circumstances time of day. That's when the professor put the pieces to all his puzzles together. He rarely answered the phone or went out after breakfast except for a walk with Mickey.

So Ray kept digging. He never stopped investigating. Never stopped learning. The only change in his daily routine since he retired was the replacement of police headquarters with his daily visits to city hall and the county courthouse. However, since police headquarters was now part of the overall Coastal Rivers County/Morgan City Government Center, he usually stopped in to pass the time of day with Chief Hornig.

Ray waited until ten am to call the county solicitor's office only to find the solicitor had left for Columbia for a meeting with the Attorney General of South Carolina. The solicitor had anticipated Ray's call and left instructions with his secretary to speak with Georgia Sawyer, a prosecutor Ray had worked with in the past and had a good relationship.

Ray leaned back in his chair as he chatted with Georgia. "So, did the boss tell you what we've been up to?"

Georgia moved some papers around on her desk. "Yeah, he dumped it all on me. Don't mind though. Even if he was still here, we'd be havin' this conversation. You know the boss well enough. He'll jump back in if he thinks it'll help him in Columbia."

Ray laughed, "I'm not surprised. He likes the high-profile blood and guts stuff. Always did. Eyes tended to gloss over when a paper-heavy corporate case showed up. But you like that stuff, don't you?"

"That's why he gave it to me. Actually, I volunteered. When I heard about the tax sale and Mrs. Averille, I couldn't resist."

"Come up with anything?"

"Yes I did, but have a few more things to check on this morning."

"Me too," Ray paused. "I'm meeting with Sidney Lake at the Café for lunch at noon to go over what I've found, can you join us?"

Georgia took a quick look at her calendar. "Long as I can get out of there by no later than one-fifteen. Have a meeting back here at one-thirty."

"Don't see a problem. Should work out fine. I have a bunch of calls to make and I should have more info for us by noon."

ↄﬣↄ

Ray showed up first and secured a table in a back corner. The City Hall Café had lots of back corners. The Café played to the government center crowd and served as their cafeteria and off-site conference room. They were all there—the mayor, council members, city and county administrators, police, fire, and EMS. Table hopping, laughter, and serious talk was everywhere. The café staff kept certain inside tables available by encouraging tourists to use the umbrella tables on the rear patio.

Sidney came limping in a few minutes after Ray. They were both early. Sidney pulled the chair out to sit at the rear of the table, his usual place of late, as he could protect his leg from getting in the way of the waitress. Sidney greeted him with, "You must have come in from a different direction. Didn't see you on the way over."

Ray got up and shifted the table slightly to accommodate Sidney. "Was over at the library for the last hour or so. Research."

Sidney sat down. "Ah, research, my favorite word. Oh, I told Tillie to join us. Talked with her this morning and she found out some interesting bits of information after she dropped off the other names with you yesterday."

"That'll make four. Georgia Sawyer's also joining us."

"She's that prosecutor that handles the non-violent

crimes, isn't she? Read about her. Like to meet her."

"Well here's your chance," Ray said seeing Georgia come in the back door and speak with a waitress who pointed her toward their table.

As Georgia approached, Sidney made an effort to get up from his chair to greet her. "Oh, don't do that. I heard about your leg. Please. I assume you're Professor Lake?" She held out her hand, which Sidney took while smiling appreciatively at her and giving her a slight bow of his head.

"A gentleman to a fault," said Ray.

Sidney looked up and saw Tillie come in the front door. "Looks like we're all here."

Sidney and his little group of information seekers were not the only such group having lunch this day. Table hopping, moving from one spot to the next, switching groups went on all around them. Most of the tables had four or five people engaged in active conversation. Men with open briefcases and others with open file folders took notes. He spotted one or two women but they were a distinct minority. It was not just the City Hall crowd, but local business people as well. Tourists were not catered to in this part of the room. There were no specials that offered catchy-sounding names or sandwiches named for pirates. Groups of women diners tended to avoid the café. It was not their sort of place. For the most part, they could be found at the Rose and Thorn two blocks away. It was clean, nicely decorated, and served healthy food. Sidney preferred it to the City Hall Café most of the time, except for breakfast. Breakfast was for greasy bacon, sausage, eggs, shrimp with grits, and gravy and biscuits. Healthy food could be had for the rest of the day. But for breakfast, well, breakfast was sacred.

The conversation began with Georgia introducing

herself to Sidney and Tillie. "I feel like I've met you both before, I've heard so much about you. Ray everyone knows." She pointed to him as she spoke. "I think Ray's more visible around City Hall since he retired than when he worked there. And Professor Lake, you seem to be acquiring the same reputation. Tillie," who sat next to her, came next. "I know Tillie by reputation." Georgia turned and spoke directly to her, "I'm delighted to finally meet you."

The general conversation continued for another few minutes. Once the waitress took their orders they got down to the topic at hand.

Ray began, "This whole business of the tax sale has opened a can of worms. We've run into this in the past, but it was always a local attempt to acquire property. By that I mean a local builder trying to fill some gaps in a development plan for a cheap price. Trying to get waterfront access for a marina or expand a clubhouse, add some tennis courts and that sort of thing. That's probably why Casey Yarbrough got involved in the bidding. Once the door was opened he just jumped in. This time, though, what I'm finding is out-of-state people actively involved."

Georgia agreed, "Yeah, Casey's always on the lookout for a bargain. Our search has come to the same conclusion you did. There seems to be a strong push to get control of the Pirate Islands. Normally this would be done quietly over a longer period of time. It's unusual for them to be so overt in their efforts."

"I think I know why." Sidney looked over his glasses as he spoke directly to Georgia. "Under the previous administration in Washington, D.C., the Department of the Interior had a number of meetings with groups in the Lowcountry Tillie, didn't you attend a few of them in

Beaufort and Edisto?"

Tillie spoke up. "Yeah, been almost three years ago now. They was talkin' about turning the Pirate Islands into a national park or monument or sompthin'. I think they decided on monument but I'm not sure what the difference is. We heard about it and was worried about what would happen to the people that been livin' there all their lives—like Miss Ester. Understand all the paperwork was done an they was set to make the announcement. All we wanted to do is make sure they was protected. But it didn't happen. Got held up. Some other stuff got done an we is still waitin.'"

"Right," said Sidney. "But the new people at the Interior Department are more likely to eliminate National Monument designations than add to them so the Pirate Island designation is on hold. When they began the process, they stopped all new development and it's been that way for the past three years. However, it's becoming clear that longevity is not going to be a hallmark of the current people and philosophy at interior and, with only a few years left until the next election, I believe the proposal to make the Pirate Islands a national monument will be thrown out sometime soon. I also believe someone is banking on that happening and is hedging their bets by trying to put a big piece of land together with development in progress before the next election."

"And get grandfathered by having started whatever they're going to build." Georgia shook her head in agreement as she spoke. "Yeah, I've seen a lot of that. Town council people and state representatives get a little too cozy with local builders who then find out about proposed rules and regulations they can use to their advantage. The average citizen doesn't realize what's going on. Wouldn't know what to do about it if they did."

Lunch started to arrive. No one paid much attention to it except for a few 'thank-yous and acknowledging smiles. The server knew they were engaged in business talk and worked at getting the food to the right places and being as invisible as possible.

Tillie spoke as she shifted her chair so the server could get around her. "Happened over on Deer Island a few years back. Built a bunch of houses that was bein' bought up by people from the north. That builder musta brought five hundred trucks of dirt into that swamp. Got the roads and sewers put in just before the state said the area was to become a protected wetlands. Developer sold out to a house builder and built the houses because they was grandfathered."

"Yeah, that's the way it works." Georgia tapped Tillie's wrist. "Bet the Gullah community never built there because they knew what the land was really like."

"You're right. Place flooded every time it rained. Still does. Always will. God made it that way. Lot a people think they's smarter than God and can make the land do what they want. God usually wins."

Sidney smiled.

Ray laughed, "You have that right."

Georgia continued. "They're a pretty slick bunch those developers and builders. The big ones rarely get caught with their pants down. They hedge everything. Before the first load of fill shows up, they've already secured options from home builders. They work out density and environmental plans. Hedge those against different designs. Homebuilders do the same. Set up a master plan for land they don't own. Only acquire it from a developer when they open a new section. Never buy in a development where the builder promises to build the clubhouse, pool, tennis court, and extras later on. Always get them upfront."

Ray took a bite of his bacon cheeseburger while Georgia spoke, then raised a question. "You just mentioned the word 'hedge' and I did earlier as well. I came across the name of a 'hedge fund' in the list of LLCs I researched. Have you come up with anything like that?"

"Now that you mentioned it," said Georgia, "I did trace a name back to a Wall Street firm."

"Wouldn't have the name 'Rostov' attached to it would it?"

Georgia, about to finish off a part of her BLT stopped in mid-air and put it down. "Rostov, yeah, that's the name. The Wall Street one. In fact, I remember a note the Solicitor wrote alongside the list when he looked at it. I didn't get a chance to ask him about it before he left for Columbia. It just said 'Rostov' with a question mark after it."

"Rostov?" said a startled Tillie. "That's a name I was gonna mention. Got a call this mornin' from one of the people I couldn't reach yesterday. They said they remembered sompthin' one of the lawyers said when she objected to the offer he made. He said, 'Gruber and Rostov ain't goin' to be happy.' Said she remembered 'cause she never heard the names before."

While the two women and Ray talked, Sidney sat quietly, ate his sandwich, and sipped at his cup of tea. He remained interested in the tax-sale resolution and that Ester Averille had her home back, but he regarded it as a problem solved. If Ray and Georgia Sawyer wanted to take the matter further that would be up to them. He could not see a need for his continued involvement. Sidney wanted to focus on the information they uncovered yesterday on Skidaway Island so he just barged ahead and interrupted the flow of the conversation asking Ray, "Do you remember the lawyer I asked you about the other day, the one who was involved with General Brewster's uncle? You know, the one we spoke with about the books the general inherited? I believe he was also the one who generated the computer inventory list."

Although taken by surprise with Sidney's moving to a new subject, Ray, knowing how the professor's mind worked, understood that chasing after a missing book would be more important to him than a real estate transaction. "Eh, yes. That was a few years ago. What brings that up again?"

"As you know, Hattie and I were on Skidaway Island yesterday speaking with the appraiser of the Brontë book and thought it would be useful to speak with him in an effort to begin to establish a *provenance* for it. The lawyer, Mr. Springwood, may have been the one responsible for acquiring it for Brewster's uncle and could tell us where and how he came across it. I..."

Georgia Sawyer's eyes popped. She put down her fork, which she had been using to clean up some of the loose ends from her sandwich, "Did you say 'Springwood?' 'Howard Springwood?'"

"Why yes. Do you know him?" Sidney answered.

She put down her fork. Everyone looked at her. "I've never met him but the name was with some of the material the solicitor left me. The Attorney General's office in Charlotte is looking for information on him."

"Has he done something?"

"Not lately. He's just been found murdered."

TWELVE

Walterboro had always been a quiet, sleepy place but that all changed with the arrival of the interstate highway system in South Carolina. The Walterboro exit on I-95 became known for its gas stations and fast-food restaurants. The road through town once served as part of the main route to Florida. No more. Once the interstate opened, all the travelers and traffic disappeared. The local cafés and restaurants closed and then, with the expanding suburbs of Charleston—which became closer with the new high-speed roads—suburban shopping malls took all the business from the shops on Main Street.

After many years of being ignored, Walterboro found a way to reinvent itself. Originally settled in 1783 by the Walter family as a safe and healthy location away from the coast, where malaria and other diseases were common among the plantations there, it became a favorite location for the building of classic southern mansions and became known as the front porch of the Lowcountry. It now championed the world of collectors with the establishment of The South Carolina Artisans Center, the official folk art and craft center of South Carolina. Many of the original shops on Main Street converted to antique stores, gift shops, and art galleries. Billboards filled I-95 announcing all the bargains that could be found in undiscovered Walterboro. They catered to tourists passing through to points south as well as serious collectors looking for a bargain. Now there were auction houses and art shows for entertainment, shopping opportunities for all wallet sizes and hidden treasures to be searched for by amateur and professional collectors alike. Walterboro had reinvented itself as a destination, and home to large art and craft fairs held on Saturdays just outside of town

Sidney Lake and Tillie James had been here many times before, although Sidney's focus had always been the used bookstores and some shops on East Washington Street while Tillie liked the hustle and bustle of the craft fair. Many people from the Lowcountry frequented the fair on Saturdays to both buy and sell. Some had tents and tables displaying wares of their own as well as serving as an outlet for friends and neighbors. Tillie liked the noise, the laughter and the good-natured bargaining that permeated the large, crowded field. She also knew it was a good idea to get your business done early and get home, as the fair sometimes had a dark side, as such places did. Late in the afternoon the drinking and the good-naturedness often turned ugly. Arguments lost their jousting and playfulness and turned to shouting and shoving. The police presence increased around three in the afternoon and Sidney's plan had them on their way home by then.

Tillie did the driving but they went in Sidney's car. It needed a good run now and then as Sidney couldn't drive it with his bad right knee. He asked Tillie to take it out at least once a week. The plan was for Tillie to drop Sidney off in town and then for her to head for the big field next to high school and the craft fair's parking lot. Sidney would make his way around downtown going from antique store to bookstore to ask about old books. They would keep in touch by cell phone and Tillie made sure he had his turned on before she left.

"I know how to turn it on," he said sounding like a seven-year-old telling a parent to stop treating him like a child.

"What gets me is you had it turned off in the first place. Why'd you do that?"

"We didn't need it on yet. Why waste power unnecessarily?"

Tillie gave him an exasperated look. "Okay. But you make sure it stays on. Maybe we'll find sompthin and maybe we won't, but we need to talk if we do."

"Yes, Tillie," said a duly chastised Sidney, as he opened the passenger door of the car.

Tillie had put his cane in the back seat. She reached back for it and then made her way around the car to his side with the cane in her hand, before he managed to swing his legs around to the side. She handed it to him and helped him up. "It's about ten-thirty. How bout I come back right before noon and pick you up. Have some lunch at the food tents and wagons at the fair. It's better and cheaper than whatchew gonna find around here." She waved her hand toward the string of shops along the sidewalk.

"Yes, I think that's a good idea. I don't doubt you'll have more luck out there than I'll have here anyway."

When they parted, Tillie kept an eye on Sidney as he limped along the sidewalk toward his target bookstore. Sitting behind the wheel of the car, she spoke out loud to herself as she watched him. "Man, we got to talk you into seein that doctor. You startin to look like an old man an you ain't. Tillie, you an Miss Hattie gotta get a plan together."

Inside the bookstore, Sidney wasted no time getting to the point and raised the question about the book.

"Yes," the bookseller said, "I did see that show the other night. Sure wish I had those three volumes. Would have known what they were right away."

"That's the mystery of it all. I would have thought any serious collector would have known."

The door chime sounded as they spoke and both men turned to see who came in. Sidney recognized him right away. Burke Mansfield.

"Why Burke, I thought you couldn't make it." Sidney limped toward his newfound friend. A broad unedited smile on his face.

"Sidney, I...knew this would be your first stop." Burke extended his hand as he closed the gap between them taking the hand in his. "I just couldn't let this opportunity pass. I tried to call you on your cell phone but couldn't reach you."

"Oh, yes, well. I must admit I didn't have it turned on." And then lowering his voice, "I'm glad Tillie didn't hear that. I'll introduce the two of you later and would appreciate you not mentioning that point."

"Certainly. I'm looking forward to meeting her. I've heard so much about Miss Tillie. Is Mrs. Ryan here as swell?"

"No, she's occupied at her church this morning." They walked toward where the bookseller stood watching them.

"Ah, too bad. A very nice lady, Mrs. Ryan. Very learned. It's not very easy to find such people these days." Coming up to the bookseller he said. "And you are the owner? Mr. Boyle?"

"Yes.'

They shook hands

"I'm Burke Mansfield of Sackville-Bedford."

"Oh, yes. We've had some dealings with your firm.

Rare books isn't it?"

"Yes, as well as other rare objects, I've just joined them. Today, Professor Lake and I are here on the same mission." Turning to Sidney he asked, "Have you told him about the book?"

"Yes. We just started to discuss it. He has seen the show."

The bookseller then exclaimed, "Wait. You're the book expert from the show. I thought you looked familiar when you came in. But I thought you might have been in the shop before and then when you mentioned Sackville-Bedford I thought that was the reason you seemed familiar. But no, it was the television where I saw you."

"Yes, I was delighted to have participated."

Sidney decided to get down to business. "So tell us, Mr. Boyle, have you ever seen that young man from the show before? I understand he's from nearby."

Burke added, "We found out that the ticket to the show he had was stolen from its legitimate owners. The name he gave was a fictitious one. Although his first name may have been real."

The bookseller thought for a moment. "Thinking back to the show, at the time I thought I recognized him but the name you called him, Danny, wasn't it?

"Yes, that's the name he gave me."

"Well, it didn't fit. I'm sure he goes by the name of Larry. I don't know the last name but I'm sure the local police do."

Sidney was taken aback. "The police?"

"Yes, Larry's one of the local boys who's been mixed up with the gang problem we've had around the area."

"Gang problem? In Walterboro? That's hard to believe. I would never have thought of such a thing. Gangs are supposed to be a big city problem."

"Yes, I know. They're not local. For some reason, they've decided to make Walterboro their battleground area. They've been coming here to settle their disputes. The local chamber of commerce has been trying to keep it low profile—all the tourists and such—but...it's becoming quite scary."

"I should say so," offered Burke.

Sidney continued, "Do you believe Larry's story about buying *The Tenant of Wildfell Hall* at the fair down the road?"

"Not for a moment. I'm sure he stole it. More than likely he was trying to sell the volumes rather than buy them."

"Have you ever mentioned this to the Police?" Burke asked.

"No. Why would I? It's just a thought on my part. Nothing's been reported stolen. I don't know that much about him other than seeing him hanging around near the shop. I would just shoo him and his friends away, as I would any of the other boys. I think your best bet would be the police. Ask them about Larry. Yeah, I think that's your best bet in finding out more about him."

Sidney and Burke continued their discussion with the bookseller for a short while, but realizing he could not offer them anything else, they left. Outside on the sidewalk, they decided to make one more stop before heading for the craft fair to have lunch with Tillie. However, before moving on, Sidney called her about Burke's arrival and let her know Burke would drive him over so she wouldn't have to come and get him. He also let her know their focus had changed and rather than looking for someone Larry bought the books from they were now looking for someone he tried to sell them to. Tillie, had already figured that out and even discovered his name was Larry and belonged to a White-only group called the Heritage Rangers. The one event that hadn't changed was their meeting place: lunch at the food tent aisle.

As they headed for the next antique store, Burke suggested he and Sidney visit the local police to inquire about Larry, but Sidney rejected the idea. Recognizing how defensive and closed mouth Morgan's Police Chief Hornig had become with him, he assumed the police chief of Walterboro would be no different. Nobody liked amateurs, especially ones from out of town. He told Burke he was welcome to try but also suggested a better plan: have Ray Morton make whatever inquiries might be needed. Ray had the connections and was a known factor to them and could learn a lot more than they ever would.

At the next shop, Sidney and Burke were unable to learn anything new. They did get confirmation of what the first bookseller said with regard to the gang problem. Sidney dropped the Heritage Rangers name but received no reaction other than the owner saying he didn't care what they called themselves, he just wanted them away from his store.

Forty-five minutes later Sidney and Burke were at the craft fair looking for directions to the food aisle. The scene looked like pure bedlam. The only sense of order came from the requirement that all tents and canopies had to be white and sit behind the white lines painted in the dirt to define the aisle grid. They eventually saw signs that pointed to where the first-aid station and sheriff's tent were located. A little farther on there was a sign for the portable toilet center and just above it an arrow pointing to where the food trucks could be found.

They pushed on. People were everywhere. Every aisle was packed. Children running. Parents yelling after them to slow down and be careful. People were buying and selling everything imaginable. The dealer selling lampshades was next to the one selling comic books, who was next to the knife collector, who was across from the vinyl record dealer, who backed up on a tent filled with Christmas village items. There were old newspapers and magazines for sale, teacups, China, furniture and Halloween costumes. One table caught Sidney's eye as they specialized in wood carving and had a large collection of hand-crafted walking sticks and canes. He even stopped to try out a few given the table was on the route to the food tents and trucks.

At the food court, Tillie had secured a small picnic table for them and quickly finished off a conversation with a man and woman as the two men approached. Sidney glanced at the receding pair and made a point to ask about them if Tillie didn't offer the information.

While Tillie listened to Sidney make the introductions, she took a hard look at Burke Mansfield. Hattie had told her about the similarities and she observed they both wore jackets and ties in the summer heat, the glasses were the same—loose enough on the bridge of the nose so they could be looked over—and they both spoke in long sentences. However, Mansfield was taller and thinner and probably younger. He also had a bit more hair.

"That was Andy Cottonwood and Miss Ellie his wife. They got a table down the aisle over there. Said that Larry fella wasn't tellin the truth. They don't let no van's an stuff around the tables after openin' time. Worry about him an' his family. Rowdy bunch. Cause trouble sometimes. Said they also seen him in Morgan. Does odd jobs and runs errands for someone on the islands. Don't know who though. Said it might be Crow Island. They's a close-knit bunch a rich White folks out there. Don't use a lot of local people when they need sompthin. Haven't figured them out too much yet. Lot of the places out there are new an' the people come from up-state and North Carolina. Bring their own help with them."

Sidney eased himself onto a white plastic armchair and asked, "So he wasn't here on a book buying expedition?"

"Bet against that. Appears to be the type never read a book much less ever spend money to buy one. No, I think—after talkin to people here—he just used the craft fair as a cover story. Speakin' of covers..." Tillie looked toward the darkening western sky. "I think we gonna need some soon. If we gonna have some food, better grab it now. What can I get you, Professor? How about you too, Mr. Mansfield?"

Sidney answered. "I see the local Rotary Club has a food truck. Good fundraiser for them. Do you know what they have?"

"Kinda thought you'd spot that. Mostly hot dogs an' stuff only they ain't hot dogs. They got good stuff. Johnsonville brats. Put 'um on a big bun with some of that good mustard an' fixins."

"I'll take two," said Sidney. "And a cold Vienna lager if they have it."

"I'll do the same...only make it one brat, not two. And it's on me." Burke gave her a twenty-dollar bill he had at the ready. "And if you'll excuse me, I have to make a side trip here." He pointed to the arrow directing the needy to the portable toilet aisle.

"Go right ahead," said Sidney.

"They's two rows, if I remember right," Tillie looked in the same direction Burke did. "Take the ones in the second row in the back. Better. Don't get used as much."

"Why thank you, Tillie," Burke smiled and gave a quick laugh. Tillie giggled.

All their assignments in place, Burke following nature's call as Tillie made her way across the open aisle to the food truck and Sidney sat at the table, which had a large market umbrella.

Burke Mansfield followed a familiar path. He had walked the aisles at the craft fair in Walterboro many times. Everything had its place along the well-traveled grid. Over the years he had been to every outdoor antiques and craft fair in the triangle of Charleston, Columbia, and Savannah. While the new wealthy built their grand air-conditioned homes on the waterfront, the old, stately mansions of the nineteenth and twentieth centuries fell on hard times. They were inland. The old grand main street became the decaying center of a town where the railroad no longer provided service and the new highways were built elsewhere. Estate sales gutted the old houses and the leftovers showed in the local shops and at the craft fair. Burke knew that the deemed worthless often contained a treasure or two.

As he reached the portable toilet center, he didn't hesitate in heading for the back row. He smiled as he thought of Tillie giving him guidance as to where he should "do his business." She was right, of course, but he too had learned the procedure.

His choice of toilet was the second one from the end of the back row. A six-foot wooden fence formed the border between the craft fair and an adjacent field running perpendicular to the row of toilets. It made a left turn behind the final row. They did not sit up against the fence Instead, a space of four feet was left so they could be maneuvered for cleaning after the event.

Burke carefully opened the door but before he had a

chance to close and lock it behind him, he heard a shout.

"You little shit. What did you do with them?"

A frightened second voice said, "Nuthin.' I ain't got 'um. Lucy, don't hurt me."

"Don't give me that bull shit. You stole them from the island house. I know you did."

There was a loud noise as something slammed against the back of the toilet and shook it violently.

The second voice cried out, "Lucy, Don't hurt me. Don't hurt me."

Burke, inside the chamber, lost his footing and fell against the sidewall.

"Then tell me. Now! Or you'll never tell anyone anything again."

The toilet shook as the owner of the second voice was slammed against the back of the toilet again. Fighting back he yelled, "Don't do it, Lucy! Don't do it! I put 'um back! I put 'um back!"

"You lying son of a bitch."

As Burke tried to get to his feet he heard the second voice cry out again followed by two popping noises.

Burke called out, "What's happening out there? Who's there?"

Burke heard no more, as a bullet came through the back wall of the thin metal booth and into his shoulder, followed by a second one that hit him in the abdomen. He stumbled back against the partially open door and fell out of the portable toilet onto his back.

Two men coming down the aisle saw him fall and ran toward him. Seeing the growing blood stains on Burke's shirt and jacket one of the men yelled, "Shooter! Shooter!" and ran in a panic out of the aisle continuing to yell.

All pandemonium broke loose. The yell was repeated

and carried like a wave across the entire tented area. Everyone ran. Tables were turned over. Tents and canopies knocked every which way and trampled down. Parents grabbed children. Men and women hid behind overturned tables. Craft fair treasures went flying. Grills were turned over in the food aisle starting fires.

The paramedics in the EMS first-aid tent at the entrance put out a call for help. Security staff tried to see where the shooter was. The county sheriff had a tent nearby and also made calls while two of the deputies determined the area the panicked crowd was heading away from and ran in that direction.

Sidney Lake dropped to his knees and crawled under the table where he had been sitting. He knew running was not an option.

Tillie had just made it to the front of the line at the food truck when the panic started. Someone in the line behind her yelled, "Take cover." And gave her a push to the side and forward. He told her to get down behind the truck. More and more people were trying to do the same thing. She looked over her shoulder before falling down. She couldn't see Sidney. He wasn't at the table.

As the crowd of frightened people eased and the first of the sheriff's deputies went past her, she got to her feet and started toward where she last saw Sidney. She felt a hand on her shoulder and jumped.

"Best stay down for a little bit, ma'am," said the paramedic from the first-aid tent, who was following in the path of the deputy sheriffs. "You don't want to make yourself a target. Let the deputies clear things out a bit. It'll be okay."

She looked at the black hand holding her down and turned her head up to see the face of the young man who encouraged her to stay in place. "I got to get to the professor. I know he's hurt."

"We'll go together. Doan worry. How you doin'?" he said seeing a fresh scratch on the back of her hand.

Tillie knelt down again. "Oh, I'm okay." She pointed across the way where Sidney's table laid upside down with its legs pointing straight up in the air, another victim of the panic. "He was right over there."

As they remained in their position, voices could be heard all around, but now they were the controlled commands of law enforcement rather than the excited panicked yells and screams of the attendees of the fair.

"Just hang on ma'am. Sounds like they're getting everything under control. They're calling for me now. You stay put a little longer. I gotta get up there. More people commin' up behind me. Wait a few more minutes. I'll go past where your professor friend is supposed to be." He got up. "Now you stay put."

Tillie did as she was told and watched the young man move through the debris that now littered the open area between the food trucks and the dining tables. A gust of wind caught the smoke from the burning trucks twenty yards away and covered the area. Her view of the paramedic now obscured, she stood up.

As another gust of wind caught the smoke and lifted it up, she saw the paramedic by Sidney's table. He raised his hand and yelled, "Looks like he's okay. Told him to stay down." He turned and headed for the portable toilet area.

There was an eerie quiet hanging over the entire food service aisle as Tillie finally made her way to Sidney. She decided to move when she felt the first few drops of rain. The storm clouds were off to the southwest and moving quickly. A gust of wind tossed debris into the air and a dust devil danced around the open area where the dining tables and umbrellas had been. People were beginning to move about. As the sky darkened, the lights from the police and emergency vehicles became pronounced. The momentary quiet disappeared into thunder, flashes of lightning, calls for help, and a wave of police moving toward the toilet area. Panicked shouts were replaced by sobs and the cries of relief as family members found one another.

Sidney was unconscious when Tillie found him under the overturned table. She straddled Sidney's legs and saw that the right one was at a strange angle. Grabbing hold of the table, she lifted it off Sidney as though it was made of light plastic instead of heavy wood. Tillie looked down at Sidney and dropped to her knees and then carefully sat down beside him. She snuggled closer, took his hand, and then looked at the side of his head. Shifting again she got his head off the ground and gently put it in her lap. Sidney had a large cut on his head. His shirt and jacket were covered with blood. Tillie had tears in her eyes as she said, "Don't you die on me, Sidney. Don't you die on me. Helps commin'. We gonna be all right." A paramedic saw her caressing Sidney and rushed over. Tillie continued to hold Sidney's hand as the young man got to his knees and checked Sidney's vital signs.

"Nasty cut ma'am. We'll take care of him. How're you doin'?" He waived to another paramedic as he spoke.

"I'm okay. It's the professor I'm worried about." She rubbed Sidney's hand as she spoke. "He kinda got run over by the crowd. Not sure what hit him in the head. Musta been the table. Has a bad leg and can't move too good. Don't know where his cane is."

The second paramedic was on the radio now calling for help as it started to rain in earnest.

"There was another man with us. Don't know what

happened to him. He was at the toilets."

"It's okay ma'am, we'll take care of it from here."

෧෨෧

Ray heard the breaking news report come in over the radio in his car, while Hattie heard the sirens and saw the emergency vehicles and police cars that rushed to serve as backup. She immediately called Ray. They talked for a while. He relayed some of the information he'd learned, but went silent and looked to the northwest when the news reporter mentioned there was an active shooter at the craft fair. He saw the darkening storm clouds. He told Hattie to go home. He would go to Morgan police headquarters and learn all he could.

Two hours passed before they began to find out what had happened. The news reports were everywhere. The information changed over and over. The first report said there were an unknown number of shooters and then settled on a single shooter who was unidentified. Another hour passed as hospital reports came in. One young man dead from gunshot wounds and an older man in critical condition from similar wounds.

The storm eased and the speculation started. It didn't look like a random shooting. A reporter suggested it might have been a dispute between the older man and the younger one. No weapon had been found. The shooter could still be on the loose. An older man may have the key to what happened but no one had been able to speak with him. The county sheriff continued as the police official in charge and kept the lock-down order in place as they assumed the shooter was still in the area.

Hattie went to police headquarters and found Ray sitting at an unassigned desk in a large open room with the Chief's office and his secretary at the far end. He had left instructions at the entry desk to let her in and she found him talking quietly on the phone while he made notes on a large yellow pad. He waved her to a chair alongside the desk.

As soon as Hattie sat down, Ray ended his call and asked, "Hattie, has Sidney called?"

"No. But that may not mean anything. You know how he is. Never can tell if he had his cell phone with him or not. What bothers me more is I haven't heard from Tillie. Her phone is permanently attached to her."

"There's no hospital news yet. No idea how many injured or where they've been taken."

"Ray," called Chief Hornig's secretary from her desk, "Tillie James is on line two."

Ray grabbed the handset and punched up the call. "Tillie, you okay? Where's Sidney?"

"I'm okay. Few cuts and bruises. Kinda shaken up. We're at the emergency room at the county hospital. The professor's banged up pretty good." Tillie went on to explain what happened, interspersed with prodding questions from Ray and a few from Hattie. She then said, "Mr. Ray, I think I know who the man was who got shot. I got a description from some of the staff people. I'm pretty sure it's Mr. Mansfield. You know, the bookman from Skidaway."

"You sure? Thought he wasn't supposed to be there."

"Yeah, I'm sure. No, he wasn't supposed to be here. Didn't get a chance to find out why he was. The professor met him in downtown Walterboro. Got a description of what he was wearin' from one of the nurses when I said we was all together. She said the police have his wallet but they ain't tellin' anyone yet."

Ray turned to Hattie, "Get Karla over here."

Hattie gave Karla an urgent wave and the chief's secretary quickly came over to Ray's side.

"Hold on Tillie. Karla, where's the chief now?"

"In the mayor's office. There's a regional conference call going on about Walterboro."

"Get him on the phone. We know who the victim is. He was there with Sidney Lake and Tillie. Hattie knows him too. Burke Mansfield. They both spent some time with him earlier in the week in Skidaway. We know why he was at the craft fair."

"Got it," she said and ran back to her desk.

"What's that, Tillie?" Oh, yeah. I'll tell her. Here's my cell number. Since you lost your phone, I can't call you. Check in every half hour. I'll see what I can find out about Sidney from here. I know they can't tell you anything. You gotta be a relative…Oh, yeah, I know you have your connections. I'm sure Sidney will ask for you as soon as he can. But it may be a while before they let any information out or outsiders in. Just stay close." They talked for a few more minutes and hung up.

"So what's happening?" Hattie asked.

"First things first. Tillie said to make sure you take care of Mickey. She's sure Mickey knows something's going on. Said Mickey would know there was a problem from a thousand miles away."

"Don't worry, I'll take care of her. What about Sidney?"

"Concussion. Nasty head cut. Reinjured his knee. On medication. Lab tests. X-rays. That's what she got from the hospital staff. The head nurse's mother lives on Deer Island. So Tillie has everyone watching over him."

"Ray," Karla called from her desk. "Chief's on." She held the handset up over her head. "Line one."

Ray picked up the phone and after a moment or two,

handed it to Hattie, who explained who Burke Mansfield was and why they were at the craft fair.

While Hattie Ryan spoke with Chief Hornig, Ray spoke with Hornig's secretary. "Karla, need you to do me a favor."

"Sure."

"I need to know who the lead FBI agent is who's been assigned to the Walterboro shooting. Chief will eventually need to know it anyway."

"No problem, Ray. I'll check with their office in Columbia."

"Thanks."

When Hattie finished with Chief Hornig, she hung up the phone and, referring to Ray's request of Karla, asked, "What's that for?"

Ray took a deep breath and sat back in his chair. "I have a feeling there's something else going on here. You've met Burke Mansfield, he's a book guy like Sidney, isn't he?"

"Yes." She hesitated, "he is."

"Think he's the violent type who might carry a gun around with him just in case he might need it?"

Hattie was taken aback by the question. "Oh, my, no. No, I don't see that at all."

"Didn't think so. I'm not so sure there was a confrontation between the murdered guy and Mansfield. Besides, if Mansfield didn't have a weapon, there definitely has to be a third person involved who did. Mansfield's being shot could just be an accident. Being in the wrong place at the wrong time. The only thing that could shake things up would be if they found a connection between Mansfield and the person killed. With any kind of a shooting like this where it results in a riot of some kind, the FBI will be all over the place.

Which is why I want to know who at the FBI is involved, as I'm sure it's going to be in their lap one way or another before the day is out."

At the hospital, Sidney was being Sidney and protested that he be released. The emergency room doctor said no. She had no intention of taking any guff from anyone. The hospital was overrun with people. Every bed in the emergency was full and their mandate focused on stabilization. Everyone rushed and ran everywhere. As soon as they finished the preliminary evaluation and had the patient's condition under control, they shipped them upstairs to a vacant room. Further evaluation and testing were done from there. Sidney authorized that Tillie be allowed to stay with him and she used her best logic to keep him in place.

"Professor, you gotta stay put. You got to be here overnight so we can find out about Mr. Mansfield."

"Burke? Is he here? Is he all right?"

"Now see, you got that bump on the head an you ain't rememberin' right. As I tole you, Mr. Mansfield is one of the people who got shot. They still workin' on him. Got two bullets in him. Other fellas dead."

Sidney looked at her, trying to remember. He squinted up his eyes. "I sort of remember that." He gently shook his head from side to side in the hope he could move the memory pieces into the right order.

"The nurse man said you got a concussion. Head's all scrambled up like a football player. You wanna go back in the game but you better not or you're gonna be out for good."

Sidney quieted down and again asked, "Is he all right?"

"Yeah, they think he'll make it, if that's what you mean. Nurse mam's from Saint Helena. Over in Beaufort.

His Aunt Mary lives over on Deer Island in Morgan. I see her at Publix a lot. He said Mr. Mansfield been shot twice once in the shoulder and the other went through his stomach. Lost a lotta blood but the bullets missed all the important parts. I think you might want to see if you can talk to him before you leave here. Find out what happened after he left us. Police may want to talk with you too. They haven't been able to talk much with him yet. Maybe you ought to have the doctors take a good look at that bad leg of yours again." Tillie thought back to her conversation with Hattie about finding a way to get Sidney to have his leg looked at again. "Be a good excuse to hang around. Besides, you can probably get everything covered hundred percent since you was hurt in the riot."

The mention of the riot triggered his memory as he visualized the people rushing at him yelling and screaming. He remembered being pushed and knocked to the ground. Some people tripped over him. His leg was caught under the chair and then the table was flipped over and hit him hard on the head. He came awake while they transported him to an ambulance. Tillie by his side talking to him. He took a deep breath and sat quiet. It was all coming back.

THIRTEEN

Within hours the shooting incident became known nationwide. For a while, it gained status along with the other mass shooting sites around the country, until the targeted nature of the first casualty could be revealed. But no one knew it at the time. Panic and fear were everywhere. The 'it can't happen here' crowd was again shocked with the realization there was not a single location in the country that was immune. And it was getting worse.

The incident had been added to the news lexicon because twenty-eight people were hospitalized and five attendees of the craft fair lost their lives.

The initial reports claimed it was a mass shooting and comparisons with Las Vegas were made. The first official reports confirmed one unidentified White male died from gunshot wounds and another was in critical condition in the local hospital. During the panic, another person lost his life when a gas tank behind a food truck exploded. The resulting fire and hysteria were responsible for all the other deaths and injuries. Although the assembled law enforcement teams were as certain as they could be that they didn't have a mass shooting on their hands, they kept the lockdown in place until the following morning.

The police finally had the opportunity to speak with Burke Mansfield for a short period of time. They pieced together that they were dealing with a personal dispute of some kind between the still-unidentified young man and his alleged killer. Their main problem continued to be the lack of a description of the shooter—if there was only one. They found the portable toilet with the bullet holes in it but hadn't as yet been able to say the same gun used to kill the young man was also used on Burke Mansfield.

The speculation about what happened didn't get clarified until the following day when the FBI spoke with the critically injured Mansfield. At a news conference headed by the county sheriff, a prepared announcement clarified that a mass shooting did not occur. Except for the two gunshot victims, all the other deaths and injuries were attributed to the panic caused by fear. They confirmed that the original shootings were a result of a personal dispute. The sheriff stated that the first responders made a heroic effort in keeping the hysteria from spreading farther than it did. He would say no more other than to announce a formal press briefing would be held at noon and then turned over the microphone to the doctor leading the response at the county hospital.

The initial formal statement kept the twenty-four-hour cable news programs alive with speculation and analysis of the fear factor in the United States.

Tillie made out well except for a cut to her hand and bruises on her arm, where she had been stepped on. Sidney was diagnosed with a severe concussion and had further damaged his kneecap. He also tore up just about every ligament around it when his leg became ensnared in the chair. The table fell on his leg and he was kicked and stepped on by fleeing fair goers. He also had a cut to his head that took eight stitches to fix. His glasses were broken and he had bruises and scrapes in a variety of places.

The FBI's Nora Sullivan spent her time in the background of the investigation. She let the county sheriff continue with the lead. As the special agent in charge of the Columbia field office, she made herself available in any way possible until it became clear what type of incident they were dealing with: local dispute resulting in a homicide or a mass shooting. If it proved local and the sheriff said he could handle it, she would step back with the understanding the full resources of the FBI would be available, if needed. However, when the FBI's Columbia office notified her that Burke Mansfield had been accompanied to the craft fair by Sidney Lake and Tillie James, she became intrigued and decided to interview Sidney since he was listed as a casualty and occupied a room on the third floor of the hospital.

Peeking into Sidney's room, she saw him propped up in bed writing on a large yellow pad. The county hospital only had single-occupant rooms. The old building dated back to the 1950s, an era when segregation of patients by race was normal procedure. The idea of having Black and White patients in the same room proved to be a medical care challenge. The problem took care of itself by putting all patients into private rooms.

"Professor Sidney Lake?" Nora asked after a soft knock on the door.

Sidney looked up and saw a woman in a dark-colored business suit standing in the doorway. "Yes, I'm Professor Lake."

Nora entered the room, "Professor, I'm Nora Sullivan of the FBI. Do you feel well enough to answer some questions?"

"Ah, I'd be delighted to. Perhaps you could answer some of mine as well."

Nora smiled. She immediately felt comfortable with the man in the bed. "How are you feeling?"

"Oh, I'm fine. A few aches, pains, and bruises. A bit

of a bother with my leg, but it will all work itself out. Just being held over for tests. Please sit down."

"Thank you," she moved a straight-backed metal chair into position. "I just wanted to ask you about yesterday and your relationship with Burke Mansfield."

"He's coming along all right, isn't he? I heard he was awake and doing quite well, under the circumstances."

"Yes, he's doing remarkably well for someone having been shot twice. I understand you were there together?"

"Well, yes and no." Sidney went on to explain how they met in the bookstore downtown and then went on to outline the meeting on Skidaway Island.

Nora took notes and became intrigued with the story of Anne Brontë's missing novel. "I don't think I've read *The Tenant of Wildfell Hall.*"

"Make a note to do so. As a professional woman, I believe you will find it quite interesting."

"I'll make a point of it. Do you know for sure that Mr. Mansfield came here to meet with you?"

Sidney hesitated. "Why...yes. It never occurred to me he would be here for another reason."

"We're just trying to determine if he knew the man who was killed. If, perhaps, a meeting had been planned between Burke Mansfield and Larry Carter?"

"Larry Carter?"

"Yes, that's the name of the young man who was shot and killed."

"Larry?" Sidney sat straight up in the bed and leaned forward away from his pillow. "Larry. Are you sure?'

"Yes, he's been positively identified. The name hasn't been released to the press yet. You know the name?"

"I...I don't know." Sidney closed his eyes for a moment and looked as though he was in pain. "I'm trying to remember." He opened his eyes but squinted them.

"Some things are a bit fuzzy. Concussion, they say." He paused again trying to remember. "Larry? That's not the name...the name from the craft show. The name of the person who owned the Brontë book was a Danny something...No, that's not right." The eyes closed again. "The bookstore owner." His eyes popped open. "Yes, the owner. On East Washington Street. He said his name was Larry. Not Danny. He was a troublemaker."

Nora had a confused look. "Who?"

"The bookstore owner on Washington Street. He identified Danny as Larry a troublemaker. Told us to check with the local police as he, Larry, was well known to them."

Now Nora perked up. "So Mansfield did know him."

"If it's the same one. He told me he didn't remember his last name. This is most disturbing. What does Mr. Mansfield have to say?"

As Nora had not been present when the sheriff's detectives interviewed Mansfield—the doctors limited the number of people in the room—she deflected the question. "We haven't completed the interview yet. He's still listed as 'critical but stable.' Detectives will be in to speak with him further as the medical team gives us the approval."

" Yes, I understand. As it turns out, we were all here for the same reason."

"Which was?"

"To see if we could find someone who knew this Danny person." Sidney related the discussion with the bookstore owner who knew the now identified Larry Carter, and the reputation he had in Walterboro."

"And all this related back to the Brontë book?"

"Oh, yes."

"Are you aware the FBI has specialists in the art fraud

area who could be of help?"

"Yes. Ray Morton had made inquiries for us in that area." Sidney had gained his composure. The strained look left his face.

"Ray Morton? Oh, yes. He's the person who notified our office in Columbia about your being up here with Mr. Mansfield. He's the retired police detective. He's well known to our people in Columbia."

"He made some inquiries but found out that, since the missing book had never been entered into your database, as there was no evidence the book was authentic and no one could put a value on it, they were not in a position to help."

Nora continued to make notes. "But you believe it is and does?"

"Burke Mansfield and his fellow appraisers believe it may be and they've had the best look at it."

"So tell me what you've discovered thus far?" asked a now very interested Nora Sullivan.

Sidney thought for a moment as he looked down at his notepad. "You know that's exactly what I was doing when you came in. I was trying to document for myself the known history of this particular book and its three volumes." He looked at Nora and realized how comfortable he felt with her. There was something in the way she asked her questions that made him feel at ease. "Let me give you an idea of where I am." He began to read from his notes.

"One–the book was acquired by the uncle of General Lawrence Brewster of Morgan, South Carolina." He looked up and said, "Unfortunately, I don't remember the uncle's name."

"Don't worry, we can get that. Go on."

"Two–we do not know from whom the uncle acquired

the book but believe his attorney Howard Springwood does. Mr. Springwood provided General Brewster with a summary of a detailed database of all the books the general inherited upon the death of his uncle.

"Three–The books were stolen from General Brewster's home in Morgan.

"Four–The book was discovered in a used bookstore and taken into the custody of the local police as evidence.

"Five–All three volumes of the book disappeared from a police car before they were properly recorded as evidence in the theft at the General's home.

"Six–Nothing was heard of the Brontë book until just recently when it appeared on *The National Arts and Crafts Show* under the ownership of a young man identified only as 'Danny.' The appraiser on the show was Burke Mansfield.

"Seven–Danny claimed he obtained the book from a vendor at the craft fair outside of Walterboro for twenty-five dollars and was trying to find out if it had more value.

"Eight–Yesterday we determined that Danny—who we now know is Larry Carter—had been trying to sell the books at the craft fair and not buy them." Sidney again made a side comment, "The show, by the way, was recorded more than a month ago."

He continued, "Nine–Larry had a reputation as an unreliable person and a police record as a troublemaker. Although that information has not been verified."

Nora said, "I think the local police have now verified that."

"Good. Ten–Howard Springwood was recently found murdered at his home in Charlotte, North Carolina."

Nora looked up from her notes, "Wait, the lawyer, the man who may know the origin of the now missing book was found murdered?"

"Yes, we just learned that. It could be a coincidence."

"Let me look into that." She made some additional notes. "Going back to my earlier question, are you sure Burke Mansfield came to the craft fair yesterday in the hope of meeting with you and not to meet with Larry Carter?"

☾☙☾☙

On the evening of the shooting, Tillie made sure Sidney had been settled in for the night at the hospital and then took Sidney's car and went home to Morgan. During the day she kept in constant contact with her family and assured them she was fine. She lived with her brother on Deer Island. He'd moved in with her last year after he retired from the Army and her granddaughter left home for school at the University of North Carolina-Wilmington. It was supposed to be a temporary arrangement until he found work, but they got along well and he stayed on. He eventually found a position as assistant director of security at one of the new gated developments outside of Beaufort.

Her two sisters met her at the door when she arrived, and her brother waited anxiously inside. She explained everything to them, but there were some things that dealt with her relationship with Sidney Lake and Harriet Ryan that she kept to herself. It was a long evening after a tiring day, but Tillie was up at the crack of dawn and went over to Hattie's for breakfast, as they both planned to head to Walterboro to collect Sidney. Ray Morton said he would take care of Mickey and wait at Sidney's until they returned.

When Tillie and Hattie exited the elevator on the third

floor of the hospital, they saw Sidney Lake at the door of his room. He was dressed and ready to go, but clearly missing his socks, and his shoes were untied.

Tillie spoke first, "Boy, you look like you're itchin' to get outta here."

"Morning, Sidney," said Hattie as she breezed by him into the room.

"Good morning. I thought you would both be here sooner."

"They still got security set tight downstairs. Never did catch the fella who started all this." Tillie gave Sidney a questioning look as she passed him. "I got all fresh clothes for you. Whatcha doin' wearin' the stuff from yesterday? We ain't getting outta here till you got the doctor's say-so—in writin'. An' I don't see that comin' too soon this morning." She handed him a small canvas bag with fresh underwear, a clean shirt, and slacks. "Look at that." Tillie pointed to a rip in the pants he wore. The cut sliced across the right knee area where he fell. "You can't leave like that. They'll think you're tryin' to escape an' bring you right back in. You get behind that curtain there and get dressed so you're decent."

With a sneaky smile, Hattie asked, "Do you need some help?"

Sidney's reply was accompanied by a stern look, "No! I don't!"

Tillie giggled.

Sidney pulled the curtain around part of the bed and Hattie finished the job.

Hattie pulled up a chair. "Did you find out anything else last night after Tillie left?"

The curtain rippled as Sidney sat on the bed to take his clothes off. "Actually I did. Had a visit from the FBI. Remember the young man we were looking for? Well, he's the one that was killed."

"Oh, my.". Hattie answered. "They know his name?"

"Larry Carter."

"Have you told Ray?"

"No, couldn't call him. I think I lost my cell phone in all the scuffling yesterday. It's not in my jacket."

Tillie also found a chair. "Nurse up front probably has it. Sometimes take the phones away from the patients now. Found mine over at the food truck where I hid. They'll bring yours when they bring the wheelchair for you to get outta here."

Hattie grabbed her handbag, pulled out her phone, and said, "I'll call Ray right now."

Sidney spoke from behind the curtain, "I'm not goin' anywhere in a wheelchair. I have my cane." He looked around the room.

"No you don't, Professor. You forgot, you lost it yesterday. You got no way to get outta here except by the nurse an me pushin' you."

Sidney did not answer but some muttering could be heard coming from behind the curtain, which now flapped instead of just giving off a rustle.

While they waited for Sidney to finish changing his clothes, a male nurse came to the door and motioned to Tillie. She walked over to him.

"Miss Tillie, thought you might like to know, they're lookin' for a woman as the shooter."

"That don't sound right. Ladies don't do this."

He whispered, "I was in the room this morning when the police and an FBI lady talked with Mr. Mansfield. He was more awake this time. Said the last thing he heard was 'Lucy, don't do it.'"

"Sompthin' don't sound right, but thanks, Oliver. I appreciate the info."

"You bet." He then turned and went away.

"Professor, you decent yet?"

Sidney pushed the curtain aside and appeared with the new pants on and a clean shirt. However, he still didn't have socks on. "Yes, I am. But I'm afraid I need some help with these." He looked down and wiggled his toes.

"Sit yourself down on the bed an' I'll give you a hand with the socks and shoes." Then with a smile, "I also got you a new cane." Then a stern face, "But I ain't gonna give it to you till we get downstairs."

Sidney looked at her and gave a small chuckle as he shook his head slowly. He then turned to Hattie and said, "Let me talk with Ray when you're finished."

Hattie nodded in response.

Tillie moved her chair over in front of Sidney's position on the bed and started to help him with the sock for his right foot. The right knee was bandaged in such a way that he couldn't bend it. She said as she worked, "Just heard the police are lookin' for a woman instead of a man for doin' the shootin' yesterday."

"A woman? Funny how you always think of a man doing the shooting when you hear of something like what happened yesterday. A woman. Interesting. What do they base that on?"

"Mr. Mansfield told them."

"He did? He must be feeling a lot better this morning. So he said it was a woman. Hmmmm."

"That's what my man said. Said Mr. Mansfield heard the young man say, 'Lucy, don't do it.'"

Hattie, on the phone, immediately relayed the information to Ray who asked her to repeat it, which she did.

Hattie gave a wave to Sidney, "He wants to talk with you." She held up her phone and walked it over to the bed.

Sidney and Ray spoke quietly for a moment and then Sidney turned to Tillie, who was now tying the laces of his right shoe, and said, "Tillie, Ray wants you to find your nurse informant and ask him again about what Mansfield said. Also find the FBI agent, Nora Sullivan, and tell her I need to speak with her."

"I'll go right away." She left Sidney sitting on the edge of the bed with one shoe on and the other off.

Hattie asked, "What's going on, Sidney?"

FOURTEEN

When Sidney Lake left the hospital, he felt encouraged at learning his new friend, Burke Mansfield, had been taken off the critical list, but they never had a chance to speak. Burke continued to be considered "serious" by hospital standards, a routine precaution given the nature of his life-threatening injuries. The troubling problem for Sidney revolved around the question Nora Sullivan of the FBI raised: did Burke Mansfield come to the craft fair to find Sidney or to meet up with Larry Carter? Sidney needed to know the answer to that question and it bothered him all the way back to Morgan. He participated in the general banter with Tillie and Hattie Ryan but the question of Burke's motivation never left him. It didn't matter what others told him. Sidney wanted to be in the same room with Burke, look him in the face, and ask him pointed questions.

Ray Morton kept his word and stayed with Mickey all morning. He knew he could have left but he gave his word to Tillie and Tillie was not someone you wanted unhappy with you. Mickey was perfectly capable of staying alone in the house. She often did. On the other hand, Ray knew of the bond that existed between Sidney and Mickey, especially after the death of Sidney's wife. The two of them were inseparable. Dogs were funny creatures in their attachment to human beings. And, as Tillie said, Mickey would know something was wrong from a thousand miles away. How? No-one knew. So Ray spent the morning using both his own cell phone and Sidney's land-line. He filled the dining room table with pages and pages of notes. He thought of using Sidney's office and the separate table Sidney used for his own research, but he didn't want to disturb what Sidney had laid out there.

Ray spent his time making calls to the county solicitor's office, the Beaufort County Sheriff's Office, the FBI field office in Columbia, the chief of detectives in Charleston and an old friend at One Police Plaza in New York. In most instances he left messages but in South Carolina everyone was at work on this Sunday because of the craft fair riot. Ray had become obsessed with finding out who would evict a ninety-year-old woman from a two-room house for the sake of making a few more dollars for themselves. He would find out who they were and he would find a way to stop them.

Sidney arrived at 111 Howard Street just after four in the afternoon. Ray had no time for pleasantries. He asked how Sidney felt, chatted with Tillie and Hattie, said goodbye to Mickey, and ran out the door headed for a meeting with Georgia Sawyer at the county courthouse. He told Sidney nothing other than to say he had developed more questions than answers.

Sidney was tired and hungry. They all were, including Mickey, so Tillie went into the kitchen to fix lunch. Hattie got him comfortably arranged in the living room overstuffed chair with the ottoman and brought over a side table for him.

"Hattie, would you bring me those papers Ray left on the table, I've got to figure out what he was doing. I know he'll tell me later this afternoon, but I'm dying to find out how what sort of a tie-in he thinks he's found between Ester Averille's tax sale and the killing of Larry Carter. I know it seems a bit far-fetched to him but, who knows, he might have found something."

As Hattie gathered up Ray's papers, Tillie carried a collapsed TV table from the kitchen and brought it to Sidney. While setting up the table to his side, Tillie could see Sidney trying to appear oblivious to what went on around him. He supposedly disliked being catered to but secretly enjoyed the attention and was only too aware of his good fortune in having the friends he did. He often wondered how he ended up with such people being nice to him when he knew his uncompromising approach turned off so many others. But it was the uncompromisingness that attracted people to him. He saw injustice and could not let it stand. He observed unethical conduct and could not be quiet. He saw "right" and "wrong" in their simplest form as being either "right" or "wrong." To say nothing in the face of injustice, for Sidney Lake, was injustice itself. His late wife, Cynthia, had been a steadying hand for him. She forced him to consider all sides to an argument before embarking on one of his crusades. He learned a lot from her tempering guidance. With her gone, Tillie stepped into her place but Tillie didn't have the softness and objectivity that his wife did. Tillie, at times, could be as uncompromising as he was only without the logical element. Tillie had intuition. She "knew" what was right and wrong and could be more vehement than Sidney when injustice came along. Harriet Ryan, on the other hand, could see all sides and played the role of devil's advocate whether she agreed or disagreed with Sidney's premise. He truly enjoyed their company and support.

As Tillie brought out lunch for the three of them, Sidney sorted through Ray's notes. Sidney liked the logic and detailed way Ray evaluated a problem. He used drawings and diagrams. Boxes were all over his pages. Names and initials were inside and outside of them. Lines went every which way. Arrows pointed up, down, and sideways. Question marks and exclamation marks were everywhere.

"Look at this Hattie, Ray has linked New York, Washington, Charleston, Charlotte, Morgan, Hilton Head, and Atlanta. What I can never figure out are the initials he uses. Sometimes they refer to people, sometimes places, and sometimes companies and groups."

"Let me see."

Sidney handed three sheets of paper to her and she laid them out on his TV table.

"It looks as though he's made three geographic groupings. It's not set out the way a map would be as the locations are not in the right places. On one sheet New York and Washington are close together side by side with a bunch of initials around them. Then we have the second sheet with Atlanta and Charlotte along with initials and then the Lowcountry from Charleston to Hilton Head. And look," she pointed to each page as she spoke. "The same initials appear around some of the locations but not all. When is Ray due back?"

"I believe he said it would be a few hours."

Hattie continued, "I can assume some initials represent people such as the SL and the BM and probably the EA. And what do the question marks mean? We definitely need a translation from Ray."

Tillie looked at the papers, shook her head, picked one of them up, and said, "None of this stuff makes any sense. Sure it'll make a lotta sense someday, but right now it ain't doin' anythin' for me." She put the papers down. "Professor, did you ever tell Mr. Morton about what Oliver tole me. About the sheriff lookin' for a woman?"

"No. He was in such a hurry I never did."

"Good. 'Cause they ain't. Changed their minds. Said they lookin' for a man now. Musta had another chance to talk with Mr. Mansfield an he told them sompthin' else."

"Not surprised. It usually takes a day or two to sort out these shooting events."

Hattie added, "What I find sad and depressing is that we know how things work. We all know the routine and the procedure. We seem to have something like this every month. It shouldn't be like this."

"No, it shouldn't," Sidney answered. "But we do, and it is. I'm sure there isn't a police department in the country that doesn't practice for a mass shooting incident response."

"Well, it ain't gonna get any better. When I was in school, we had air-raid drills for atomic bomb attacks. People were building bomb shelters for themselves where they could hide out. Storin' food an can goods. Don't change. Just different. Yeah." She turned and walked slowly away toward the kitchen softly saying, "Don't change. Just different."

Sidney watched her and with a touch of sadness in his voice spoke softly, "Yes, just different. This time we're doing it to ourselves."

∽∾∽

The sheriff's detectives in Walterboro did get a chance to speak with Burke Mansfield just after Sidney started his trip back to Morgan. This time Nora Sullivan of the FBI was present. She had asked the sheriff if he knew of Sidney Lake, and he admitted he did. He had never met him but he knew Ray Morton very well as they had worked together over the years. During the interview, Burke again explained where he was and what had happened but this time he remembered more. He said he never saw anyone and had no idea who they were. One man was very angry and the other scared. It seemed there was a fight of some kind going on and the whole portable toilet shook so much he thought it would fall over. All he heard was a popping sound. He didn't know anyone was shot. He said he didn't know he was shot until after he woke up in the hospital.

The good news for the sheriff confirmed he didn't have a mass shooting on his hands while the bad news was he had no idea who the victim, now identified as Larry Carter, had the argument with. But he could deal with that; it happened all the time. A fight that turned ugly. They would find out who didn't like Mr. Carter.

Burke Mansfield didn't see the other man and neither did anyone else. The portable toilets adjacent to the one Burke occupied had been empty and there were no security cameras in the toilet area. There were cameras at the main entrance and at the food area but no others. The craft fair venue had no fences around it except where it bordered on private property and the fence surrounding the high school sports fields. The backs of vendor tents served as the boundary of the event. Sheriff's detectives had already begun to review the camera tapes in the hope of finding Larry Carter and whomever he interacted with during his time at the craft fair.

The one piece of information that gave the detectives some hope revolved around Burke Mansfield's further recollection of what he heard, in the hope that someone spoke a name and he would recall it. Nora Sullivan having questioned Sidney Lake also added another dimension to the investigation that they planned to follow: the theft of a very valuable three-volume book and its whereabouts, which could be the centerpiece of the dispute between Larry Carter and his killer.

Ray Morton had something very different in focus, he wanted to stop the person who had tried to take Ester Averille's home from her. He knew it had to be someone from out of the area, someone who had no real idea who Ester Averille was and didn't care. Someone focused on making a large amount of money and willing to do whatever was necessary to achieve his objective. People were not important to such a person. People like Ester were obstacles to overcome. If they were foolish enough to reject his very generous offer for the property then he would use the courts as his partner. Ray knew that every move such a person made would be within the law, but he would find a way to stop him. What he didn't know was that Ray himself had been identified as an obstacle and had become a subject of a number of lengthy meetings at Zutter Industrial Alliance, LLC in Florida.

When Ray Morton left Sidney Lake's house in a rush he had a long list of questions for Georgia Sawyer at the solicitor's office and didn't notice the car that sat down the street with a single occupant who watched his every move.

Georgia had done her homework. Ten properties in the Pirate Islands had quietly changed hands over the past year and others were believed to be under some form of legal agreement to be acquired. Ester Averille's sat right in the middle of everything. A keystone that would make everything else work.

"Ray, it looks to me like we have a major land speculation underway. Up until now they have been quiet and careful." Georgia and Ray were huddled around a series of maps and papers in a small conference room in the county solicitor's office. "Staying under everyone's radar. Everything legal, naturally. The move at the tax sale brought them into the open."

"Why do you think they're suddenly becoming active in the open?" Ray leaned over and looked at the maps as he spoke.

"Lot of weird stuff going on in the Interior Department in D.C. of late. You've seen some of the headlines about conflicts of interest at the highest levels. About some protected lands suddenly losing their protected designations—like the Pirate Islands. In this case, I think someone believes there's a shakeup coming at Interior soon and the protections will be put back on. A lot of time, effort, and money have been invested by someone. Someone who doesn't like to lose or maybe can't afford to."

"Any idea who?" Ray looked up and dropped the map onto the table.

"Not yet. We have some names. Some of the ones you've given us. We've added a few more. Everything we've seen is all legal. We expected that. We've seen it before."

"Any chance of doing some sharing?"

"We don't have a formal investigation underway." She shifted a specific piece of paper that was under another. "There's nothing here that's under any special designation."

"What would it take to have something change the designation?" Ray put a finger on the paper and turned it toward him so he could read it.

"If someone from Justice would show up and start asking questions about the Pirate Islands land sales in relation to the Department of the Interior designations...we would be required to clam up."

"And that hasn't happened I take it?"

"Not to my knowledge."

Referring to the paper he had his finger on Ray asked? "Mind if I borrow this?"

Georgia got up from her chair, "Be back in a few minutes. Just remembered a call I have to make." She left the room.

Ray took out his notebook and began to copy the information on the sheet of paper. It contained a list of law firms and specific lawyers related to the land transfers. Another group consisted of companies located in New York, D.C., and Atlanta. Some of them he recognized.

There were a couple of lines of inquiry that Ray wanted to pursue and they were the grey area ones. The tax sale of the Averille house and land had been dealt with, so Ester kept her home, but the troubling part revolved around the deception, the attempt to defraud her by downplaying the failure to pay the taxes, as the new mortgage they promised would take care of everything. Ester Averille looked at the tax problem as being behind her but Ray saw it as a danger signal related to the crime of scamming the elderly. Being retired and in his mid-sixties, taking advantage of the elderly did not sit well with him as it now hit too close to home. In the near future, he knew he could be a target as the scammers were unmerciful in their efforts to defraud those who couldn't protect themselves. So Ray took what happened to Ester personally.

When Georgia came back into the room she noticed the papers she left had been moved but ignored them. "Sorry about that."

"No problem. Tell me, what are you folks prepared to

do about what happened to Ester Averille?"

Georgia sat down. "I want to get my hands around the neck of that lawyer."

"Is it realistic?"

"I have no intention of letting this go. My mother is in her eighties and lives alone. She's as independent as hell. I don't want this to happen to her. She's now getting at least one scamming phone call a day. The telecommunications companies could stop it, as could the social media sites, but they won't unless forced to by government regulations. State and especially federal legislators won't do anything, they're all into tax cuts and fundraising so it's up to the justice system to use what laws and resources we have to go after the bad guys."

"Well, good luck with that. I may be a private citizen now but I'm not going to be put off by politicians. Not this time." Ray got up from his chair.

"Ray, I'll support you wherever I can, but watch yourself on this one. My gut reaction is that there's something else going on here, especially if we're dealing with inside information and leaks coming from the Department of the Interior." Georgia got up and extended her hand. "I know you're pretty close with Pete Hornig and Pete and I get along very well. I intend to let him know what I'm doing and I'm going to ask that he assign one of his detectives to be the point person on the mortgage scam."

Ray took her hand, "What about the Sheriff? The Pirate Islands are in his jurisdiction."

"I know. You know how it works. I want Hornig and the Sheriff to work things out between themselves and be ready. If this leads its way back to Interior, the feds will be all over the place. We all need to be ready for this one."

"Okay," He picked up his notebook. "I have to go back to Sidney's again. I didn't get to talk to him about what went on in Walterboro yesterday."

"He's all right isn't he?"

"Yes, a bit banged up but okay. Has a concussion and reinjured his knee. The knee I think is going to be his biggest problem. Some strange things went on up there yesterday and, as usual, he seems to be in the middle of it. This book dealer he was with was one of the people shot. Assuming it was an accident but it probably needs a bit more explanation. I haven't spoken with anyone up there yet. They've been a bit busy. Once I've had a chance to talk with Sidney and Tillie I'll know more." Ray finished packing up and got ready to leave.

Georgia also stood up and opened the door to the room. "Ray keep me up to date on what you find out. It could be out of my jurisdiction, but you never know about these things."

"Sure, maybe you could do the same?"

She paused, "Yeah, whatever I can."

"That's fair."

ഇ∽ഇ

The man sat quietly on the bench in the small park across from the county administration building. His legs were crossed and his body turned slightly to the left. He had the newspaper he read opened to its full width, which concealed his face from the camera positioned to capture an image of anyone entering the building. While he read, he peripherally monitored the people coming and going. When Ray came out, the man stood up and turned his back to the front of the county building. Ray walked down the street to where he parked his car. The man stepped behind the bench onto the grass and walked parallel to Ray.

FIFTEEN

The following few days were dedicated to recuperation and reflection. The aches and pains came to the fore—the real, the imagined, the remembered. Sidney Lake stayed up in his bedroom. Once he had negotiated the staircase to get upstairs, it became impossible for him to get back down. The injured leg and concussion proved to be a safety issue for him, and it kept him immobilized. He dearly wanted to get downstairs to his office and his library but every time he put pressure on his right leg the pain hit him and the movement to get up made him dizzy. Tillie envisioned him losing his balance and falling down the stairs. She moved in and took control of the upstairs bedroom down the hall. Despite her own aches and pains, she cooked, cleaned, chastised, and catered to him. Mickey rarely left the room except for short walks with Tillie or Hattie.

While "Murder at the Craft Fair" continued to be the catchy tagline for cable news shows, the general news media began to move on. It became clear that what happened was a targeted killing that prompted mass hysteria. Larry Carter, the victim, was profiled over and over. The gang violence in and around Walterboro and the psychology of fear in the country proved too big an issue to be ignored. By Tuesday evening the White House and politics righted itself and took center stage once again.

The last major public briefing by the sheriff occurred

on Tuesday at noon. No one had been arrested. The investigation continued. They were following numerous leads. Police work was a slow, careful business. Television news needed action pictures, newspapers needed quotes and analysis to fill their pages. By Wednesday morning there were no front-page headlines or "Breaking News" to report. The story went quiet while the investigation intensified.

"Damn," Sidney said while looking through *The Morgan City Times.* "There's nothing in here." The paper rustled as he went from page to page.

Tillie entered carrying a tray filled with his breakfast. "Then there ain't nothin' new. How you doin' this mornin?" She put the tray on the card table she had set up for him next to the bed. It served as his temporary desk and contained the research he continued to do despite the medical directive he had received about not reading too much, as it might exacerbate his occasional bout with blurred vision.

"I need more information. There's a connection here between the Anne Brontë book and the murder that no one has picked up. This is not a *gang hit* as *The State* newspaper suggested. That's too simple a reason for what happened and they know it."

"They gotta say sompthin' an' the police ain't talkin' no more. Don't forget Mr. Cunningham of the *Times* will be here this mornin." She got the bed covers straightened around as she spoke and then placed a tray in front of him. His coffee, she placed on the card table.

"Yes, I know. He wants to do a story called *Eyewitness view of the craft fair terror.* "

"Gotta feelin' you gonna ask more questions than he does." She turned to leave the room and suddenly stopped. "Oh, almost forgot. Mr. Morton called an' said he's comin' over around eleven this mornin' and he's gonna have that FBI woman from the hospital with him. Miss Sullivan, I think it was."

"Oh, very good. That talk I had with her is a little fuzzy in my memory. I've got some questions for her too."

Tillie smiled and shook her head as she went out, "I'll bet you do."

While confined to his bedroom, Sidney had been reading up on concussions. He hoped the meeting with Cunningham and then Sullivan would stir things up and get his head back on track.

The session with the editor of *The Morgan City Times* turned into a rehash of what everyone knew. Sidney wasn't much help as he made it clear that being unconscious made him an unreliable witness. He stayed away from his association with Burke Mansfield, although he did mention they had met. He didn't have to bring up Larry Carter as the murdered man had been profiled in the national media. Sidney didn't mention the association with the Anne Brontë novel either. Tillie filled in the information that Cunningham wanted: the eyewitness view. The whole interview should have been about Tillie's experiences, but that's not the way it worked. The editor wanted Professor Sidney Lake's story. The pictures accompanying the article showed Sidney sitting on the end of his bed holding his new cane, his leg covered in bandages, and a separate one on his head. Sidney's shelved his plan to interrogate Cunningham when it became clear that the editor knew nothing of value.

When Ray Morton came by with Special Agent Nora Sullivan, the tone of the conversation changed. Based on their hospital conversation, Sidney assumed something occurred over the past few days that changed her position in the investigation.

"I suppose you could say that," Nora answered. "The sheriff's people up in Walterboro still have the lead and they're actively pursuing Larry Carter's gang member associates as the prime avenue of investigation…"

Sidney interrupted. "But…you think there's more going on here."

Ray Morton, who sat in one of the two card table chairs Tillie brought in for them, smiled.

Nora paused and looked at Ray, who had told her earlier in the car that Sidney would assume something had changed when they called to see him.

Sidney continued, "The Brontë connection."

"Hmmmm," replied Nora.

Sidney again, "Howard Springwood?"

Now Nora had a look of surprise on her face but stayed cool. "What makes you ask that?"

Sidney shifted in his bed so he sat more upright, clasped his hands together, placed them on his midsection, and looked over his glasses at the FBI agent. "I always believed he knew about *The Tenant of Wildfell Hall* being in the group of books that General Lawrence Brewster inherited. He also knew its value."

Nora looked at Ray as she said, "Ray has been telling me about your involvement in solving the George Reed murder."

"Yes, well, I always suspected there was more going on behind the scenes but could never figure it out. The books were stolen, and the police were embarrassed, but they had their killer, so Chief Hornig shut everything down. Tell me, how do you see a connection to Howard Springwood?"

"You started me down that road with our discussion in

the hospital about the Brontë sisters. Ray put me in touch with Georgia Sawyer, the assistant solicitor, who gave me access to the Reed murder investigation records. I spotted the name Howard Springwood. We know he was recently found murdered at his home in Charlotte. Larry Carter, we have learned, did odd jobs for Howard Springwood at his home on Crow Island."

While the conversations continued in Sidney's bedroom, Harriet Ryan came in the back door and saw Mickey lying down at the front door.

"Mickey did they forget all about you?"

Mickey got up but did not come to her. She looked over at Hattie and then looked back at the front door.

"Ah, need to go out do you? And nobody's paying attention. I'll take you."

Hattie took Mickey's lead from the hook on the clothes rack and they went out to the porch. She closed the door but didn't lock it. "Which way this afternoon, Mickey?"

Mickey did not hesitate. She led Hattie straight down the steps and to the left. The tall maples on both sides of the street were well known to every dog in the area. Mickey headed right for the second one up and began to check who had been there since early this morning. She sniffed and sniffed.

Hattie's phone rang and in the process of looking for it in her purse, she dropped Mickey's lead. She immediately bent over to pick up the end which landed near the passenger side of the door parked at the curb. While bent over she looked up and saw the car was occupied. A blond haired man sat in the driver's seat with a notebook in his lap and looked right at her. His look startled her and she jumped back up.

Getting her composure, she leaned over again and said

to the man, "Oh, I'm sorry. I didn't know you were there."

He immediately started the car. Looked away. Said nothing and drove off.

She watched as the car went to the corner and made a right turn.

"That was a little strange, wasn't it Mickey?"

Finally looking at her phone, she checked the log and spotted Tillie's name and number. Hattie called her back.

"Hi, Tillie. Sorry about that. Dropped my phone getting it out of my purse."

"That's okay. Thought it was you who took Mickey. She knows how to open the door, but I don't think she can get the leash off the hook yet."

Hattie laughed, "She's probably working on that."

"You commin' back in soon?"

"Be right there. Is there something going on?"

"Yeah. The professor's meetin' with Mr. Morton and an FBI lady. They want to talk with all of us together. Sompthin' funny goin' on."

"Be right there."

When Tillie ended her call, she went back upstairs to the bedroom with Sidney, Ray, and Nora Sullivan, who had just raised a question for Sidney, who had begun to answer it, "You asked me this the other day at the hospital, and I've given it a lot of thought since then…I haven't changed my mind. I don't think Burke was there to meet Larry Carter." Sidney gave his usual look over his glasses to Nora. "I do believe he had the hope of seeing him, as I did. We knew he had been there before, which is why we came, even though it was not together. Remember, we had originally planned it that way."

"Yes I know. It's just that the coincidence factor is interesting."

"Coincidences do happen."

With an intense look, Sidney responded, "Yes they do. Keep in mind that being in Walterboro on a Saturday—or any other day—would not be an unusual event for Mr. Larry Carter. He lived nearby around Smoak and had a reputation for being a troublemaker in Walterboro. The odds of finding him there were probably very good."

"Well, I will give you that."

They all heard the front door open and close.

"That'll be Mickey and Hattie," Tillie announced. "I told her to come up when she got back."

Sidney used the pause to take control of the conversation with, "If I may, I'd like to get back to something I'm curious about. I know we both agree with the existence of a connection between Larry Carter and Howard Springwood being the Brontë book, but you said Mr. Carter sometimes worked for Mr. Springwood. Why would a reputable lawyer want to hire a young man of such dubious character?"

Ray, who had been mainly a listener thus far, couldn't resist jumping in, "Sidney, the answer may be in your choice of words. Perhaps Springwood was not as reputable a lawyer as you assumed. I had a grandmother who often warned us grandchildren with 'Tell me who you go with and I'll tell you who you are.'"

"Smart lady," offered Tillie. "Round here we been sayin' 'You lie down with dogs an' you get up with fleas.' Not much difference. Seems like all grandmas is related."

Hattie walked in with Mickey and saw the smiles all around the room. "My, my. A room full of cheerful philosophers."

Sidney made the introduction. "Special Agent Nora Sullivan meet Professor Harriet Ryan. Hattie here is with

Morgan College and a very good friend."

They shook hands.

Sidney continued, "Ms. Sullivan is with the FBI and wanted to speak with all of us about not just what happened last Saturday but the theft of the Anne Brontë book as well. She's also coming around to the same conclusion we have, the possible involvement of Howard Springwood, the Charlotte lawyer." Sidney then posed another question to Nora, "Would it be fair to say you are aware of Mr. Springwood for another reason, other than his connection to a missing rare and valuable book?"

Nora didn't answer right away. She seemed to be trying to decide how much information to reveal. "Well, let's just say we have been aware of him, not because he had done anything wrong—that we know of—but because of the choice of a number of his clients."

Tillie couldn't resist, "Got some fleas on 'um, hah."

Nora now looked a little unsettled as she responded, "It would be a possibility. But you have to keep in mind that lawyers that defend disreputable people are not necessarily disreputable themselves. They're doing the job they were trained to do."

"Yeah, he got some fleas on 'um all right."

"Well, be that as it may, there is something related that I wanted to caution all of you about. We believe the killing of Howard Springwood was a professional one. It was originally billed as a robbery, but the Charlotte police department is still actively pursuing other avenues. We've asked that ballistics people do a comparison of the bullets that killed Springwood and Carter. If we get a match…"

Ray said, "All bets are off. You know, I haven't been focusing too much on this although the shooting at the craft fair has brought me around. I'm still deep into what's going on out at the Pirate Islands and the solicitor's office has been digging up some interesting information, but if there's a link between the killing of Carter and Springwood well...I have to believe our noseying around is going to make someone very nervous."

"My point exactly," said Nora. "I don't want to alarm you all, but please be cautious. If a link is determined I'll let you know. In the meantime watch yourselves. Don't take any chances on your own. Call us. Although we're not officially involved, we're always officially involved. You're welcome to call me at any time. Don't keep anything to yourselves. Everything is routine at this point. I'll be speaking with the sheriff of Coastal Rivers County before the day is out as that's where Crow Island—Springwoods residence down here—is located."

Hattie thought for a moment while Nora spoke, waiting for her to finish before interrupting. "This may be nothing, but when I was outside a few minutes ago with Mickey..." She told them about the man and the car.

Ray and Nora spoke in unison, "Did you get the license number?"

e⁄ɔe⁄ɔ

A few blocks away, the man who had been sitting in his car outside Sidney Lake's house, made a call on his cell phone. "Somethings going on. Have been watching Morton but I think we have another party of interest. Sidney Lake. Retired college professor. Both Morton and the FBI woman showed up at his house...Yes, I'm sure it's the same one...No, don't have any information on Lake...Okay, tonight in Savannah." He ended the connection and drove off.

e/ɔe/ɔ

Ray stood up and walked over to Sidney's bedroom door. He turned around and stood a moment before he spoke. "So it's possible that Springwood was mixed up in something shady and Carter did odd jobs for Springwood."

Nora nodded in agreement.

"If you don't mind," interjected Sidney, "I wonder if the sheriff in Walterboro, in connection with finding out about Larry Carter's background, has asked Mr. Carter's local associates, who enjoy terrorizing the local businesses with him, if they know the nature of the work Mr. Carter had been doing for Mr. Springwood?"

Nora answered. "I haven't seen any of the reports of their interviews as yet. I also haven't shared my thoughts about Springwood with the sheriff, as everyone is focused on the shooting being the result of a personal dispute between two local troublemakers."

"So they're not making a connection to the shooting and the Brontë book?"

"We still don't know if there is one."

Sidney continued to press the point. "But it is a valid line of inquiry, isn't it?"

"Yes," said Nora, "That's why I'm here."

SIXTEEN

Another day passed and while Sidney felt better, he remained unsteady on his feet. The headaches didn't bother him anymore but his knee wouldn't support him. He had almost fallen twice while he made his way to the bathroom. He relied on the cane Tillie provided although he knew he didn't have the experience or skill to use it properly. He envisioned spending the rest of his life with a walker and shuddered at the thought. Besides, that wouldn't solve his problem of getting up and down the stairs. Tillie spent the night again but how long could she keep doing it? He decided he would get himself down the stairs this morning and just stay there as he had done once before when he originally injured his knee last year.

"Don't you worry about me, we'll get you downstairs," assured Tillie.

"Who's we?"

"Mister Morton's comin' over."

"He's not coming just for that is he?" Sidney sounded embarrassed. He had no intention of being considered an invalid and he didn't want to be a burden to his friends.

"No, don't you worry, you ain't imposin' on him. He said he needed to talk with you about the Pirate Islands, so I figured I'd put him to work as long as he was here. We'll get a system worked out for movin' you around before the day's out."

Sidney looked at her with a smile on his face. "Tillie, I

don't know how I'm ever going to repay you for all of this."

"Friends don't have to pay one another. That's what bein' a friend means. When I got my house cleanin' hat on that's one thing and when I got my friend hat on that's another. Don't you worry."

Tillie helped Sidney to the bathroom and then made the bed and got out a fresh set of clothes for him to wear. Since he would be downstairs, she made sure he would be presentable to receive visitors. She knew he would want everyone to believe he was back to normal, even though he wasn't.

Ray Morton arrived at nine o'clock, a time he and Tillie had agreed upon. She knew Sidney would be ready by then. Negotiating the stairs proved to be as difficult as Tillie expected. She walked in front carrying the cane while Sidney grabbed the railing with his right hand and Ray shored him up on the left side. It was slow going.

"You ever consider moving to a single-level place, Sidney?" asked Ray. "I have to believe this has to be a tough climb even with two good legs."

"I've given it some thought, but no, I'm not leaving here. I've been told there are a number of mobility alternatives available to me. I may decide to explore some of them."

Tillie stopped at the bottom of the stairs and handed Sidney his cane. "Don't you worry, Mr. Morton, me an' Miss Hattie have some ideas for him. We'll get it all fixed up."

Once Sidney had settled into his oversized chair with the hassock, Ray took his place in the living room on the sofa.

Tillie said, "How 'bout some fresh coffee for everyone?"

"Make sure you bring a cup for yourself, I want to talk about the status of the Pirate Islands and could use your input."

"Okay, be right back."

Ray turned his attention to Sidney. "Remember that person Hattie saw in the car the other night?"

"The blond fellow."

"Yes. One of the thoughts I had was it could be a reporter continuing to nose around. Even though the craft fair is off the front page, the topic of fear in America has replaced it. One of the cable news outlets is even using 'Fear in America' as a tagline for a regular feature. The craft fair riot itself may have gone into the background, but I think they've tapped into a nerve that's in the back of everyone's head and they intend to exploit it. I can't say they're wrong. I guess it's just another case of the new normal. Anyway, I made some calls to the TV networks about their having someone snooping around and also have Jim Cunningham check some of the local papers."

"How are you doing this? I mean you have no authority. Why would they respond to your questions?"

"Ah, yes. Well, it seems the solicitor's office is a bit understaffed at the moment, as are both Chief Hornig and the sheriff's office—have no one they can lend her—so Georgia Sawyer offered me the job of Chief Investigator for the tax sale scam. Couldn't resist. I've done some work for them in the past and since I was already deep into it, it made sense. Marie's not too thrilled."

Sidney deadpanned his answer as he took the opportunity to needle his friend, "Don't be so sure. She's probably happy to have you out of the house."

Tillie came back into the room carrying a tray with a full coffee service and placed it on the table in front of the sofa. A TV table had been placed next to Sidney's chair earlier.

Ray looked up and laughed, "Ha, Tillie you're a wonder. Sidney, you ought to hire her full time. What else are you going to do with all your money?"

"Don't you give him any ideas. He gets enough of those all by himself."

Sidney smiled and said to Tillie, "Pull up a chair and sit yourself down."

Tillie poured the coffee and gave them each a cup: a little cream with no sugar for Ray, heavy on the cream, and two sugars for Sidney. She moved a straight chair over from the other side of the room, placed it across the table from Ray, and poured a half cup of black coffee for herself.

Sidney suddenly looked confused. "Ray, where were we? Don't remember if you said what you learned from…"

Tillie saw the look on Sidney's face and said, "That's that concussion thing again. Memory gets a bit fuzzy for a while. Nephew had a bad one. Football in high school. Rang his bell pretty good. Didn't remember anything about the game or bein' hit bad for three days. Came all back in pieces. He's okay now."

Ray immediately saw how Tillie eased Sidney's confusion and knew what she was doing. "No, no, haven't gotten to it yet, Sidney. You haven't missed anything. The reporter thing is a long shot. Had to give it a try though. Doesn't mean some freelancer might be working on something. Nothing from the mainstream people though."

Sidney looked relieved. "So it didn't mean anything? I mean what Hattie saw. The man was just startled by her and took off?"

"I think we'll just have to leave it that way for now."

"All right. So what about the Pirate Islands?"

Ray leaned forward from his position on the sofa. "Ah, that's another matter. We're not dealing with locals this time. That law firm in Washington is definitely in the middle of this and I'm becoming certain there's a Department of the Interior connection here someplace. Have a feeling someone's leaking information they shouldn't. The solicitor's office has started making some quiet inquiries of the Justice Department."

Tillie very deliberately placed her coffee cup on the table in front of her and reached out and touched Ray Morton's arm, "Just you hold on here a minute."

Sidney and Ray froze and looked at her.

She continued, "Don't know where my head's at. Forgot all about it with what happened at the craft fair. The blond man. There was a blond man with one of those lawyers tryin' to buy up Pirate Island land. One of the people I spoke with mentioned it. Man didn't say anything. Just watched. Kinda creepy like."

Sidney said, "This only happened once? Only one of the people you spoke with mentioned it?"

"Yeah, think so. Doesn't mean he wasn't there other times. With some of the others. They just didn't mention it."

Ray rubbed his chin. "Could just be a coincidence."

They all went silent for a moment. Then Sidney spoke. "Coincidences. I don't like coincidences. I don't believe in coincidences."

Ray looked at Sidney as he said, "You sound like Nora Sullivan of the FBI. I heard her mumble the same thing only she also added, 'Too many coincidences.' What the hell is going on here?"

While the conversation about the Pirate Islands continued in Sidney's living room, Burke Mansfield laid in his bed at the county hospital. He had been very lucky. A few inches either way would have produced a very different outcome. He had five separate interviews with the detectives of the Sheriff's Department, and they had become convinced that he didn't participate in the dispute that resulted in Larry Carter's death. They were finished with him. Their attention focused on Carter's gang connections. Mansfield became categorized as an innocent bystander who chose the wrong toilet at the wrong time. But Nora Sullivan became convinced there was more going on than simply gang violence. She kept looking at the bigger connection. Sidney and Burke Mansfield were both at the craft fair because of the Brontë book. Larry Carter at one time had the book and may still have it. He also worked for the recently murdered Howard Springwood, the attorney who once, also, had the book. A coincidence? No, Nora Sullivan didn't believe in coincidences. With Burke, Carter, and Springwood all having touched and pursued *The Tenant of Wildfell Hall*, she became absolutely certain there was a connection and she was going to find it. She also wanted to know who else Carter worked for.

Once Ray Morton left Sidney's house, Sidney refocused on the missing Brontë book. Since the professor left the hospital, he had not been in contact with Burke and began to have second thoughts about the man. He didn't know him that well. His contact with him had only been the one time in Savannah and again in Walterboro. They got along extremely well and seemed to have a lot in common but the questions being asked by Nora Sullivan bothered him. Was she right to question

Burke Mansfield's motives? Should he as well? Did Burke tell him the truth about his reason for being in Walterboro on Saturday? Is it possible he did come to meet with Larry Carter and make an offer for the Anne Brontë novel?

loes

A short while after Ray Morton left, Sidney pushed, shoved, twisted, and pulled until he managed to get up from his chair in the living room. Tillie had made up the sofa bed for him in his library so he wouldn't have to negotiate the stairs to the second floor, an impossible task for him now with his knee bandaged and the dizzy spells from the concussion. This was the second time in two years that he had to move into his library. He began to wonder if a two-story house had become too much for him. He seemed to be questioning everything lately. The doctor told him he would be out of sorts for a few weeks and Tillie made her usual comment, "Oh, that's good news. It means he's getting' back to normal."

The Burke Mansfield questions were getting to him. He had to sort them out. But how? As Sidney grabbed his cane and stood on his own, Mickey looked up at him from her position next to him. She rarely left his side. Their routine had been disrupted with Sidney coming downstairs so late in the morning and, although Mickey had been through it before, she knew this was different. Sidney's voice had a strange sound. It didn't have that assured confident tone.

"I've got to stay out of this chair. I've got to move around more," Sidney said as he stood and shifted his weight to get around the hassock in front of him. He took a firm grip of the new cane Hattie Ryan bought for him.

It was black and had the carved head of a Labrador retriever for its handle. "Just have to be careful when I get up. Don't want to fall over. Tillie told me to stay put and not do anything until she got back from her chores. Mickey, I think she's babying me too much and I've got to move around more. I don't want to disappoint her, but it's time to get back on track."

He inched forward and Mickey got up and out of his way. She gave him a look that said, "Tillie isn't going to be happy about this."

Sidney looked at her and said, "I know. I know, but I have to do this. We'll be all right."

Finally standing up and facing the direction of the kitchen, he let out a sigh of relief. "Okay, I've got some cooking to do."

Sidney was right. When Tillie came in the back door and found him in the kitchen seated at the breakfast table she was not happy. He had assembled some ingredients in front of him as he intended to use the area as his workspace. Normally he would do his prep work on the island in the center of the room but that would mean standing the whole time and he experienced some slight dizziness after he moved around for a while so he just sat down.

Tillie put the two bags of groceries on the island and looked at Sidney, "Just couldn't stay put could you."

Mickey gave her a look from her spot in front of the island that said, "I told him to stay put but he wouldn't."

"Not your fault," she said to the dog. "I'm sure you told him to stay in that chair." Mickey got a pat on the head.

"Tillie, I just can't sit still anymore. I've got to work some things out."

Tillie looked at the ingredients assembled on the table.

"Need to do some cookin'." She paused a moment. "You probably right." Sidney's cookbook sat on the table among some potatoes and carrots. "Shepherd's pie? I don't think so."

Sidney looked at her questioningly.

"No. Too easy. You need to give that head o' yours a test. Make it perk up." She turned around and went over to the bookcase by the refrigerator. Looked around for the book she thought had the right recipe. Found it. Took it down and thumbed through the pages until she found what she wanted. Sidney and Mickey remained silent but watched her carefully. "Okay, I got it right here." She had chosen *Mary Berry's Baking Bible* and a recipe for basic scones. The book had been a gift from Hattie, since they were all fans of the PBS program *The Great British Baking Show.* She passed the book to Sidney as she said, "I know this ain't too complicated so how 'bout you do it the way she wrote it. The English way. Grams an' stuff. Cook it usin' the centigrade temperature."

Sidney got a smile on his face. "What a great idea."

"Yeah, I'll even be your helper. That sou sompthin'. Get mixin' stuff out. You can't go crawlin' around on the floor to get bowls and pans. Betcha we can even get sompthin' for Mickey to do."

"Tillie, you're the best nurse anybody could have. Sous chef it will be."

They started right in and when all the equipment was ready Sidney asked, "What do you think of Burke Mansfield?"

"Seems like a nice man. Only saw him that time at the food court. Hard to tell." Tillie positioned the food scale a little more to Sidney's right to make it as convenient as possible.

"Yes, but you always have a first impression."

Tillie thought before answering, as though she was visualizing last week's meeting. "Well, maybe a little guarded. Like he was holdin' sompthin back. You do the same thing when you're tryin' not to give too much away to someone new. Not sure of them."

"Hmmm. I suppose you're right. Could be nothing." Sidney winced.

"Headache again?"

"Yeah, but not as bad as it has been."

"Doc said it might take two weeks to get all cleared up."

"I know."

"You worried about Mr. Mansfield?"

Sidney thought before answering. "No. It looks like the doctors have everything under control. He's going to be fine."

"Not what I meant. Talkin' 'bout worried as in *can you trust him*?"

Sidney began to read the recipe as he talked, "Good question. That FBI agent, Nora Sullivan, put some ideas in my head. Not sure which way to go with it. What if he was playing me along? What if he had Larry Carter checked out and knew Carter would be at the craft fair and that's why he told me he couldn't go with me? What if he knew the Brontë book was stolen and he wanted to buy it on the sly? What if they were both in the toilet area because that's where they were supposed to meet?" Sidney winced again.

"What if you thinkin' too hard? Doc said you got to relax. Let's bake some scones an' if you gets an idea you write it down. Take the pressure off. When Miss Hattie comes later we'll all take a look at what you wrote an' we'll talk."

დადა

Ray, true to his word, put Nora in touch with Georgia Sawyer in the solicitor's office, to get access to the files related to George Reed's murder and the theft of *The Tenant of Wildfell Hall*. In theory, he could have done it himself now that he was working for Georgia, but he also knew that his investigator position assignment was a narrow one. He was there to pursue the evidence related to attempts to swindle elderly members of the Gullah community out of their land and nothing more.

"So, Ray," asked Georgia once Ray became comfortable at the conference room table. "What have we got so far?" They had agreed that they would meet formally every Monday, Wednesday, and Friday afternoon. This was in addition to the phone calls and messages that they exchanged during the week. "I know you had developed some information on your own about the law firms before the Walterboro craft fair crises."

"I have to admit this is very convoluted. Let's talk about motivation. This is definitely tied into the Interior Departments plan to undo the previous administration's plan to designate the Pirate Islands as a 'National Monument.' Word got out that the Secretary of the Interior was going to formally take the islands off the list." Ray looked at some papers and a notebook he had opened in front of him, looked up, and continued. "As I said, none of this is formal. The Interior Department hasn't done anything yet. It's all hearsay and 'leaked' conversations. However, the general consensus is that it's going to happen. What made this an urgent matter for some people, is the very real prospect of the current administration losing all of its clout in Congress. Interior has the ability to knock it off the list, which is what a group of investors, led by a New York hedge fund, want to see happen. But they're savvy enough to recognize that a new administration will put it right back on again. And the prospects of a new administration taking over is looking more likely as the year goes on. What this hedge fund is focusing on is getting hold of enough land for a series of resort islands to rival Hilton Head. Have the developer get its plans to the county and the state so everything can be grandfathered, no matter what a new administration tries to undo."

Georgia sat back in her chair. "None of what you're telling me is illegal, unless someone can prove there were leaks made for the purpose of the leakers enhancing their own pocketbooks and essentially amounted to bribe of a government official. And even that wouldn't involve us, as that would be a job for Justice."

"Agreed." Ray leaned forward. "It's the way they've gone about it that falls in our lap. The deception. The running of a scam to defraud property owners. There's nothing wrong with legally buying up the property, if someone is willing to sell. The problem comes in when they get resistance and tell the current residents of the property they are not the sole legal owners and infer that the other legal owners have agreed to sign over the property to the developer. This, , isn't entirely true but the current residents become frightened and enter into an agreement to sign over their rights to the lawyers acting on behalf of the developer, which is being funded by the hedge fund." He leaned back.

"We've run into this before."

"I know that. Only this time they're aggressive. The developer needs to get grandfathered."

"The name of the hedge fund?"

"Rostov Credit Partners, LLC, New York."

Georgia wrote the name down on the pad in front of her and picked up the phone sitting in the middle of the table. "Sue, get me everything you can find on a R-O-S-T-O-V credit partners, LLC. They're out of New York. Thanks." She refocused on Ray. "Who's the principal?"

"David Rostov. He was the one that was late for that meeting in D.C."

"Right, I remember that. How reliable are the people you got this information from?"

"Very. Rostov is not a liked person. He's rubbed a lot of people in New York and Washington the wrong way. No love lost."

"What's his connection down here?"

"Has one of the big places on deep water on Crow Island. Basically a summer place. Not around much."

"Ah, a county resident. Could be interesting."

SEVENTEEN

When Harriet Ryan entered 111 Howard Street and saw the living room empty she called out, "Sidney?…Tillie?…Are you here?" She turned and began to head up the stairs to the second floor when Tillie answered her.

"In here Miss Hattie. In the kitchen."

Hattie stopped and looked around the banister. She could see down the hallway and saw Sidney sitting at the kitchen table. She walked toward him. "I expected to find you resting in the living room. What are you doing?"

Tillie answered from her position at the small island, "Cookin'. Got some things to work out. You know how to how to make this oven do centigrade?"

"Centigrade?" She spotted Sidney with Mary Berry's book in front of him. "You're trying to do it the way the book is written. Why?"

Sidney answered, "Tillie thought it would make us concentrate more, since we would be forced to do conversions and measure everything differently."

Hattie walked over to the table. "Oh, I get it. A bit like driving on the other side of the road. Going down the left instead of the right makes you concentrate and focus."

"Yes," Sidney said. "I need that. This concussion has truly rattled my head. There's something staring me in the face about what's been going on and I can't make it pop out. If I stop trying so hard, it'll be there."

"So you're cooking." Hattie thought for a moment and

then nodded her head. "Makes sense. It's what you do. How can I help?"

"You can tell me how to turn this oven into an English one. Make like the Berry lady was doin' the cookin'." Tillie waved her hand at the oven as she spoke.

"Hmmm. I know this is the same kind I have. Let me think for a moment. I've done it before. It's very complicated." Hattie walked to the oven. "You have to press and hold one of the buttons. It's up near the 'conv bake' one. Let me see." She looked over the control panel on the combination microwave and regular oven. It was a combined set of controls. "I think it was the 'broil' button. This one." She pressed it and held her finger in place while she counted, "One thousand, two thousand, three thousand, four thousand, five thousand." The display window suddenly changed and the letter "F" appeared with the letter "C" below it.

Tillie exclaimed, "You got it."

Hattie smiled. "Okay. Now what do I do?"

"I guess you push the 'C' button. Only there ain't one. That don't make sense."

"Right. You can't press the display, it has to be a button but which one. Is the manual around?" As Hattie spoke the display changed and returned to its original position of showing the current time. "Damn. Oh, sorry. Modern technology does wonders for ones' vocabulary."

Tillie made a face. "Don't give you much time do they. I guess it's like cookin'. Got to get all the ingredients lined up before you start or it won't work. I think the manuals for everything are in the bottom drawer of the cabinet next to you."

Hattie reached over and pulled out at least six instruction guides and pamphlet-sized books written in three languages and dealing with multiple models of appliances. She shook her head as she looked for the one for the oven. "They're all the same. One size fits all. Make it economical for the manufacturer and a nightmare for the customer." She found it. "Here it is. Now let's see if we can figure out where the instructions would be to convert from Fahrenheit to centigrade."

Sidney suggested, "Check the index."

Tillie gave him a questioning look, "Professor, this ain't no textbook."

Hattie skipped through the pages. "Let me see if I can find something on the control panel. Ah, here it is." She read the material on the left side of the page and then the right. "Hmmmm. Well, it seems they use the 'Flex Clean' control button to change from 'F' to 'C' after you press the 'Broil' button."

Sidney, with a shocked look on his face said, "No. You have to be kidding?"

"Fella who worked this out musta had a job with the CIA creatin' secret codes before he went to work makin' ovens. The connection ain't logical. There's nothin' logical about it."

Hattie put down the instruction guide and stared at the control panel. "Let's try it. It may not be logical and it may not seem to make sense but if it does the job, well…"

As Sidney's helpers went back to square one to switch the oven over to centigrade, the professor sat quietly with Tillie's words swirling around in his head. *The connection ain't logical. There's nothin' logical about it.* Mickey, sensing the change in Sidney, came over from her position near the rear door, lay down on the floor under the table, and placed her head on his foot.

"Damn! It worked," Hattie exclaimed, as the "F" in the display switched to "C."

Tillie shook her head in dismay. "Technology stuff sure is stupid. That little scale we use has a button that says 'unit' and switches real easy from 'g' to 'p' to 'oz' to 'ml' an cost twenty-five dollars an this thousand dollar set of ovens makes you jump through hoops to set the temperature." She turned to make a comment directly to Sidney but stopped when she saw him staring off into space. She gave Hattie a look and directed her attention to the kitchen table by pointing her thumb in that direction and shaking it.

Hattie said quietly, "Sidney, what's up?"

Both women were concerned that the hit he took to the head had now caused Sidney to go into a trance. They knew his memory was off and maybe something else had now happened that caused him to sit and stare into space.

"Sidney?" She said a little louder this time.

Finally Tillie spoke up, "Professor, you there?"

Sidney looked up with a start. "Yes." He turned to look at the two women. Mickey raised her head from her position on his foot. "It ain't logical."

The two women looked at one another. Puzzled, Tillie said, "What ain't logical? The oven?"

"No, the connection. It's not logical. There's nothing logical about it."

Hattie spoke up this time. "Sidney, what are you talking about?"

"The connection."

"What connection you talkin' about. We ain't talkin' about no ovens are we?"

"No. The tax sale. The missing book. The land grab. The craft fair. The murder of Larry Carter. The murder of Howard Springwood. They're all connected."

"How?" said Hattie.

"I don't know. It doesn't make sense. It's not logical.

But I know they all go together. There's a common bond somewhere between Ester Averille's land and Larry Carter having the Brontë book. We've got to find the link."

Tillie muttered, "Eh oh, there's sumpthin' cookin' an' it ain't Miss Berry's scones."

EIGHTEEN

The scones were a success, but it wasn't easy. They agreed the size of the scones was too small so they planned to increase the size to a two and three-quarter inch diameter. The flavor was good, although Tillie thought they should have more sugar. Sidney countered that in England they purposely did not have more sugar as they were intended to be eaten with fresh jam, which provided the sweetness. "Well, we ain't in England. I like 'um sweeter," she observed.

The conversation switched back and forth from scone making to finding a connection between Ester Averille and Larry Carter. As with the scones, they felt they were on the right track but needed to make some minor adjustments.

Hattie had no sooner left on an errand when Ray Morton telephoned Sidney and told him he would be there in a few minutes. That put the making of the second batch on hold.

"You've been cooking," observed Ray, as he came into the kitchen. "Well, that means you're up to something. So am I."

"Well, don't keep us in suspense. What have you learned?"

"Spent a lot of time with Georgia Sawyer in the solicitor's office this morning." Ray made himself comfortable in one of the chairs on the other side of the island from Sidney, who continued to sit at the kitchen table. "She's been making inquiries in neighboring states about some of the people who showed up at the tax sale. In the meantime, I've been checking up on the people who were at that law firm meeting in D.C. What we've managed to piece together is that a hedge fund in New York seems to be a key player in everything. Could I try one of those?" The scones were cooling on a rack just off to his side.

"Of course. Help yourself."

He did. Took a bite and continued, "Georgia doesn't have a name yet, but is convinced it's related to someone who was at the D.C. meeting. These are good." Referring to the scones. "Could use a little more sugar, though."

"Somehow I knew you would say that. I'll be sure to send a note to Miss Berry for you and Tillie, so she can adjust her recipe for future editions of her book."

"What?"

"Never mind. Just continue on please."

Ray took another bite and did as instructed. "Well, what I found interesting is that one of the names that popped up from Georgia is Howard Springwood. It seems he and a few others have been acquiring some of the land on the Pirate Islands, although not by the tax sale route."

Sidney stiffened in his chair. Most people would have jumped out of it but given his leg and girth, any motion by the professor achieved the same effect.

Tillie saw the movement as she came in the back door.

Ray did as well and immediately responded with, "You okay, Sidney?"

"Oh yes. I knew it. There had to be a connection and you just found it."

"Connection to what?"

"A link between the Brontë book and the Pirate Islands."

"How?"

"Don't you remember? Springwood was the attorney in Charlotte who worked for General Brewster's uncle. He's the one that provided the book and now you've linked him to the speculative purchases of land on the Pirate Islands. The missing rare book and the Pirate Islands are connected."

"Yeah, but there were others as well."

"Who?"

"Casey Yarborough, for one."

"The one who bid on the Averille property? That was just opportunism. I can't see him as a major player in anything. He's just a small fish in a small pond."

Ray didn't respond. He just sat back in his chair and stared at Sidney. Tillie watched them as she placed two grocery bags on the counter.

Sidney continued, "Ray, we've got two seemingly unrelated murders on our hands: Howard Springwood and Larry Carter. The police are going after the Springwood killing as a break-in robbery and with Carter, they're assuming a gang killing. They're both off the mark. The common denominator is a rare book."

Ray leaned forward, "I don't know. I think you may be reaching a bit." He looked straight at Sidney. "Could be just a coincidence."

"There's that word again. No, Ray. It's a link."

Tillie did not move to empty the bags but turned, leaned against the counter, and listened.

"All right, let's say it isn't a coincidence, but where's the actual link? Yes, you can say they both touched a certain book at some point in their lives, but can you put them together? Can you see a relationship between the people? Lots of people may have an interest in a book, but if you can't put them together in the same room talking about it, you'll never make a case for anything other than an unrelated common interest."

Sidney fidgeted with his hands as though washing them. "Well, you're the professional detective. My job is to push you down a path to the truth. Your job is to find it. What about that FBI friend of yours? Have you talked with her?"

"Well...no. Why would I? She's dealing with the shooting at the craft fair, not the Pirate Islands. There's no connection."

"There is now."

"Sidney, please." Ray looked exasperated.

Sidney did not speak but Ray caught the look over the professor's glasses.

"Okay, okay. Maybe you have something." Ray knew Sidney did. He always did and he knew he'd be calling Nora Sullivan before the day was out.

Tillie also had some thoughts but decided not to share them. Larry Carter was from near Smoak, SC and she knew a lot of people from there came to Morgan for work on the islands and around town. If there was a connection, she would find it.

ↄↄↄ

Sidney seemed to be doing pretty well on his own, since they moved him from his bedroom upstairs into the library downstairs, where there was a sleeper sofa, so Tillie decided it would be okay to go home for the evening. She planned to be back in the morning to see Sidney had a decent breakfast and take care of Mickey.

As she drove off in her car, Tillie kept thinking of how to explore the movements of Larry Carter around Morgan. She never noticed the car parked at the end of the street, where a man with a notebook kept tr000ack of the people going in and out of 111 Howard Street. He had four names written down. Hattie left a half hour ago and Ray left for home fifteen minutes later. As Ray lived only a few houses down the street, the man managed to keep track of both of them and watched both houses until Tillie came out. He knew both Sidney and Ray were finished for the day. Because of his leg, he knew Sidney was grounded, and Ray had settled down at his dining room table for dinner with his wife, Marie. Harriet Ryan didn't seem to interest him. It was the trio of Sidney Lake, Tillie James and Ray Morton that had his attention. With Sidney and Ray finished for the day, he decided to follow Tillie on her way back to Deer Island. He would have to be careful though, as he knew she lived somewhere in the Gullah community, and he would stand out too much if he got close to her.

As Tillie drove, she kept her mind focused on Larry Carter and where he supposedly lived. The whole region around Walterboro was well known for its antipathy for the Black community even if Walterboro itself wasn't. Lots of Confederate flags and symbols dotted front lawns throughout the backroads and signs demanding *Protect our Heritage* could be seen at gas stations and convenience stores. This was Dylan Roof sympathizer country. So where would someone here like a Larry Carter get a job around Morgan? She was sure he had a pick-up truck with a confederate flag symbol on it so he wouldn't exactly be welcome on Deer Island where she lived, especially after the Mother Emanuel church massacre in Charleston. Most likely he worked for people on one of the newly developed islands popular with retirees from the North. They didn't understand the significance of the flag and the "heritage" code word as it was used in some parts of the south. They were looking for cheap manual labor and someone to run errands. She began making a mental list of people she knew who worked on Horse, Crow, and Summer islands around Morgan. She crossed the Deer Island bridge and headed for the Harriet Tubman Community Center, which sat next to the Long Road Praise House. When the driver in the car behind her saw where she was headed, he stopped and turned around.

Ray finished dinner and called Nora Sullivan of the FBI. Over dinner, he and Marie had had a long conversation about the tax sale business. Marie served as his sounding board and he always let her know what was going on so she would not be blindsided by something with which he became involved. She thought his connection to police matters would diminish when he retired, but wasn't surprised when he took on one job after another.

Nora Sullivan didn't seem to be surprised by Ray's comment that Sidney Lake believed there had to be a link between the tax sale and the missing Brontë book. As a Brontë sisters' fan, she knew how addictive the Brontë family story could be and how original Brontë material excited collectors. The question she had been wrestling with was: "Would someone be willing to kill to obtain or keep the original author's copy of *The Tenant of Wildfell Hall*?"

"So you think Sidney could be on to something?" Ray said in a surprised tone.

"I like the way Professor Lake thinks. We had quite an interesting talk when he was in the hospital. He's very good at stepping back to see the whole forest, regardless of how many interesting and dominant trees there might be around. So yes, I wouldn't rule it out. I wouldn't rule anything out. Especially since nine-eleven. Any time you try to narrow an investigation down you're bound to miss something, something that could be linked to another seemingly unrelated investigation. This is why defense attorneys and politicians are always trying to narrow them down. We've learned a lot over the past twenty-odd years."

"I'm getting the feeling you know something that may confirm Sidney's suspicions."

The line remained quiet for a moment as Agent Sullivan collected her thoughts. "Okay. You said you were officially working as an investigator for the County Solicitor's office so let me put it this way, I don't want what I say to get out just yet. In the spirit of cooperation, I'll tell you what we've learned, since you've asked the question—no one in the sheriff's office has done that yet. One—Larry Carter may have worked for Howard Springwood, as he did for other people in the area. Two—Howard Springwood was involved in land speculation on The Pirate Islands. Three—Howard Springwood is a person of interest in the marketing of stolen rare books. And four—Larry Carter and Howard Springwood have both been murdered…possibly by the same person."

When the conversation ended, Ray sat in his chair quietly. How would he keep this from Sidney? If he told Sidney, he was sure Tillie would know it in no time. Sidney wouldn't say it specifically to Tillie. Tillie found out about everything from Mickey. Not that the black Lab could speak—although she was very good at understanding and communicating—but Sidney confided everything to her. Out loud. And Tillie lurked in every corner of the house and overheard everything. Especially now that she had become Sidney's primary caregiver. Tillie, having learned something, would not necessarily repeat it, but she could accidentally blurt it out to someone else, probably in her family or someone in her housekeeper network. He could just stay away from Sidney for a few days, but that would be unusual, and Sidney would be after him immediately. *Could I deceive Sidney? Or better yet could I leave hints around that would lead him to find the links himself.* "Hmmm, there's an idea."

"What was that?" said Marie coming into the room.

Startled, Ray twisted and saw his wife looking at him as she held a dishtowel. "Oh, a thought just came to me about the case."

"Oh, good. That call to the FBI person was a good one then."

"Yes it was…yes it was."

⁕⁕⁕

The following day, Saturday, aroused memories of the Craft Fair for a great number of people. Sidney Lake would never forget the experience. There were a number of nights during the week when he awoke believing he was caught under the table in the food court area and panicked people were running across it, crushing him. Today, though, his thoughts were more analytical. He looked at the craft fair panic not from under the table but from above. He visualized the event as though he floated above the entire craft fair field, where he could see it all at once. Sidney had been told what happened. Tillie told him her story and he could see her hiding behind the food truck but he also saw her cradling him in her arms, as she sat next to him on the ground. That picture did not come from Tillie. She never said anything about it. No one did. But it was there as part of what happened. He never asked her about it.

The vision of the panic moved about and he could see the portable toilet area. There were news reports about it and Ray Morton had relayed information to him that he obtained from police sources who were at the scene. There was also the conversation he had with the FBI agent, Nora Sullivan, which filled in some of the blanks. Sidney envisioned an argument of some kind behind the toilet Burke Mansfield had occupied. He could see two men. One much older than the other. There was pushing and shoving. The young man was thrown against the back of the toilet by the older one and it shook violently. The door popped open. People were startled. A gun was drawn and shots fired. Burke fell out of the portable toilet as it shifted position and began to fall on him. The younger man fell to the ground behind the rear of the adjacent toilet. The older man anxiously watched the toilet shift, which gave him a partial view of Burke. The man hesitated. He looked first to his left at the younger man on the ground and then to his front where he had a partial view of two men near Burke. He moved out of the line of sight. Pressed his back against the neighboring toilet. He knew they didn't see him. The two men turned and ran. The man, now feeling confident, replaced the gun into its holster inside his jacket. He turned and hurriedly left the scene, making his way behind the cover of the other toilets.

Is this what happened? thought Sidney. He couldn't be sure, but it made sense. He had learned about the argument between the older and younger man from interviews with Burke Mansfield that Ray revealed. Burke had remembered the sounds of the voices and he assumed the age differences although Burke never saw either of them. The voice sounds convinced the investigators that they were mistaken about the word "Lucy" and that it referred to a woman. Burke must have been mistaken. They were sure they were looking for a man. The police decided to pursue the local gang dispute avenue, as the primary direction of their investigation. At least that was the official statement that was put out to the press. Ray knew the investigation was much wider. The police tentacles reach would have many arms. The press needed to be placated. The gang angle would keep the news cycle busy.

Sidney tried to envision a dispute between two younger men behind the toilet but he couldn't make it work.

Tillie had her own remembrances of the craft fair panic. Having made Sidney comfortable in his chair in the living room, she cleaned up the table and dishes from breakfast, stopped and stared out the kitchen window. Her view of what happened centered on reliving her own experience. She could still feel the hand of the EMS worker on her shoulder and him telling her to stay down, but the image that kept coming back was of her sitting on the ground holding Sidney's bleeding head in her lap. The words she spoke kept haunting her: "Sidney, don't you die on me." She never told anyone. It bothered her. Why did she say that? In just that way? She never called him Sidney. Never. Not even at home.

An hour away, Burke Mansfield lay in his hospital bed. They had taken him off the critical list. Never in his wildest dreams did he ever think he would be the victim of a shooting. Who shoots book dealers? He'd never even heard of anyone robbing a bookstore. It had to be one of the safest professions in existence. Yes, people did steal rare books, but books weren't like paintings or jewelry. They were personal. You had to know what you were looking for. But then the shooting didn't involve books. He, too, kept going over what happened a week ago. The police said he was an innocent victim of a dispute between two other people. So why did he keep bringing his profession into the mix? He learned from coworkers and family who came to see him yesterday that the person shot was Larry Carter, the young man he interviewed on the antiques show a few months earlier. Surely a strange coincidence? Perhaps that's why he kept thinking about a connection to books. Larry Carter and the Brontë book. It made sense. Or did it? And then it was the yelling he'd heard between an older man and Carter. At least it sounded like an older man. And why did he think he heard one of the men referred to as Lucy? Burke kept running everything over in his head. He couldn't explain was why the name of a woman kept coming into his head in connection with what happened.

Ray Morton also had the craft fair on his mind, but not a remembrance of it—as he had no personal experience of the panic. Marie left earlier for a Saturday meeting of a church group, leaving Ray with his thoughts as to how to reveal to Sidney the connection between the Brontë book and the tax sale scam. He knew Sidney had convinced himself of the connection, theoretically, but Ray had the proof. What sort of hints could he throw Sidney's way without divulging a confidence? "Something had better come to me soon," he said as he went to his front door. It was time for his meeting with Sidney and Tillie.

NINETEEN

No, we can't say that for sure," Ray said in response to Sidney's continued insistence of a definitive connection between the land grab of the Pirate Island and the theft of the Brontë book. "Yes, there does seem to be a link with regard to Howard Springwood and the Pirate Islands, but it could be an innocent one."

"Innocent? Hah!" pronounced Tillie, who sat in a straight chair on one side of the coffee table in Sidney's living room. Ray was opposite her on the sofa and Sidney held court from his comfortable chair between them.

"Not you too?"

"Yes, me too, Mister Morton. It's as clear as the nose on your face."

Sidney chuckled as he thought, *Two against one. Maybe it should be three if you've got Tillie on your side.*

"Look Tillie," continued Ray, "I understand where you're coming from but what's needed is some kind of proof. We don't have it...yet. It may be there—*I just can't tell you*—we just have to let it play out. I know you're both absolutely sure there's a link and if there is, Nora Sullivan will let me know. She's still looking into Howard Springwood's background. The sheriff in Walterboro is still looking into Larry Carter's background and his gang connections, so it's going to be a little while yet. They're moving careful an' deliberate."

"You mean slow. Betcha they still don't know that

Carter fella worked for Mister Springwood over on Crow Island."

Ray almost jumped out of his chair, "He what!"

Sidney sat back.

Tillie smiled. "Gotcha, don't I? Found out just before I got here."

"How?" said Ray.

"Missy Driscoll."

"Missy who?" Ray stared at Tillie in disbelief. "What have you found out?"

"Missy Driscoll teaches third grade at the Deer Island school an she has an uncle who works for a landscape company that takes care of the big houses on Crow Island, including' Mister Springwood's. Well, seems he had a couple of run-ins with Carter. A few days before the craft fair, the landscape workers was re-mulchin' some of the driveway plants an as Carter was leaven the Springwood place, he told one of them to get his nigger ass into the landscape truck an move outta his way. If Missy's uncle and friends could have got their hands on im, Carter would have never made it to that craft fair. He just took off for his own truck an give everybody the finger as he sped away across the mulch. He was bad, that one."

Sidney and Ray looked at one another.

Sidney asked, "Tillie have you told anyone about this?"

"Haven't had a chance. Just got here before Mister Morton. "Was gonna tell you what I heard then Mister Morton came in."

Ray stood up, "I have to make a phone call. Don't go away." He stepped into the front hallway and called Nora Sullivan.

Sidney addressed Tillie, "I'm trying to remember the

date of Howard Springwood's murder. I'm sure it was
well before the craft fair. A few weeks anyway. I wonder
what Larry Carter was doing at the Springwood place,
since it's probably all closed up?"

"No good, I'll bet. Pickin' up sompthin. Mighta had a
key. His truck was parked right in front of the place.
Lotta the real estate companies take care of the places
when the owners are away. An on Crow Island they're
away a lot. They have people just do a quick check on
stuff all the time. Lot's a times the owner calls up and
says they're commin' in for the weekend and want
someone to turn the water on and put out some porch
furniture. That kinda stuff. Betcha that's what he was
doin'."

Ray came back into the room after leaving Nora
Sullivan a message that he had firm proof Larry Carter
did work for Howard Springwood. Hearing Tillie's last
comment he said. "I could be wrong. Now that I think of
it, I can't imagine someone like Springwood giving the
likes of Carter a key. I'll call her back again later."

Sidney finally made a comment. "A break-in doesn't
sound right since his car was right out front and it was
daytime. If no one i living there Tillie could be right, he
might have had a key from someone. How about the real
estate company that manages the place when it's empty,
do we know which one?"

"We can find out. But Missy's uncle probably would
have reported him if he thought he was on the property
illegally. They have some pretty good security there.
Guards at the gate are armed and they make routine
patrols. The people that work on the island are cleared by
their employers, has anyone checked with them about
Carter?'

"Good point." Sidney looked at Ray and continued,

"You're the official investigator now. So…"

"Okay. My job," Ray sat down again. "I would assume the real estate company would notify the gatehouse that the property was empty. Security would do a periodic check of the building and should have a record of authorized people."

Another question from Sidney, "Interesting point. In addition to the real estate company, what about Springwood's family? Does he have any?"

"Another good question. I just don't know. Don't know anything about the man." Then after thinking for a moment, "Sidney, you've met him. What did you think? You had a number of conversations with him toward the end of the Reed murder case, what kind of an impression did you get of him?"

Sidney shifted in his chair and massaged his chin slowly. "It was some time ago. I remember him being a little standoffish when I first spoke with him. But that was on the phone, and he had no idea who I was so his reaction would have been appropriate, under the circumstances. I did get a chance to speak with him in person at the garden club affair." He continued to rub his chin. Remembering. "He seemed well versed in Victorian literature, I remember. Not out of the ordinary. I know many lawyers who are avid readers…and collectors. Yes, I do remember him being well versed in Victorian studies. A bit strange, now that I think of it, he never seemed to pick up on the Bell brothers."

"Bell brothers?" questioned Ray.

"That's the phony name those Brontë sisters wrote as," offered Tillie.

"Oh," Ray looked at Sidney.

"She's correct."

"Bin hanging around with the professor here too

much. I just kinda pick up things."

Ray now saw a route he could take to put Sidney on the confidential track Nora wanted to keep quiet. Time for Sidney to put some pieces together for himself. "Didn't you once say you suspected Springwood of stealing the novel from the police?"

"Yes, I did. Didn't follow it up though. The case had been solved. The missing books would be the chief of police's problem."

"Think differently now?"

Tillie looked at Sidney. "If he didn't, he sure does now. I know I do."

"You do?" said Ray feeling pleased with himself.

"Yeah, lot of those big business types on Crow Island ain't to be trusted. Got a feelin Springwood would fit right in. Somebody might want to talk with Missy's uncle. He just might have a missing piece." Tillie sat back, satisfied.

Sidney also looked satisfied, as though an avenue opened up to him, one he knew to be correct. "He should have known."

"Known what," said Ray.

"That the Bells were the Brontës. He was the one who put the list of books together that contained the rare ones. From my conversation with him on the phone, I was impressed with his knowledge of writers and titles. Hmmmm. I wonder…?"

"You wonder what?"

"I wonder if he could have been the source of the books. I wonder if he sold the books to General Brewster's uncle or, at least, was the source of them. Given that, is it possible he knew there was some question as to the validity of the notations in the margins attributed to Anne Brontë? Many questions are in need of answers. Wait a minute, didn't you tell Hattie some weeks ago that Springwood was someone the special art group of the FBI had been interested in? My memory has really gone off somewhere."

Ray sat back on the sofa, took a large breath, and exhaled slowly. "Hmmm. Interesting. There was a rumor I heard a few weeks back when I was in Charlotte." He paused. "Any thoughts on where we should start looking for those answers?" *Mission accomplished,* thought Ray. *It didn't take the crafty professor long.*

"Yes. Yes I do."

Tillie rolled her eyes and said, "Oh, oh, here we go again."

Ray pressed on, "Well, Sidney?"

"The lists."

"The lists?" inquired Ray.

Sidney shifted in his chair and moved his leg to the opposite side of the hassock. "If I remember correctly, there were two lists of books. Remember, before this whole episode of George Reed's murder, General Brewster inherited the complete library of his uncle in Charlotte, North Carolina that he had received after the uncle died. He asked me to catalog the books for him in an effort to see if there was anything there of value. Much of the collection was fiction and the General never read fiction, he was a military history buff. When I first started looking over the collection there was no list at all. Then, a list of the contents of the entire library was uncovered, which seemed to be a summary of some kind. Subsequently, as a result of my prodding, I believe, a more elaborate list was uncovered, which I never had the opportunity to see because of the George Reed murder investigation coming to a head. I would love to see those lists and compare them. Do you think our Chief of Police still has them?"

Ray thought for a moment. "Possible. Back then we had two problems on our hands, as you know. One was the murder of George Reed, and the other was the burglary of General Brewster's home. I'm not sure which case would have the lists if they have them at all."

"Why wouldn't they have been retained?"

"Looking back on it at this point, the lists themselves were not evidence of anything having to do with either the murder or the break-in. They could have been returned to General Brewster."

"I would love to get my hands on those lists to compare them. I think they'll tell us a very interesting story about Howard Springwood."

"How?" Ray said with a very quizzical look on his face.

Tillie smiled again as she said, "Oh yeah, here we go."

℆℈℆

The plan from the meeting had Sidney checking with General Brewster about the book lists and Ray discussing the matter with Police Chief Hornig. However, Sidney developed a further plan that he knew Ray would not be happy with. Tillie would get in touch with Missy's uncle and obtain access to Crow Island to confirm Springwood's house had a library. He was convinced it did and contained rare and valuable books. All Tillie had to do was peek through some windows. Depending on what Tillie discovered, Hattie's job would be to work on getting access to the house through one of her real estate friends who sang in the choir with her at St. Luke's. Sidney assumed the empty property would be under the management of a local realtor.

The plan had not been fully fleshed out yet. Sidney knew from past experience it would change and that would be fine. What he knew for sure was that Springwood was the key to everything and Sidney wanted to be part of solving the puzzle. He could usually talk Ray into going along with his plans but, since Ray had become part of the formal investigation—being an investigator for the solicitor's office—Ray had to play by the rules. Sidney had no intention of doing so, as usual.

The small gathering at Sidney's broke up just before ten am. Ray left first and headed for Morgan's city hall building and police headquarters. While most government offices in the building were closed on Saturdays, the police department ran twenty-four seven. What Ray didn't expect was the activity going on in the building. Then he remembered: *Javier* was coming. With all that had been going on over the past week, he'd lost track of the hurricane pounding the Bahamas. The original forecasts had the storm moving west across the Florida peninsular and then up toward Pensacola. A familiar pattern. It would eventually make its way back to the Atlantic but only after being knocked down to a tropical storm. Morgan would get the backwash. Wet and windy as usual. Downtown Charleston would flood, as would the poorer neighborhoods, also as usual. Those areas tended to flood in a heavy mist.

"What's going on," Ray called to a uniformed officer coming out of the building.

"*Javier* changed his mind. Decided to take a tour of the Florida and Georgia coastline rather than Disney World."

"Wow. We gonna get hit?"

"Could be." The officer pointed with his thumb to the building behind him. "Emergency management's gearing up no matter what." He continued to the police cruiser parked at the curb.

"Hornig in."

"Yup."

"Thanks."

"No problem."

Ray quickly headed up the steps to the entrance to the police department. For a Saturday, there was a hubbub of activity. Emergency management staff and volunteers were everywhere. When you live along the southeast coast every threat of a major storm triggered crisis preparedness mode. In the region, every town from Charleston to Savannah would be holding meetings, evaluating shelters, notifying volunteers, and planning evacuation routes. In the Lowcountry of South Carolina, there are occupied islands everywhere filled with not only long-time residents but also recently built housing developments and holiday resorts. The maximum elevation runs below ten feet above sea level and every coastal storm is a potential threat.

Everyone knew this. Everyone knew the risks. Everyone had been through it before, which created a problem. The area contained thousands of people who believed themselves to be hurricane savvy. They had seen storm after storm make an unforcasted turn to the right and stay in the Gulf Stream offshore. Evacuation was not for them. They would ride it out.

Then there were the new residents from the north who moved in with all their worldly possessions. They lived behind gates with armed guards but when the storms came they had their own homes and families to take care of. They would "secure" the islands and protect their own. No way were the residents leaving all their possessions unguarded. It can't be that bad, they reasoned. We're not going.

It happened every time a storm approached. This time would be no different.

Ray spotted Chief Hornig's secretary at her desk, "The chief around?"

"Emergency management meeting. You know the drill."

"Yeah. I need to check a document list from a case a while back. You have time to look it up for me or can I do it myself?"

"I'm not sure I should let you do it. I heard you're working for Georgia Sawyer but I don't think they gave you a password for the system and I can't let you have mine. Give me a few minutes and we'll look together. Which case?"

"The Reed murder."

"Oh, sure. That's come up a couple of times recently."

Back at Howard Street, Sidney kept re-thinking the plan he envisioned earlier. Tillie was out with Mickey and Harriet Ryan would arrive momentarily. He knew he had to get into Howard Springwood's library but there were probably two of them. The larger one would be at his home in Charlotte, North Carolina with the secondary one at Crow Island. He had no idea which would be the most likely place to hide rare books, especially those that might be forgeries or, possibly, even stolen originals. He would love to know what Nora Sullivan knew about why Springwood was a "person of interest" of the FBI's art fraud division and while conjuring up possible reasons, Nora Sullivan called him.

Hattie heard the phone ring as she came in. "Want me to get that, Sidney?"

"Oh please do. I forgot to have Tillie bring the phone

over before she left."

Hattie answered the phone and would normally screen the call for him, but Nora Sullivan identified herself right up front and Hattie knew Sidney would want to talk with her. "Yes, Miss Sullivan, he's right here. I'll get the phone to him."

In a whisper Hattie said, "It's Nora Sull..."

"Yes, let me have it."

She handed him the phone.

"Miss Sullivan, Sidney Lake, here. How can I help you?"

Hattie sat down

"Sorry to bother you on a Saturday morning, professor. How are you feeling?"

"Oh, I'm doing very well. It's been a week now and I'm getting back into a normal routine. The leg's a little bothersome but then it was before I reinjured it."

"Well, I'm glad to hear that. I just received a message from Burke Mansfield that he wanted to talk with me and has asked that you come along as well. Could you meet me at the hospital in Walterboro around one pm?"

Sidney placed his hand over the receiver and whispered to Hattie, "Can you get us to Walterboro by one pm?"

She nodded her head in reply.

"Why, yes. Mrs. Ryan can drive me. Is there something going on? I spoke with Mr. Mansfield yesterday and he seemed to be doing very well. There's nothing wrong is there?"

"Your call seems to have jogged his memory about something. Something that happened a few years ago, which he believes may tie into the conversation he overheard last week just before he was shot, as well as a comment you made. Something you may be able to help him…and me…with."

"I'll be happy to."

"Good, thank you, professor. Walterboro is midway between Columbia and Morgan, so we'll probably arrive around the same time. And tell Mrs. Ryan she's welcome to join us in the meeting. Mr. Mansfield has mentioned her a few times."

"I certainly will, Thank you."

Sidney put down the phone. He didn't say anything for a few moments. Then, "Burke Mansfield seems to want to see both of us. I wonder what he's remembered."

"Both of us?"

"Something has triggered his memory. There's a connection of some sort between an event a few years ago and what happened last Saturday."

"My…hmmm…I wonder…Sidney, we have to get going. With the latest on *Javier* coming this way by tomorrow night, the roads will be a mess. The route to Walterboro is an evacuation route from here."

"I agree. But I have to talk to Tillie before we leave."

"That's fine. I left my car at home and it'll take me five minutes to go over and get it."

"We could take mine."

"No, if there's going to be traffic, I'd feel better driving my own car." She got up from the chair. "You stay put. I'll be right back."

Within a minute of her shutting the door behind her, Tillie and Mickey came in.

"Ah, Tillie, we need to talk, I have an errand for you."

TWENTY

The drive to the hospital in Walterboro proved to be a lot better than the one to Savannah, as Sidney and Hattie were able to stay away from all interstates, especially I-95.

"More traffic than I would have thought," said Sidney as they stopped for a red light. "This is the second time we had to wait for two lights to get through."

Hattie inched the car forward slightly. "Everyone seems to be taking these storm warnings more seriously. We've had some nasty ones in the last couple of years."

"I wonder if we should have made an evacuation reservation at a hotel in Columbia just to be safe. Maybe I should do that now." Sidney reached into his jacket pocket and took out his cell phone.

Hattie spotted the phone. "Oh my goodness, you have it with you."

He gave her a look over his glasses. "Of course...Tillie shoved it in my pocket just before I went out the door," he confessed.

"What in the world would you do without that woman?"

Sidney didn't answer the question but asked one of his own, "How would I find out the number of one of the La Quinta's around Columbia?"

"Why don't I just pull over up here? I can get it from the internet on my phone."

"You have the internet on your phone?"

"Yes. And so do you. If you'd like me to, I'd be happy to show you how to use it?"

"No, no. That's all right. Some other time."

As Hattie pulled onto the shoulder where the road widened, her phone rang. She stopped and took it from the center console tray. She quickly checked the display as she answered, "Hi Carol. What did you find out?"

"Not listed and nothing pending," said the voice on the phone.

"Didn't think it would be. Springwood only died a few weeks ago. Know anything about the place?"

"Driven by it a lot. Sits back about seventy-five feet off Crow Island Drive. It's number 75. Nice looking. Pretty average place. Runs about eight hundred thousand I would think. Probably twenty-five hundred square feet or so. On the water but not deep enough for a dock. Can launch a kayak or canoe other than at low tide. Never met the owner. Apparently a weekend place. Doesn't rent it out. On the left side as you drive in. Gets the sun in the evening. Deck and screened-in porch. Sunsets over the marsh."

"I'm sold," Hattie laughed.

Laughter back, "Hey, I'm in real estate. Every house is a potential listing. Just ask Casey. He's got us on quotas now."

More laughter. "I'm, in the car on the way to Walterboro. I'll give you a call back later. Thanks, Carol, you're the best. Oh, by the way, do you know who has the management contract?"

"We do. Morgan Real Estate. That's how I know about it. Casey has a bunch of them on Crow." They ended the call.

Hattie spoke to Sidney as she put the phone back, "That was my real estate contact. She just gave me a complete run-down on the Springwood place on Crow Island. It's number 75 Crow Island Drive. Left side as you drive in. It's not listed, so there's not a lockbox on it. I don't believe they use them for Crow Island residents. Most people don't want them there as they're afraid of someone stealing the key from the box and cleaning the house out."

"I should think that's what they pay the armed guards at the gate to protect them from, but then, it is an island. There are unlimited places to land a boat to get around the gate."

"True, the houses have security systems as well, though."

"Ah, yes. But in the case of a house where no one resides, I would not be surprised to find the system unmonitored."

"Sidney, this is not downtown Morgan, I'll bet half the houses on Crow Island are empty most of the time."

"Possibly. There would be regular patrols of the empty ones. The residents would just notify the gate when they leave and again when they return. It's going to be interesting trying to get inside."

"Maybe not. Casey Yarborough-Morgan Real Estate has the management contract." Hattie suddenly realized why they stopped and reached for her phone again. "Almost forgot. Let me check the LQ site. Didn't we stay at the one just north of Columbia last time? The one off of route one?"

"Yes, I think we did. It has a park not far away for Mickey."

As Hattie worked with her phone, Sidney 1.

2began to think about the coming meeting with Nora Sullivan and Burke Mansfield. *What could Burke have remembered? Everything happened so fast that day. And why does he need me to be present? Do I have some information I don't know about? Well, we'll soon find out.*

"I grabbed two rooms on the first floor. Make it easier to get out with Mickey when we have to." Hattie put her phone away again and put the car in gear." We're only a couple of miles away from the hospital now." She eased into traffic. "Where are we supposed to meet the FBI?"

"Miss Sullivan said she'd like to meet in the lobby for a few minutes before we go upstairs. I'm sure she's there now. Easier ride down from Columbia. Traffic going in the opposite direction."

"Why don't you give her a call? Tell her we'll be there in ten minutes."

Hattie's estimate held true as they left the main road and lost the traffic that had been slowing them down. Sidney no sooner finished leaving Nora Sullivan a message when he saw the sign for the hospital. They parked within a reasonable distance of the front entrance so walking would be easier for Sidney. Hattie had suggested Sidney get a temporary handicap parking sticker for himself, which he, being Sidney, didn't do.

"Professor Lake, nice to see you up and around," Nora said while making her way over to Sidney and Hattie as they entered the lobby. "Leg still bothering you, though. Hope it's not too bad."

Hattie extended her hand, "I'm Harriet Ryan, the designated driver for the day."

"Ah, Professor Ryan. Yes, I expected to see you here. I believe you also know Mr. Mansfield?"

They started walking toward a series of chairs set up in a back corner of the room.

Hattie answered. "Well, yes. We met that one time on Skidaway Island. Exploring the background of the missing Anne Brontë novel."

"The book. That's what I wanted to discuss before we went upstairs."

As they approached the target sitting area, a young man got up and took a step toward them. Nora introduced him. "This is agent Kaufman. He's been doing some research on rare book thefts, and I thought it would be useful to have him here." They exchanged greetings and sat down."

"Professor Lake, why don't you sit over here," Nora pointed to the chair closest to the wall. "You should be able to keep your leg out of harm's way back in the corner."

"Thank you."

Once everyone became comfortable, Nora began, "Professor Lake, I know you and your friends have become involved in some difficult situations in the past and have developed a reputation for being accurate in judging—or perhaps evaluating is a better word—people and their motives."

Sidney sat back and folded his hands in front of him and lightly tapped his right index finger against the back of his left hand. He remained silent but gave a slight nod of his head.

Nora observed his acknowledgment and continued, "I'm aware that you have met Burke Mansfield on two occasions in your pursuit of the missing rare edition of *The Tenant of Wildfell Hall.* Are these the only times you have met?"

"Yes."

"Have you formed an opinion of him?"

"To a degree."

With that answer, Nora noticed that Hattie gave Sidney a quick look that indicated she did not expect him to provide an answer with any qualifying element to it.

"Could you share your thoughts?"

"Yes. I assume we're being informal here as you're trying to piece together the possibility of a link of some sort between the missing novel, Mr. Mansfield, and the murder of Mr. Carter. A link you haven't completely found."

"Let's just say we have some unanswered questions and coincidences bother me."

"Me too." Sidney and Nora locked eyes and held them for a bit longer than would be expected.

Hattie noticed. Agent Kaufmann did not.

Sidney shifted slightly in his chair. "All right. On reflection, I've begun to develop some questions as to why he showed up at the craft fair that Saturday. At first, he said he would not be there. He had a conflict. When we met he seemed surprised even though he said he hoped to run into me. He claimed he tried to call me but my cell phone didn't answer. That in itself would not be unusual, as Mrs. Ryan can attest. I'm not very good with electronic devices and often don't have my cell phone with me or have forgotten to turn it on. However, after I returned to Morgan and had an opportunity to think about the events that Saturday, I finally got around to checking the phone's answering system. He didn't leave a message. I was surprised. Given his initial enthusiastic reaction to joining me in looking for links to the novel, I expected otherwise. During the time we were together that morning we got along well and, again, found we had much in common. I could not see any actions or hear any comments that gave me any reason to suspect that what he said wasn't true. However, on reflection again, I began to question his leaving for the restroom area when he did. Did he have a pre-arranged meeting set with Mr. Carter?

Is this why he was unable to come to the craft fair with me? Was a meeting with Mr. Carter the conflict he referred to?"

At this point Sidney stopped, unfolded his hands, and raised them slightly in the air.

Nora responded with, "And have you answered any of those questions?"

"No, I have not."

At this point, Nora turned to Hattie and asked, "Professor Ryan, what did you think of Burke Mansfield?"

Hattie shifted nervously in her chair. All eyes were now on her. "Well...I only...met him the one time. He seemed to be very pleasant and polite. I saw...how well he and Professor Lake were getting on. They were both expressing enthusiasm about the Brontë novel. My impression of him was certainly favorable. I can't think of anything unfavorable to say. Yes, I would say my impression was favorable."

Sidney leaned forward in his chair and asked, "Agent Sullivan, let me give you an idea where I am at this point. I've expressed this concern to both Professor Ryan and Mrs. James, who, as I'm sure you know, is my housekeeper," Nora nodded, "as well as Ray Morton, who is now working on special assignment for the county solicitor's office," Nora again nodded. "I believe there is a connection between the shooting at the craft fair, which I believe to involve the missing novel, and some suspicious land purchases, or attempted purchases, in Coastal Rivers County."

Nora Sullivan sat quietly for a moment before she said, "You mean Howard Springwood?"

Sidney stared at Nora, as did Hattie. They both stayed silent. Nora noted their surprise but her expression did not change. She expected the reaction.

Finally Sidney asked, "How do you know about Howard Springwood?"

"The FBI is very thorough. We have to be. Just because we don't have enough evidence to proceed against someone, doesn't mean we ignore them. A case or an accusation may become cold, but it's not forgotten. Some years ago he was a person of interest in the transfer of some stolen rare books from a private library in Europe. Nothing stuck to him. His was just one of many names that popped up. It came as a referral from INTERPOL. The original perpetrator of the theft, a college professor," a very small smile appeared at the corner of her mouth as she said the words, "who claimed he didn't know someone had stolen from him, some of the books *he* stole from the library. Mr. Springwood's name remained in our database. When a report of his murder appeared a few weeks ago, it was linked back to the INTERPOL referral.

"Last week, you may recall, while you were here in the hospital, we discussed the missing Brontë novel. A few bells went off for me and when I looked into the case of the Reed murder investigation, there was Howard Springwood again. And a rare book went missing."

"Ah," said Sidney, "I am duly impressed. But let me ask you a specific question—what does this have to do with Burke Mansfield and why do you want me with you today when you speak with him?"

"Well, it was not my idea, but his, Mr. Mansfield's. My first instincts were to reject the idea but after giving it some thought, I realized your being here could be a real asset."

"In what way?"

"I don't want to bring up the name of Howard

Springwood. I would like you to do that. I want him to believe I'm here about the incident that occurred at the craft fair. Which I am, but right now that's still in the hands of the local sheriff. At this point the link I'm trying to make is between Larry Carter and Howard Springwood."

Sidney perked up. "I can definitely help you with that. We've already found it but...not the way you may think. The link that Mrs. James came up with is in relation to a potentially fraudulent land purchases related to The Pirate Islands in Coastal Rivers County."

Nora looked over to the junior agent who was writing furiously in his notebook. "I saw something recently on that name. Kaufman, check with the office on The Pirate Islands." Turning back to Sidney and Hattie, "One piece of information we have may relate to your land purchase query, you probably don't know, although it is public information, is that Howard Springwood was a registered lobbyist at the Department of the Interior."

☙❧☙

Tillie met Missy's uncle at a turn-off a mile away from the front gate to Crow Island.

"You must be Miss Tillie," said the handsome, tall, Black man standing by the pickup truck.

Tillie pulled up right next to him. Her window was already open. "Yes sir," she said. "You must be Missy's uncle Jerry?"

"Yes, Ma'am."

Tillie made a motion to get out but he stopped her. "No, that's not needed. I got you all set up. Here's a gate pass for you." He handed her a rectangular white cardboard sign about the size of a license plate. "I'm sure you know the drill. Just hang back until you see the left guest lane get backed up, then ease over to the right lane, creep up to the gatehouse, make sure the sign's real clear in the front window, wave and give a big smile an keep goin'. Anybody says anything tell 'um your workin' with me on hurricane get ready stuff."

"Yeah, I know how to do it. Missy gave me your cell phone if there's any questions."

"You know how to find the place?"

"Yeah, I'm okay."

"One suggestion, back down the driveway so the front of the car with the pass in the windshield is facin' Crow Island Drive. When you're lookin' around through the windows, look like you're making sure they are shut tight and the shutters are in workin' order. I don't think anybody's gonna bother you."

Tillie laughed as she said, "Tell me one thing, how'd, a nice lady like Missy get such a devious Uncle Jerry?"

"Ha, ha," he laughed with a big smile. "Don't let that sweet little girl fool ya, it runs in the family."

More laughter from both of them.

Uncle Jerry finally said, "Git yourself up there now, you'll do all right. But keep my number handy. I don't expect you'll get stopped by the guards. More likely it'll be a nosey neighbor. Don't trust anyone they don't recognize. There's lots of 'um around. Give my regards to Missy when you see her an' tell her she owes her old Uncle Jerry one."

More laughter as Tillie headed for the gatehouse at Crow Island.

TWENTY-ONE

Sidney and Hattie were both tense as they entered Burke Mansfield's hospital room. They liked the rare book dealer. For Sidney, it was not easy for him to find people he felt compatible with because of his adherence to proper conduct and formality. But here sat Burke Mansfield, as close a clone of himself as he might find—the jacket, the tie, the polite manner, and the love of old books, especially Victorian ones. Sidney did not want to learn Burke was other than what he appeared to be. However, the professor had no intention of being influenced by personal feelings.

Hattie also liked Burke for the same reason Sidney did. After all, she liked Sidney, although she admitted he drove her to distraction from time to time. She assumed Burke would as well, but he had a more appealing physical appearance. However, if the rare book dealer was found to be on the wrong side of the law, well...

Burke sat in a chair near his bed and other chairs had been brought into the room to accommodate the four visitors. A nurse straightened everything up for her patient before she left, closing the door on her way out.

Sidney began, "I am so pleased to see you up and about. For someone whose been shot twice you seem to be doing remarkably well."

"Well, I'm definitely feeling much better. After what happened, I...I'm just happy to be anywhere. And Professor Ryan, it's so nice to see you again," he gave her a big smile. "I'm so glad you were able to come along."

"I'm Sidney's driver today, but I would have liked to come anyway."

Concern appeared on Burke's face, "Oh, yes, your leg Sidney. How is it?"

"It's coming along. It's a re-injury so it's a bit more problematic. But it is coming along." He gave a quick glance toward Hattie, who merely let the remark pass.

Nora decided to take control. "The nurse reminded us that this is only your first full day out of bed and didn't want us to tire you out too much, so perhaps we should get down to business. Mr. Mansfield, you indicated you had remembered something about the shooting that you wanted to share with us."

"Ah, yes, but first I have to make an apology to Sidney here." He looked directly at Sidney as he spoke. "I wasn't entirely truthful that Saturday when I said I had a conflicting appointment and wouldn't be able to join you. I wanted to find the source of the Anne Brontë book first. It's a competitive thing you see. We rare book dealers are a small but intense group. If Mr. Carter had been telling the truth, then the source from whom he obtained the book might have other rare books as well. An estate sale with a trove of undiscovered gems, perhaps. I wanted to get to it first so my plan was to visit the antique and estate sale places before you did. I had always planned on doing it after I heard Mr. Carter's story on the television show, but never got around to it because of my employer passing away and his family deciding to close up the business. At that point, I was out of work and searching for a new position. With you in the picture, you had an advantage: you could interrogate Mr. Carter about the book where I, ethically, couldn't. My

plan was to meet up with you at the craft fair around
lunchtime after I had visited the shops in town. I hadn't
anticipated you going to the shops as well. I'm not very
good at deception so it has bothered me the whole time.
That's why I hoped you would come today. I do
apologize."

Sidney looked at Burke and smiled. "Thank you. , I
wondered about your actions that day when I had the
opportunity to review them. I didn't think they were
sinister in any way. Let's just forget it."

Hattie sat in amazement looking at the two men. *What
a pair*, she thought, *what a pair.*

The young FBI agent, Kaufman looked completely
confused, as though he couldn't understand what the fuss
was about.

Nora Sullivan took the conversation in stride and got
down to business. "I wonder, Mr. Mansfield, if you could
tell us what you now remember about the shooting, in
addition to what you said previously?"

"Ah, yes." Burke shifted in his chair. His lower half
was draped in a lightweight blanket while his upper torso
was covered with a hospital gown and another blanket
draped around his shoulders. "Well, it was just as I was
entering the toilet. I heard some raised voices but I
assumed they were from behind me. It never occurred to
me that they were coming from anywhere else."

"Where, now, do you think they were coming from?"

"In front of me. On the other side of the toilet wall."

"Go on." Nora crossed her pants suited legs and
settled back in her chair.

"They were speaking very low at first and I didn't pay
any attention to what they were saying. It was none of my
business. It just seemed like ordinary chatter. Then the
older man pushed Mr. Carter against my toilet and the

unit shook violently."

"How do you know the person was older and are you sure it was a man?" asked Nora.

"Well, I don't. It's just that the voice was deeper and there was anger in it and not fear. The other voice, who I now presume was Mr. Carter, had a higher pitch to his voice. He sounded younger and afraid."

"Okay. What did you hear the older person say?"

"Something like, 'Where is it?' It was an angry demanding voice. They could have been there for some time before I arrived and the older man was losing his patience. At least that's what I think looking back on it." Burke's face looked strained. His shoulders slumped and his face appeared whiter than it did when they first came in. He was clearly getting tired. "No...no. It was 'Where are they?' Yes. Yes...yes, that was it. 'Where are...they?' I'm sure of it."

"And the response?" asked Nora.

Sidney tensed as he waited for the answer that didn't come. Burke had his eyes closed and breathed heavily. His shoulders slumped as he exhaled.

Nora asked the question again. She also could see that Burke was now tired and having difficulty. She held back and waited. "Take your time, Mr. Mansfield."

Hattie, seeing the change got up and said, "I'll get the nurse."

Nora continued, "Mr. Mansfield?"

Finally, he said, "I...put...them...back. Lucy, I put...them back."

Hattie's head snapped around. "A woman? The shooter *was* a woman?"

ⲉⲟⲉⲟ

Tillie did as she had been told and parked her car with the front windshield facing out the driveway. She placed the gate pass so it stood out and would be clearly recognizable from the road. Uncle Jerry didn't need to instruct her to follow this procedure. She knew it well. People who live behind gates are frightened...of everything. They become that way because they feel vulnerable. Southerners, in general, don't live behind gates. Real estate developers love the word *exclusive,* which is based on the word *exclude,* the gate at the front of a new development puts a punctuation mark on the word *exclusive,* as it is designed to exclude everyone not on the approved list. A wonderful selling point. Guarantying privacy and the comfort of being among your own kind...for safety. Crow Island was very *exclusive.*

Tillie expected to be challenged when she entered a gated community, and not just at the front gate. Frightened people were everywhere and if a Black face came into view it would be reported to the security team or someone would come up to her and ask her what she was doing around a million-dollar property. The idea of someone with a Black face owning such a place would never be considered. So Tillie was happy to have the excuse of hurricane preparedness as a cover. She knew it would be helpful. She had no sooner closed her car door when a vehicle out on the road slowed to a crawl and she could see a grey-haired head straining to look in her direction. She smiled to herself and walked to the house.

The building had a large Lowcountry porch that wrapped around three sides. The structure was raised about five feet, as most island houses were, depending on the local mean high tide elevations. As she went up the stairs, and looked at the sky, the clouds were beginning to appear angry and there were occasional bursts of wind. She checked the weather forecasts an hour ago from the car and had learned that *Javier* changed his mind…again. Earlier this morning he seemed to be going to pass west of Jacksonville Florida, but the front coming from the west decided to assert itself and block the move. The storm would now stay east of Jacksonville and hug the Georgia coastline. Given the new forecast, Tillie decided to perform a cursory hurricane readiness evaluation and give it to Uncle Jerry. It seemed the right thing to do.

She started at the front door and the outside porch area. There was a sitting area consisting of a sofa, a coffee table, and three comfortable chairs. They were weatherproof cane with green pillows. *With that storm commin' somebody better get all this stuff moved outta here,* she noted to herself. Tillie then checked the two windows on each side of the front door. Both had working shutters and would fully protect the windows…if they were closed and latched together. In checking the shutters, she also took the time to have a look inside. What appeared to be a parlor was to the left. It had a fireplace on the left wall and some bookshelves at the back. The shelves were filled with various display pieces and ceramic ware, but no books.

On the right side of the front door were a matching set of windows with shutters. She inspected them and then looked inside. It was a formal dining room with a crystal chandelier and a table and chairs for ten. No books.

Around the right side of the porch were some more chairs that needed to be moved to safety and three windows with appropriate working shutters. Two windows gave light to the dining room and the third revealed a butler's pantry. The porch ended here, as the building jutted out, concealing the kitchen beyond.

As she came back around to the front of the building, a woman stood at the front door. "May I help you?" she asked in a firm tone that said, *What are you doing here?*

Tillie didn't skip a beat, "Checkin' the house for the storm."

"Oh. You're supposed to be here?"

"Ma'am, jus' look at what's on this porch." Tillie pointed to the chairs, table, and cushions. "The wind hits and these things are goin' right through those windows. I sure hope you got good shutters on your place. Shutters ain't no good if they can't be closed an' locked."

"Well, yes we do. Do you think the storm is coming this way?"

"Sure do. Gonna come right up off the coast. The islands is gonna be shut down. Everybody gonna have to go." Tillie purposely spoke with a stronger than usual accent in order to fit the stereotype the woman expected. "Yes Ma'am, it's comin' an' it ain't gonna be pretty. You better get you-self back home an get your place ready and go lookin' for a place to say till it's over."

The woman now looked worried. "You mean we're going to have to leave everything...unprotected?"

"Guess you ain't been here too long. Don't you worry none. They shut down the gate and block the roadway with some a the heavy garden stuff and trucks. Block it all up so nobody can drive by. Don't wanna be stuck inside when that happens. You betta get home an' get ready. If you need some help come back and get me an' I'll help."

"Oh, thank you. My husband's away in Boston and won't be back until next weekend." She now had something more pressing to worry about. "I'll go right now."

Tillie watched her make her way down the steps and

get to her car that she parked next to Tillie's. She gave the woman a wave as she drove off.

Back to business, Tillie headed for the left side of the porch. The first two windows were the mirror image of the right side, bracketing the outside of the fireplace that was in the parlor. The rest of the porch was different, it extended beyond where the other side ended by at least fifteen feet. The wall space had only one window. Tillie looked inside. The library looked back. "Wow," she said out loud. "Professor Lake would love this room." It was three times the size of Sidney's library on Howard Street. There were floor-to-ceiling bookshelves everywhere. She gave the room a careful examination. There was a fireplace next to the window where she stood. What caught her interest right away was a section of the bookcase that had glass doors on them and below another section that had solid wood doors. All the doors were lockable. *Sompthin' important in there I'll bet,* she thought. Then remembering what she was supposed to be doing began to inspect, close, and lock the shutters, all the time she concentrated on committing the room to memory. Every inch of it she could see.

There was only one more place she hadn't looked: the rear of the house that faced the water. As Tillie made her way back to the front porch stairs, a tall, slim, man with short blond hair made his way carefully through the wooded area on the right side of the house. He was clad in a black three-piece suit and focused on getting to the house without Tillie seeing him.

એએએ

The nurse assigned to Burke Mansfield's room advised everyone not to worry. Burke's dozing off was not unusual and was common given the medications he took just before they arrived. She checked him and said, "Just give him a few minutes and he'll be fine."

Everyone left the room except for agent Kaufman who offered to stay and alert everyone when Burke woke up. Sidney and Nora stepped just outside the room to chat while Hattie went over to the nurse's station.

Sidney leaned comfortably on his cane as he said, "Seems rather interesting how a dead man, with no apparent link to the tax sale, and the missing rare book have become catalysts in both crimes. There is something I wanted to mention that has been bothering me. It has to do with two lists, or catalogue of books, that Mr. Springwood came up with when I was involved with trying to determine if books of value were stolen during a break-in a few years back. I'm sure if the Anne Brontë book had been on the first list I was given, I would have spotted it."

"The connection to the Reed murder case, yes, I've reviewed that in connection with Springwood's involvement. Although he was never much of a factor from what I can tell."

"True, I thought the same at the time. Now I'm not so sure." Sidney hesitated but then decided to go on. "Have you been to Springwood's home in Charlotte?"

"No I haven't. His death was deemed a local matter and the investigation is still in the hands of the local police. No reason for the FBI to be involved. Why do you ask?"

"The connection to stolen rare books. You said he was a person of interest at one point."

"Yes, but nothing ever came of it. INTERPOL never sent us another inquiry so we never had anything to pursue."

Sidney had a slight smile on his face when he said, "I think an analysis of his personal library in the house in Charlotte might be very interesting."

Now it was Nora's time to hesitate before responding. "You believe the Brontë book might be the beginning of something and Springwood is in the middle of it?"

Agent Kaufmann peeked out of Burke's room. "He's awake."

As Nora and Sidney walked back into Burke Mansfield's room, Sidney's cell phone rang. They stopped as Sidney searched for the phone.

Nora seeing him fumble around pointed to his left jacket pocket. "I think it's coming from there."

Sidney, now flustered, retrieved the phone. In trying to answer it the phone slipped from his grasp and hit the floor at his feet. Nora immediately bent over and grabbed it. In handing it over to him she looked at the display "It's Ray Morton."

"Hello? Ray?" He acted as though he had never used a cell phone before.

Nora just smiled and pointed toward Burke's room. "I'll see you inside."

Sidney nodded his head as Ray spoke. "Sidney, good. You have your phone with you. Can you talk?"

"Oh. Yes."

"Bad news. Cannot find any record of a book inventory list among the exhibits for the Reed murder case."

"Neither list?"

"No, I can't imagine why they wouldn't be kept. Could be they just gave them back to General Brewster. The Brontë book was never part of the evidence since it was stolen before the police had a chance to enter it into evidence, so the lists wouldn't matter."

"I suppose I can just ask the general...wait. We could be looking in the wrong place."

"How so?"

"The book lists wouldn't relate to the Reed case but the break-in and burglary at the general's. A separate case. The general also made an insurance claim where the lists would be important."

"Sidney, as usual, I think you're right. Let me go down that route and I'll call you back."

Sidney had been inching toward the hospital room door as he spoke. "Good. I think the Springwood connection is starting to loom larger."

With the call ended, Sidney entered Burke's room as the injured man offered an apology. "I'm so sorry. I seem to be doing a lot of that lately. It's very embarrassing."

"Not to worry," offered Nora.

Burke suddenly perked up. The chair he sat in moved visibly as he asked, "Did I hear you say the name Springwood just now."

Sidney responded with an immediate yes. "You know the name?"

"If it's the same person. An attorney by the name of Howard Springwood was a customer of my former employer in Savannah. Nice man. Very knowledgeable about rare books. I believe he has a place in your neck of the woods, Sidney. One of the residential islands near Morgan. Have sent material to him there. The address is in my files."

Nora jumped in to take control. "Did you sell rare books to him? Or was he trying to find a buyer for something he had?"

"Actually a bit of both. Although I believe he represented someone else. His inquiries were on behalf of one of his clients. Someone from New York or

Washington. He didn't mention any names. Met him at a few auctions also. Again, representing a third party. It's a very common practice. More activity happens over the telephone at auctions rather than on the floor, that's where the theatre part of the auction occurs. The business part is on the phone."

"Did he come into your place of business often?"

"No, not really. I had sold him one or two things over the years, but he usually came by to ask questions and to have me do some checking with ABAA, that's the Antiquarian Booksellers' Association of America. He wasn't a member, which is why I made the inquiries for him. Is it the same person you were speaking about?"

Nora gave Sidney a look. "Yes, yes from what you have described I would say that your Howard Springwood and ours are one and the same."

"Oh, and something else. If it means anything? On the way to the toilet, I also saw Ryan Bedford. My new employer. The owner of Bedford-Sackville. We didn't speak as I had some urgent business to attend to..."

Hattie, who had just come into the room, turned her head away and did her best to suppress a smile.

"...but promised myself to find him after I'd finished. Mr. Springwood is also a customer of Bedford-Sackville, and, I believe a close friend of Mr. Bedford's."

TWENTY-TWO

The elusive book lists were found with the burglary file. Georgia Sawyer and Ray moved to the open conference room nearby and put the papers on the table in front of them.

"Sidney was right," Georgia said as she began to spread the papers about with the shorter list above the larger one. "Copies of these were made for General Brewster so he could file an insurance claim."

"One thing I've learned about Sidney is that he's usually right. Sometimes it doesn't seem like something works, but in the end, it does."

"I'll keep that in mind. So, what did he say to look for?"

Ray picked up the first page of the abbreviated list and looked at it. "He said that if he's right, there should be more names on the shorter list than the one with the more extensive descriptions."

"Did he say why?"

"Ah…Sidney can be a bit mysterious sometimes. He said something about finding books that shouldn't be there. I'm not entirely sure what he meant. All I know is he believes the role of Howard Springwood in all that's been going on will prove to be a catalyst for everything else."

Georgia reached over and took the first page of the extensive description list. "Okay, let's put it to the quick test."

"Sidney said to start with the Anne Brontë book. See if it is on the shortlist first."

Georgia was now enthusiastic. "Remember, it should be under Bell, Acton not Brontë." *My God*, she thought, *why am I so excited about all of this? But why wouldn't I be, searching for something touched by a member of one of the greatest of all writing families? A hundred-and fifty-year-old mystery.*

"Oh, right." Ray picked up the first page of the shortlist. "Yeah, okay. I got it. It's here."

As Ray spoke, Georgia glanced over the first three pages of the long list. "Don't see it. Checking both Bell and Brontë. No…No…It's not here."

"All right. That was easy. Sidney said to go after the giants of the Victorian age, Dickens, Hardy, Eliot, Stevenson."

Georgia looked at the papers in her hand and said, "Okay, let's look for a Dickens, and then we'll do Hardy. If we can find a few more of these with just a spot check we should be able to get authorization to see what Springwood has in his own library in Charlotte."

"Might also justify getting a look at his client list."

They found four Dickens novels but they appeared on both lists.

"All right, let's do Thomas Hardy?" Georgia couldn't believe the excitement in her own voice. "I believe *Jude the Obscure* was his last book. He quit writing after that one. A first edition with a personal inscription should be worth quite a bit." She flipped through the pages she had but couldn't find anything. "What do you have?"

ര⁊ര

Two nurses came into the hospital room and

interrupted Burke Mansfield, who looked very tired.

"I think that's about as much as we should do for a while." The male nurse addressed Nora, assuming her to be in charge. "We've got to get him back into bed now. I think he's had enough exercise for a while."

Nora then addressed Burke, "Thank you Mr. Mansfield. You've been very helpful."

Suddenly Burke brightened up and became agitated. "Yes, yes. Put them back. He said put *them* back."

"Who did?" said Sidney.

"The young one. I remember...yes. That's what he said. I put them back. Just before the shots were fired. Mr. Carter said, 'I put them back.'"

Sidney smiled, "I was right."

"What do you mean?" Nora looked at Sidney and then Burke.

"The libraries," Hattie exclaimed. "Springwood's libraries."

It was clear that Nora didn't understand.

Sidney explained, "The best place to hide a book is with other books. I believe Howard Springwood was dealing in stolen rare books and temporarily hid portions of his inventory in his client's libraries. Assuming they would not know they were there. The Brontë book was hidden in the Brewster library in Charlotte. There must have been more than a thousand books in there and they were all shipped to his uncle in Morgan before Springwood was able to retrieve the three volumes of *The Tenant of Wildfell Hall.*"

As Sidney spoke, the two nurses began to move Burke Mansfield to his bed. He put his arm on the hand of the nurse to his left. "Wait. Just a moment. Sidney, I mentioned to you that my new employer, Ryan Bedford, was also at the meet on Saturday and he was well acquainted with Mr. Springwood."

"*Well* acquainted? I thought you said he knew him as a customer? Was there more to the relationship?"

"On reflection," Burke leaned back into the chair. "They were very friendly. Sometimes went to lunch together. I don't know if there is a stronger connection. I believe the relationship was more than just a good customer of the store and the owner."

Nora joined in, "How well did you know Mr. Bedford before you joined his company?"

"Only professionally. We knew one another from Savannah. From the antiquarian book world. We were not friends. We moved in different personal circles."

"And his relationship with Springwood was more than that?"

"It certainly seemed so."

Sidney and Nora looked at one another. Sidney spoke first. "Sounds like the cultivation of an entry point into the antiquarian book world." Addressing Burke, "Do you believe Mr. Bedford was representing his own interest, or was he strictly acquiring rare books for his clients?"

Burke again looked tired. "I...can't speak to that. I...personally...had no direct dealings with him."

"I'm sorry folks," the male nurse cut in. "We've got to get him back into bed. Give him some time to rest. You can all get together later today if you need to."

"Oh, ," said Nora. "Of course. Mr. Mansfield, thank you so very much. You've been very helpful. We will be in touch again, I'm sure."

Sidney got out of his chair with the help of Hattie who stood by it the whole time. "Burke, thank you for your candidness. We'll get together again once you're feeling better."

"Thank you both. I'm glad I could be of some help.

And Professor Ryan," a big smile from Burke, it's so good to see you again. I'm only sorry it couldn't have been under better circumstances. Perhaps we can get together as well."

"Oh, that would be lovely. Just concentrate on getting well for now. We'll stay in touch," Hattie replied with a warm smile as well.

As they went out the door, Sidney gave Hattie a little nudge in the side, "I do believe Burke is quite taken with you."

"Oh, Sidney," she said with a laugh. "Mind your own business. By the way, have you heard anything from Tillie yet?"

ℰↃℰↄ

The outer bands of the storm were getting stronger and more frequent. *Javier* continued to grow as it moved up the coast and began to drift toward the Gulf Stream. The winds came into Morgan from the east. The tide had just begun to come in and would be much higher than usual driven by the winds. Coastal flooding would be everywhere. Many of the roads through the marshlands of the coast were dirt roads and would begin to disappear under the tide. They always did. But it would not happen for another four hours, or at least that's what Tillie planned on.

After leaving Crow Island, she instinctively checked her rearview mirror. A dark SUV followed her out the gate. The driver didn't turn in a day pass so she assumed it belonged to a resident, although they could have forgotten to put it in the pass return receptacle. Being a natural skeptic, she kept watching the car. She didn't feel comfortable. The ride home to Deer Island would be about twenty minutes, if she went the regular route. But there was another way. It was through the marsh. Was she being too cautious? The storm didn't look good. Like everyone in the Lowcountry, she knew the tide. It had just passed dead low. Plenty of time to take the old sugar mill cut off before the water started to come up.

She came to the stoplight that intersected with the road to Morgan and Deer Island. The dark car came up behind her. An outer band of *Javier* exploded over them with high winds and heavy rain. She switched on the rear wiper of her SUV and could see the man in the driver's seat of the dark car behind her. He was wearing aviator-type sunglasses. He had his right turn signal on just as she did. Who wears sunglasses in a hurricane? She decided she would take the back road.

She took off around the corner as quickly as she could. The turn-off for the old sugar mill was a half-mile ahead. The black car stayed behind her. She could feel her heartbeat quicken. She never signaled or slowed down when she made the sugar mill turn. Her car splashed through a large puddle and skidded slightly. She saw the car behind put on its brakes as it went past the cut-off. Her foot went to the floor as she raced down the dirt road. Her next turn would be a half-mile away: Promised Land Road. This time she manually shifted into second gear so the car would slow without her putting on the brake lights. She also turned off the headlights. She thought she saw the black car turn onto the road to follow her just before she made her turn onto Promised Land. She kept going and didn't look back. The rain and wind swirled every which way. She hung on. Tidal marsh was on both sides of the road. She reached a grove of oak and palm trees on a small rise and decided to take a quick look back and peeked at the rearview mirror. That's when the palm frond hit the windshield. She tried to hold on to the steering wheel but the road went left and the car went straight ahead. The car hit a rise at the edge of the road and then the left front fender bounced off a sturdy live-oak tree. Her head slammed against the side of the car. Her hands came off the wheel as she hit another oak on the right side. She was snapped to the right as the airbag exploded and then to the left where she hit her head again. The SUV partially turned over on its right side and settled in the mudflat of the marsh bed.

಄಄಄

The mantle clock struck five as Sidney, Ray and Hattie sat in the living room reviewing what they had learned. Ray had spread out some note pages that he brought with him from the solicitor's office and sat in one of the dining room chairs he brought into the living room. Sidney had moved the hassock away from his chair so he could see what Ray had set up on the coffee table. Sidney's landline rang.

"I'll get it." Hattie got up and walked over to the small table at the far end of the sofa.

"Ray, it's Georgia." Hattie brought the phone over to Ray.

"Georgia, did you find any more names on the lists?...Really?...Do you mind if I put you on speaker?...It's just Sidney and Hattie. We haven't heard from Tillie this afternoon...Don't worry it won't go any farther than this room." Ray looked at Sidney and Hattie. "She has an update on the Pirate Islands. We're not to mention this to anyone. I'm turning on the speaker." Ray placed the phone on the coffee table in front of the three of them. "Go ahead Georgia."

"Ray, as you know, we've been tracking down the names that you provided to us and Sidney's theory about the Interior Department's plan to withdraw the application for national landmark designation has turned out to be right. I've just learned the FBI in Washington has arrested an Interior Department senior member for leaking information to certain business interests for pay. One of the names mentioned is a New York hedge fund by the name of Rostov Credit Partners. David Rostov is one of the people you identified as being at that meeting in Washington. The one run by the law firm that bid on property at the tax sale. As usual, it's all convoluted."

"Not surprised," said Ray.

"Miss Sawyer, this is Sidney Lake. Can you tell us anything about the principal of Rostov Credit Partners?"

"A bit. I'm sure the FBI has quite a lot more. All I know is that David Rostov's been in trouble before. I looked him up and the SEC, that's the Securities and Exchange Commission, has sanctioned him a number of times. Interestingly enough, he has a summer place on Crow Island."

Silence.

Then Sidney thought out loud, "I wonder if he is an acquaintance of Howard Springwood?"

Ray reacted with, "Wow, wouldn't that be a coincidence."

Hattie reached over and touched Ray's arm. "Ray, everyone on those islands knows everyone else. I've been to dinner at that clubhouse of theirs. There are no strangers."

TWENTY-THREE

Sidney and Hattie sat while Ray paced. The three of them were trying to make sense of the information from Georgia Sawyer.

Sidney broke the silence, "What could the connection be between Howard Springwood and this David Rostov person? It seems Rostov has an interest in the Pirate Islands, which makes sense given the nature of hedge funds, but where does Springwood come in? Although he does seem to be the only one with a link to both the Pirate Islands and the Anne Brontë book. But wait, didn't Ms. Sullivan of the FBI say Mr. Springwood was a registered lobbyist with the Interior Department? And didn't Burke Mansfield say he knew the name from his company, Sackville-Bedford?"

Hattie leaned forward from her position on the sofa and said the obvious, "But he's dead. How does a dead man fit into what happened to Larry Carter?"

Ray stopped pacing. "It's a puzzle, Hattie. I suppose it could be a coincidence that Springwood is in the middle. Lawyers often have a diverse clientele, but they usually work within an area of expertise. Guys who do wills and estates don't usually take medical insurance cases or get involved with the criminal justice system. Real estate lawyers just stick to what they do best and have a tie in with a couple of real estate agencies."

Sidney responded, "Exactly the point. We don't know what Howard Springwood's area of expertise was. All we know is that he had General Brewster's uncle for a client. Why? What did he really do for him? Ray, that client list of Springwoods could be an eye-opener. Who do you think has the best chance of getting hold of it?"

"Probably Nora Sullivan of the FBI. What happened to Springwood up in Charlotte had nothing to do with Georgia Sawyer and the County Solicitor's Office. Admittedly, Springwood had a residence over on Crow Island, which puts him in the county, but that doesn't have anything to do with his death in Charlotte. Besides, Nora did say the FBI would try to make a case for getting that client list."

Sidney winced as he shifted in his chair to get a better look at Ray. "I wish you'd sit down. The pacing isn't getting us anywhere."

Mickey, at this point got up from her position next to Sidney's chair and walked toward the front door.

"I'll get her," Hattie said as she got up and then asked, "Whatever happened to Tillie? As anyone heard from her? To be honest, I'm starting to get worried. This storm isn't going away too soon and we haven't heard a word from her since she went exploring on Crow Island. That was this morning. She should definitely be back by now."

"Ray, while Hattie takes Mickey out, could you go into the kitchen for me and get the telephone address book that sits under the wall telephone. I have a phone number in there for Tillie's brother. Since she's not answering her cell phone, maybe he knows why."

"Sure Sidney," Ray started to turn and stopped. "Who was that person she was supposed to meet this morning?"

"I'm not sure."

Hattie called into the room from the front door, "Missy's uncle. Don't know his name but I'll bet Tillie's brother does. Ask him for the uncle's number. She was to meet him before she went through the Crow Island gate. He works out there so you could ask him to check with gate security to see when her gate pass was turned in and left, if she did."

"Good idea."

While Hattie walked Mickey, both Sidney and Ray made a number of phone calls. Sidney focused on Tillie's whereabouts while Ray decided to call one of his contacts in the Charlotte police department and do a little snooping about Howard Springwood. Sidney managed to get a name for Missy's uncle, Jerry Simpson, and his cell phone number but struck out when his call went into Simpson's voice mail. Ray had luck with his Charlotte police contact who indicated Springwood was not a trial lawyer but mostly handled business contracts and acted on behalf of clients who wished to be anonymous in one way or another. He also served as a financial manager for business people in Europe who needed US dollar accounts but didn't want it known they kept funds in the US. His contact indicated that such services were being handled by a number of Charlotte law firms, since the city had become a major financial center. The FBI and Treasury Department were aware of the firms but they were all pretty careful about following the law and not crossing over the line. He knew of nothing bad about Springwood but admitted that people who trade in secrets often get caught up in them.

Ray decided he needed to talk to Georgia Sawyer in person and when Hattie came in with Mickey, he told her not to take her rain gear off. "Hattie, could you give me a lift over to the county center? That rain's a little too much to be walking over there in. Marie's got my car."

"That's not rain anymore, that's a deluge. Mickey decided that a walk was not a good idea and did her business right near the front steps. She's no dummy. Sure, I'd be happy to."

Sidney, while waiting for Simpson to call him back, decided to call Burke Mansfield to follow up on something the book dealer said.

"Burke, so they let you take calls now. I guess we didn't tire you out too much earlier."

"No, Sidney, I needed the exercise. Need to keep my mind going. They say the toughest part of surgery is the recovery and I'm beginning to see why. The anesthetic seems to be the worst of it. How can I help?"

"Something you said that I hope you can clarify. Your new employer, Ryan Bedford. Can you give me a little bit more on the relationship of Ryan Bedford and Howard Springwood?"

"Oh, yes. To be honest, I'm not sure what it was I mentioned. My memory seems to be all over the place with the anesthetic playing games with my head."

"That's all right. Just start over."

Burke paused for just a moment while he tried to get his thoughts together and then began, "Well, as I may have said before, I was not well acquainted with Mr. Springwood, but Mr. Bedford most certainly was. As I understand it, Mr. Springwood represented quite a few clients that were book collectors and some of them were from outside the US. He served as the intermediary between the client and the store. It's not uncommon, especially when wealthy clients are involved. You see it all the time at auctions where they're always on the phone making bids on behalf of their employers. Well, the same goes on in the rare book business. We at Sackville-Bedford have a large auction house as part of the business and often people such as Mr. Springwood would be on a preferred list of people to advise of a coming estate sale. They would be able to preview the potential items and make an offer on something of interest prior to the sale catalogue being created."

"Ah, that seems quite consistent with what I've recently learned about Mr. Springwood's business interests. Would he be considered quite knowledgeable in the area of rare books?"

"Oh, I would think so. You're welcome to check with Mr. Bedford. I've mentioned you to him and I'm sure he would welcome a call. I have his private number in my cell phone right here."

"That would be quite helpful."

After obtaining the number, Sidney and Burke talked for another five minutes and agreed to get together for lunch in either Savannah or Hilton Head, once Burke was on his feet again. He also asked if Hattie Ryan would be able to come along. A question Sidney found very interesting.

Sidney no sooner put the phone down when it rang. It was Missy's uncle Jerry. Without making any polite conversation with someone he was talking to for the first time, Sidney, uncharacteristically, jumped to the topic, "Have you heard from Tillie?"

"Why...no. Is something wrong?"

"She's not answering her phone, and no one has heard from her since she went to Crow Island."

"Well I was with her just before she went through the gate. I know she got through all right. Maybe something is wrong with her phone. I can't believe she's still on the island and surely not at Springwood's. I'm nearby and I'll take a run by the place to make sure her car is gone. The only possibility I can think of is one of the neighbors saw her walking around in the rain and reported her to the front gate and they detained her. Although it's been five hours...that wouldn't make sense. Especially as this storm is picking up and the guards are all over the place making sure everything is tied down. I'm pretty sure there's going to shut the whole island down shortly."

"Could you do me a favor?"

"Anything for Tillie's favorite professor."

"Ah...well thank you. I'm concerned about Tillie. She thinks she's invincible sometimes and can talk her way out of anything."

"That's Tillie."

"Well look, could you check with the gate and see if her pass has been turned in? At least that way we'll know she left the island."

"Oh sure. Be happy to. They're pretty good about keeping track of the passes. They even time stamp them when people leave. Keep track of who's on the island that way. Residents here are a cautious bunch. Can be real touchy about strangers wandering around. Understand there have been a rash of minor thefts of late. Fact is there's a guy just a few houses up from the Springwood place has his own security people."

"My, must be a celebrity of some type."

"Don't think so. Never heard of him. Russian name. Lots of money."

"Russian?"

"Sounds like one. Rostov. Did some landscape work there once and had this big blond guy watching over us the whole time. Creepy."

Sidney remained silent for a moment before he said, "Mr. Simpson, I doappreciate this. Please let me know what you find out."

"Sure, professor, not a problem. I'm sure she'll be okay."

As Sidney ended the connection, he was really

worried now. He picked up the phone and called Hattie."

☙☙☙

The ride to the county center took longer than expected. It rained so hard Hattie couldn't see more than ten feet in front of the car. She white-knuckled it all the way. As they pulled into the almost empty parking lot, Ray could see that Georgia Sawyer's space was empty. "She's gone. Not surprised. Don't know what I was thinking. This is the kind of weather nobody wants to be out in. Besides everybody's scrambling around with this storm."

Hattie's phone rang. She asked Ray to take the cell phone from her purse and answer it as she turned the car around. A gust of wind hit the car and the windshield wipers flapped furiously at their high setting. It was Sidney on the phone and he and Ray spoke while Hattie carefully maneuvered the car around the parking lot. Sidney explained about the conversation he had with Jerry Simpson. "Hold on Sidney." Then to Hattie. "You up to a ride to Crow Island."

She looked at him and stopped the car. "In this?"

"Sidney said Tillie's still among the missing and he thinks something must have happened to her on her way back home. Could be stuck someplace or worse. Also, the mysterious Mr. Rostov is a neighbor and your blond-haired friend may work for him."

"Oh my. I hope she's all right." Reacting to the wind and rain hitting the car she added, "This is not a day to be stuck anywhere."

Ray spoke into Hattie's cell phone, "Sidney, we're heading for Crow Island. We'll keep you posted." He ended the call and turned to Hattie. "This fellow Simson is checking on Crow Island security for Tillie, so I figure we should start at the security gate and work our way toward Deer Island. We'll just go the same route that Tillie would have taken."

"I hope we can still get through. The governor called for a voluntary evacuation so traffic around the islands may be allowed in only one direction and that will be away from the islands not toward them."

"Ray, should we call Chief Hornig and report her missing?"

"It's only been a couple of hours. Besides, with this storm, believe me, he doesn't have anyone available to go looking for anyone."

"I'm sure you're right. The rain is easing up." She looked through the windshield at the sky ahead and could see some bright spots.

"The band is moving on. Let's make the most of it and get moving before the next one hits."

As soon as Sidney finished the call with Ray, he turned his attention to the Springwood connection and the idea that the lawyer acted as a catalyst for everything that had been happening: the providing of the book to Brewster's uncle, the theft of it afterward, the connection to Larry Carter, the connection to Sackville-Bedford rare books, and the link to David Rostov and the Pirate Islands. But Springwood was dead so what is the next link. Sidney turned to Mickey, who sat by his chair as always. "Mickey, let's think about this a bit. Lawyer Springwood seemed to touch everyone. He had the rare book involvement and he was trying to buy up property on the Pirate Islands. Now who else touches both rare books and land speculation? Larry Carter, the young man who was killed at the craft fair, had the connection to the rare book and the connection to Springwood, but he's also dead. Could he have been involved with running errands for both Springwood and for Rostov on Crow Island? And maybe someone we don't know about. Could young Mr. Carter have been foolish enough to steal the Brontë book from Springwood, get caught in the process, and kill Springwood?" Sidney gave Mickey a look to see if she was listening. The Lab was stretched out on the floor with her eyes closed, but every time Sidney spoke, her ear twitched. Sidney continued, "Okay, although it's a possibility and I can see Carter as a thief and a troublemaker, I don't see him as a premeditated killer. Maybe an accidental one. How about this, Mickey, Carter steals the book from Springwood, but Springwood didn't own it. He was hiding it for someone else until it could be delivered, which is why it was in the Brewster library and not in his own." Sidney stopped, leaned back, and looked up at the ceiling, as he thought and tried to visualize the Brewster library. Mickey, no longer hearing the droning of Sidney's voice, lifted her head and looked toward Sidney. She then put her head down again, but the eyes remained open this time.

"Ryan Bedford." Sidney looked down from the ceiling and focused on the front windows. The rain had stopped. It was eerily quiet. No wind. No sound. "Ryan Bedford and Howard Springwood, could they have had something going between them in the area of stolen or forged rare books? Why was Mr. Bedford at the craft fair? Was he there to meet with Larry Carter? I wonder."

Sidney picked up the phone on the small table next to him. "Why don't we find out, hah Mickey?" Sidney dialed the number for Sackville-Bedford on Skidaway Island.

The phone rang three times before a woman's very anxious voice answered. "Hello, this is Sackville-

Bedford. We're closed at the moment."

"Oh, I'm sorry. The storm. This is professor Sidney Lake."

"Professor Lake, yes. I'm afraid Mr. Mansfield is still in hospital and Mr. Bedford is in the process of moving books to the mainland. The Island is being evacuated."

"I won't keep you. I was looking for Mr. Bedford. I'll call back after the storm."

"I'll tell him you called. He's outside. We're loading up the van."

"Well good luck to you both and please be careful and stay safe."

"Well, Mickey, I guess that will have to wait." Sidney ended the call." I wonder if we're going to be evacuating."

TWENTY-FOUR

Ray looked toward the sky as they pulled away from the Crow Island security gate. The clouds to the southeast were dark and menacing. The evacuation order for coastal South Carolina had come and the gate staff had closed down the entrance lanes. Ray met with Missy's uncle Jerry in the small parking area by the gatehouse and took notes, as the man gave him a rundown on both the Springwood and Rostov properties and what he knew of their owners. Simpson had also been able to estimate the time that Tillie left the island from the gate pass she turned in. She had been missing for just short of three hours, based on the gate pass time stamp, which could be off by more than a half-hour as the security people were concentrating on island safety issues and had left the returned gate passes uncollected for long periods of time. Lack of communication from Tillie for that length of time was unheard of. Something was definitely wrong.

The rain had restarted as a full downpour when they reached the traffic light for the road that would take them to Deer Island. Ray continued to speak on his cell phone with Police Chief Hornig, "You sure using the auxiliary people is a help?"

"Ray, you know how strapped I am with the budget they gave me. I have to use them. Besides, they'll just be doing traffic reporting and gate checks. Gives me some extra eyes and ears during the storm. They're all volunteers and they have orders to pull back with everyone else for safety purposes. I'll get the word out to them about Tillie. You know these people, Ray, they're lifetime locals. They know everyone and everything about the Lowcountry. Hell Casey Yarborough will be using the storm as an excuse to scout the region for real estate deals."

"You still have him doing this stuff? I thought you were going to tell him to resign after that gun incident."

"Gave him a good talkin' to. He'll be all right. Just gets excitable sometimes."

"Hope you know what you're doing. Using the auxs too much is what got Sheriff Joe in trouble in Arizona. Only he called them his posse."

"I know. I have it under control. They're good people. They'll keep an eye out for Tillie. And you be careful yourself. You know how bad these storms can be. You get yourself hurt and Marie will kill me as well as you. Tillie's probably in one of the shelters. She's a smart lady. Ray, I gotta go. Keep in touch."

Seeing that the call ended, Hattie made a suggestion while they waited for the light to change. "I think I'll just focus on the driving and you do the looking for her car. If she did break down she'd be on your side of the road. Although I can't believe she would stay with her car in this storm. But where in the world would she go?"

"I'm assuming she may have tried to drive through water that was too deep for her and the car stalled out. It happens all the time."

"But that wouldn't explain why she wouldn't call someone. Besides, this is the main road to both Morgan and Deer Island and it doesn't have a history of flooding. They fixed the flooding problem when they widened it to four lanes five years ago,"

Ray thought for a moment. The light went green and Hattie eased around the corner and stopped on the side of the road. The traffic was mainly heading away from Morgan and there was little traffic going in their direction. "Hattie, let's think this through. Do you have a map?"

"I have the GPS."

"No I need a map that will give me a large overview of the area. GPS is great if you know where you're going, not if you're trying to figure out where to go."

"Well, I do have an old gas station map in the glove compartment. It has to be at least ten years old."

"That's exactly what I'm looking for." Ray opened the glove compartment and pulled a bunch of miscellaneous material until he found a map of Coastal Rivers County. "This'll do just fine." He unfolded the map and laid it across his lap. "What I'm looking for is turnoffs that would serve as a local shortcut to Deer Island. Around the Lowcountry there are always dirt roads that only the locals know about and use. The Sheriff's Office and EMS use them all the time to find places that still don't appear on the automated systems. Let me see. Ah, here we are."

While Ray looked at the map, Hattie kept looking at the rain and the now fiercely blowing wind. The car shook from side to side as a gust of wind grabbed hold of it from a totally different direction from the way the rain was falling. "I sure wouldn't want to be out in this today. I'm glad Sidney and I have hotel rooms reserved for a few days. The trick may be in getting to them."

Ray looked up. "I think I found something. Just drive up ahead about a mile, after the road curves to the left there's a road that comes in on the right. I've been on that one a few times in a police cruiser. It heads through the marsh and then goes directly to Deer Island. Let's give that a try. I also want to check in with Sidney.

As Ray and Hattie made their way to Promised Land Road, Sidney made himself comfortable in his chair and started his thinking process again. "Mickey, I need to cook something, but this damn leg is hampering everything. I need to concentrate. Maybe Tillie's right and I need to go back to the doctors and have them put a plan together for me." He crossed his arms in front of him and let out a long breath of frustration. "Mickey, what in the world has happened to Tillie?" The phone on the small table rang and interrupted his thoughts.

"Sidney Lake," he answered.

"Professor Lake, this is Ryan Bedford of Sackville-Bedford on Skidaway Island. You called a little while ago."

Sidney perked up. "Mr. Bedford. Oh, I didn't mean for you to call me back today. I understand you're trying to pack up and secure your inventory and I didn't want to interrupt."

"No, no. It's perfectly all right. To be truthful, I needed a break. I'm not as young as I used to be and books can be very heavy. How can I help you?"

"Ah, well, as you may know, I've become an acquaintance of Burke Mansfield. In fact, I was up to see him around noon today. He's doing quite well."

"Yes, I spoke with him this morning and let him know we were evacuating."

"It was quite an experience, the panic at the craft fair. I understand you were also there."

"Much earlier. I was long gone before the shooting started. I spent the night in Columbia and, as it was Saturday, I thought I'd stop at the fair. It's a wonderful place to look for rare books. Didn't stay too long."

"You certainly made the right decision. I wonder if I could ask you a question or two." While speaking, Sidney began to formulate a track he wanted to take with Bedford.

"Yes, certainly. Happy to help."

Over the phone, Sidney could hear the wind whistling and windows rattling. "Are you sure you have the time."

"Yes, been through this before…too many times. No, ask away."

"Well, it seems the name of a lawyer by the name of Howard Springwood has come up a number of times in relation to the missing copy of Anne Brontë's *The Tenant of Wildfell Hall*. Mr. Mansfield had indicated that Mr. Springwood was a regular customer of yours. I'm curious to learn if his interest was on behalf of himself or another party."

"Howard was a very personable man. I assume you know of his death?"

"Oh yes."

"It's most unfortunate. I came to enjoy his company. He was very knowledgeable when it came to rare books, and he seems to have quite a collection. We would often have discussions about authors and the publishing business of the nineteenth century."

Sidney pressed the point he wanted to make. "So his interest was personal and not business related?"

"Not entirely. Because of his knowledge and expertise, he did represent some collectors who wished to remain anonymous. That's quite common in the business."

"Did you ever learn who any of them were?"

"One or two. He did mention one client he said he would no longer represent. Said he felt uncomfortable around him. He had been forced to sign a non-disclosure agreement with the man swearing he would not reveal any of the treasures he had seen in the client's possession. Also mentioned a security person. I think it was the client's bodyguard."

"Did he mention the man's name? The one he was representing."

The line was silent for a moment. "Eh...no, but he did say he was a Wall Street type. Lots of money. Had a number of homes in different places. Don't know anything else."

"Well, Mr. Bedford, you've been very helpful. I don't want to keep you. It certainly sounds as though that storm is closing in."

"They said we should have at least another five hours before the leading edge gets here, but this is an island, and if it comes too close the storm surge will sweep right over us."

"Well, please stay safe. We have to evacuate here as well and even though we're almost five miles from the coast, the nature of the Lowcountry make us very susceptible to rising water and driving winds."

"I guess, as they say, it comes with the territory. Oh, one more thing I just remembered. Howard said that his client was a neighbor."

"Here or in Charlotte?'

"That he didn't say."

"You've been very helpful. I hope we have a chance to meet quite soon."

"That would be very nice. Goodbye, Professor Lake."

Sidney put down the phone very slowly and looked at Mickey, "I think we've found the final link."

୧ୠ୬

On the other side of Morgan, Ray gave up trying to

reach Sidney and finally put his phone away in order to concentrate on Promised Land Road. He said to Hattie, "Keep it as slow as you can. It's difficult to see with the way the wind is driving the rain." The clatter of the windshield wipers forced him to speak louder than usual.

"The debris on the road isn't helping either." She held onto the steering wheel as tight as she could and began to have bad thoughts about the decision to go down Promised Land Road. "Have you seen anything at all yet? The water in the marsh is getting awfully high."

"Tide's coming in and I haven't seen any traffic coming this way. It could have washed over the road up ahead. The road turns to the left and there's a small rise coming up. Pull off to the side when we get up there. We may have to make the decision to go back."

As Hattie rounded the curve Ray called out, "Wait! I thought I saw something over there." He looked out into the marsh on the right side of the car. "Just stop it here." He opened the window to get a better view. The rain and wind eased just a bit but he still got a blast of it as he stared off to his right. "I'll swear there's something out there." He closed the window and opened the door. "Stay here." His lightweight jacket and jeans were soaked instantly as he stepped onto the shoulder. Looking down he could see the outline of tire tracks carved into the soft earth. They were filled with water but were recent as there was no vegetation growing in them. He lined up behind them and looked into the marsh. There was definitely something out there, half-submerged in the water. He moved forward. A tan SUV up against a large white oak loomed ahead. The car tilted to the right so the driver's side sat mostly out of the water but the passenger side had water almost up to the window. He could see the first three letters of the license plate, "TIL." He turned back to Hattie and yelled. "Call nine-one-one!" Ray raced to the car. He could see Tillie sitting at a strange angle in the driver's seat. He slipped and went down into the water.

Hattie notified the nine-one-one operator and gave her name and Ray's and explained where they were and who was in the car.

"Miss Tillie's in the car? Don't worry. Help's commin'. Tell Mr. Ray to be careful."

Hattie turned on the flashers of her car, got her umbrella out of the back seat, and made her way down to Ray. He had managed to get the driver's door partially open but no more than a foot. Tillie was awake but clearly dazed. She was partially submerged. Her right arm was clearly broken, and she couldn't get out of the seatbelt. She had hit her head at least twice and had cuts on her forehead. Her right foot was caught under the brake pedal.

"Mr. Ray, you must be the angel I been prayin' for. An' I've been prayin' a lot."

"We'll get you out." Ray pulled hard on the door and slipped again. Hattie tried to cover him with her umbrella. Wind slammed the door closed again.

As Ray got back up Hattie said, "How far away is the EMS station from here?"

"There's one just outside the Crow Island gate. It's no more than ten minutes away."

They could hear a siren in the distance and looked back toward the road. Ray looked up. "That's a police cruiser siren. Figured they'd be here first."

Hattie handed the umbrella to Ray as she said, "I'll go back to my car to make sure they see us."

"Keep the umbrella. I'm so wet now it doesn't matter. I'll keep Tillie company."

Ray again turned to the car and made another attempt to get the door open. He looked at the scene around him. With the wind driving the tide, it was already rising all around them and it looked as though they sat on the edge of a great lake.

Meanwhile, Sidney sat in his chair making notes about the conversation he had with Ryan Bedford. As he looked up for a moment he spotted the house phone's message-waiting light flashing as it sat on the small table next to him. Seeing the missed call was from Ray he called him back.

"Have you found Tillie?" he asked with great concern in his voice.

"Yes. Phone's all wet. Me too. Surprised it's working at all."

On the other end of the line, what Sidney heard was: "Yes, *squawk crack* too….at all."

"Is she all right?"

No answer.

Sidney yelled into the phone, "Ray, is she all right?"

Ray heard only part of Sidney's question but assumed what it was. The call was breaking up so Ray just continued talking. "She's okay. She's okay. She's okay. Accident. Accident. Accident. EMS here. EMS here. EMS here." The connection dropped.

Sidney understood. He tried Hattie's number and left her a message. Outside, the storm raged. The lights flickered but stayed on. "Mickey, looks like we're going to be riding this one out by ourselves. I'm glad Tillie's okay. Let's get some flashlights and candles. It's going to be worse than forecast." As he and Mickey made their way to the kitchen, he could hear the wind and rain pulsating against the house. Porch furniture banged against the railing and a window shutter came unlocked and began to slam back and forth. The lights flickered again. "Mickey, the first sign of a lull, I'll let you out the kitchen door. Don't fool around out there. Just do what you have to do and come right back." Mickey gave a wag of her tail and looked at Sidney, who grabbed hold of his cane as they both walked slowly to the kitchen.

❧❧❧

The sheriff's deputy who arrived at the accident scene was fully outfitted in his rain gear. He told Hattie to stay in her car. She watched as the deputy and Ray used a crowbar to get the driver's side door open wider. When the EMS truck arrived, everyone worked on getting Tillie out of the car. It took them twenty minutes. They hand carried her to the truck and got her inside. A second deputy showed up and talked with Ray and Hattie. He also gave them an update on the storm. It had grown to a category four and was heading for Savannah. They expected it to stay offshore and make its way up the coast with a landfall in the outer banks of North Carolina late tomorrow. The highways were jammed with traffic heading inland. It should hit the region at low tide but the current rising tide will just stay where it is, as the surge and high wind won't let the water out. Everything in the region is shutting down. Power was already out in most of Morgan, Beaufort, and Hilton Head.

TWENTY-FIVE

The world turned upside down. Two days ago Sidney Lake used every argument he could think of to get out of the hospital early in Walterboro and Tillie parried his every thrust. Tonight it was Sidney's turn to do the same for her in Morgan.

"What I got to stay here for? So my arms broke. Happened before. They fixed it. Time to go home."

Sidney sat in a chair near the side of Tillie's bed. "They will let you out when they agree you're ready. That right foot of yours isn't working very well either."

Tillie's two sisters stood silently at the other side of the bed with a look of disbelief on both their faces as they listened to the back and forth between Tillie and Sidney. This was not the conversation they expected to hear between Tillie and her employer.

"Right foot nuthin'," Tillie continued to argue. "Hasn't worked right since the axident twenty years ago. So it's a little banged up again. Hospital's for sick people. I ain't sick. Just needed some repair work. And it's done. Time to go home."

"You can't go until the doctor signs the release papers. And you know that's not going to happen until tomorrow...if then. It's almost midnight. There's a hurricane making a mess of everything. You're not thinking clearly, Tillie. Just relax."

Tillie's sister standing closest to her started to say something and Tillie cut her off. "Don't you start. Bad enough I got him to push me around. Don't need it from nobody else. Damn, I can't stand sittin' around. I feel fine. I don't like hospitals."

Sidney began again, "The only reason you feel fine is because of the medicine they gave you. You're not fine. You've got a broken arm, a sprained ankle, and a nasty cut on your head. You're not fine. Besides, you can't go home. All the traffic is stopped going onto the islands. Everybody's evacuating. Can't you hear all that racket going on out there?" He pointed to the window where the wind and rain slammed against it in continuing sheets. We're both stayin' here tonight."

"Hrumph," came Tillie's reply as she tried to cross her arms and failed because of the bandages.

Tillie's sister nearest the bed finally got a word in, "You two can fight it out amongst yourselves. I gotta get back to work. The county may be closed but the Red Cross ain't an that's where I'm workin' till the storm passes."

"Me too," added the other sister. "I don't think you're goin' anywhere till tomorrow. We'll be back first thing. Spendin' the night where we're workin'. You pay attention to the professor here."

Both women moved forward and gave her a kiss on the cheek.

"Professor Lake," said the first sister, "Thank you for caring for Tillie like you do. You're a good person." She walked around the bed to Sidney, who seeing her coming tried to get up from his chair. "No, no. You stay there," She took his hand in hers and then gave it a pat with her other one. "Thank you."

The second sister followed suit.

Tillie said with a smile, "Don't be too nice to um. Gotta keep him under control."

Everyone laughed.

Hattie and Ray came into the room just as the sisters were leaving and exchanged greetings.

Ray turned his attention to Tillie and said, "Well, you sure look a lot better than you did earlier."

Tillie smiled, "Got you and Miss Hattie to thank for that."

Hattie walked over to the bed and gave Tillie a kiss on the cheek. "Have to protect our most valuable asset."

"Whatcha gotta do is get that guy with the short blond hair. He was followin' me when I went off the road. Stupid thing to do. Shoudda known better."

Hattie looked surprised and said, "The same one that was outside Sidney's the other day?"

"Gotta believe so."

Ray had a steely-eyed look as he took the lead from Hattie, "Did you tell the police?"

"Never got the chance. EMS people brought me right here. Police have their hands full with the storm and evacuation and took off someplace else."

"Have you told Sidney what happened?" Ray looked at Sidney.

Sidney spoke up, "We just got here. Hattie let me off out front while she parked the car and I came in a few minutes ago. Tillie's had family here and I didn't want to interfere. Tillie, what did happen?"

Tillie explained about her looking around the outside of the Springwood house and the extensive library she spotted inside. She also mentioned being challenged by the woman and then being followed by the man as she left the gate.

"He had on those aviator sunglasses. Some folks think they's cool to wear all the time, but if you're wearin' them in a hurricane you ain't being cool, you tryin' to hide yourself. And yeah, he was definitely followin' me. Creepy. Got a pretty good look at him as we slowed down at the gate. Didn't hand in a gate pass so the car he had musta had a decal. Definitely blond hair. Cut short. Big black car. Ditched him when I turned down Promised Land."

Ray's phone rang. "Hold on just a minute, Tillie."

The call was from Georgia Sawyer of the county solicitor's office. Ray stepped away from the bedside as he spoke with her.

Sidney continued the conversation with Tillie. "When you looked in the window and saw the library, did you notice if there were any boxes around that would indicate someone was moving any of the books?"

"No. It was clean. Everything nice and neat."

"And all the bookshelves were full?"

Tillie thought for a minute before answering. "No. It didn't look like anything was moved."

"Interesting. With the storm coming, I would have thought someone might try to close up the house. Possibly remove any books that were valuable."

"I closed some of the shutters. Did it for the library windows. Told that lady that came by that's what I was there for. So I did. Make it look all proper."

Ray ended his phone call and joined the group. "Georgia. Big meeting set for tomorrow afternoon about the Pirate Islands. Keep it quiet, but the leaker at the Interior Department just caved. Admitted he took a bribe. Implicated this guy Rostov and also the owner of Zutter International, P. L. Zutter. FBI looking for both of them to serve warrants. Nora Sullivan's coming down from Columbia. The storm should be out of here by morning. Power is out just about everywhere. Expect it to start coming back around noon, if not before. By the way, learned that Rostov has a personal bodyguard. Big tall guy. Blond crew cut."

Sidney said, "Aaah," and sat back in his chair. "What time is the meeting?"

"Four o'clock. At the county offices. This storm is complicating things."

"I wonder where our blond haired fellow fits into all of this? If he does."

"Don't know. My gut reaction is that his interest is in whatever this guy Rostov wants it to be, so I put my money on the Pirate Islands."

Sidney made a face that indicated disagreement. "Hmmm, I'm not so sure. I'm still convinced the book and the Pirate Islands are tied together in some way."

"That may be, but there's no official investigation going on about the book."

"What about Springwood?"

Ray looked at Sidney for a moment before saying, "Well, you might say there's a link to him, but it could be a personal one. It might not have anything to do with the book or the Pirate Islands."

Sidney gave the answer some thought. "Ray, if I gave you a series of questions for both Nora Sullivan and Georgia Sawyer could you weave them into your meeting somehow?"

"I could certainly try."

"That's all I ask." Sidney reached into the pocket of his jacket and pulled out a small notebook. While Ray waited, Sidney created three pages of questions, tore the pages out of the book, and gave them to Ray.

The Coastal Rivers County command center for the storm emergency made its headquarters in the basement of the county building complex. With the police and EMS headquarters nearby, and all their communications facilities, it was the one place in Morgan that was fully staffed and operating. The rest of the complex had shut down and all non-essential staff were sent home. The previously jammed roads out of town were eerily empty and quiet. The surprise turn to the northeast by *Javier* caught everyone off guard. The grade schools on the islands were always ready to become shelters, given the number of storms that come through the Lowcountry, but a larger than usual crowd was expected. The same held true for the high school in Morgan. So Ray wasn't surprised when he entered the conference room and didn't see representation from the sheriff's office or the Morgan police department. Georgia Sawyer, the assistant solicitor, and Special Agent Sullivan were the only ones around the table.

"Looks like we're the only expendable ones in town," Ray said in greeting.

Georgia responded, "Not entirely. Chief Hornig and the sheriff said they agreed on a single representative for both of them. One of Hornig's detectives who's on education leave from the department but currently in town. Said he knows the Pirate Islands better than anyone."

"I think I know who you mean," Ray heard the door open behind him as he spoke and turned around. "Sam Cashman. I thought so." He extended his hand and had a big smile on his face as he greeted the tall, young, Black detective. "Great to see you. How's everything in Columbia?"

Nora Sullivan stood up from her position at the table and extended her hand. "I'm Nora Sullivan of the FBI's Columbia field office."

Sam took her hand. "Sam Cashman."

Georgia, who sat at the table across from everyone

else, waved her hand at Sam as she said, "Hi, Sam. Take off that wet jacket and have a seat." She indicated the chair next to her.

Everyone got settled around the table and the small talk continued. Georgia explained to Nora that Sam was from the Gullah community on Deer Island and also mentioned he was now on leave to attend the University of South Carolina in Columbia under a new program the state had initiated. Georgia, the official host of the meeting, finally got around to the reason they were assembled by asking Nora Sullivan to tell them what had been going on.

Nora opened a folder in front of her and explained what happened in Washington last week. The FBI had been interviewing people at the Interior Department and hit gold in one of the assistant secretaries who admitted he was the source of the leaks. He had been feeding information to a number of contacts and had been paid handsomely for doing so. The Pirate Islands was not the only project that was being taken off the national monument list. There were also properties in Utah and Arizona. The difference being that only the property in South Carolina involved an active plan for land acquisition and development.

Nora Sullivan then outlined the actions underway, "The four main locations for which warrants have been issued are New York City, Washington, D.C., Hilton Head, South Carolina and Naples, Florida. The corporate entities are Rostov Partners, LLC, Zutter Industrial Alliance LLC, and the law firm of Cavanaugh, McKnight, and Pazzini. The New York, Washington, and Naples locations were hit this morning. Hilton Head was held off because of the storm."

Ray asked, "Who has the office on Hilton Head?"

"Magnolia Development Projects, LLC. It's an affiliate of Zutter Industrial Alliance. The company is headed by P. L. Zutter. They're the resort building arm. As we understand it, Zutter would be the developer of the Pirate Islands through the Magnolia company."

Georgia spoke up, "Shouldn't Beaufort County be represented here as Hilton Head is in their jurisdiction?"

"They were asked but couldn't because of the storm. It's a good deal more difficult to get from Beaufort to Morgan at this point. They're being kept informed. As the storm clears out of Morgan and Beaufort this afternoon, the move will be made at Hilton Head tomorrow morning. The element of surprise has been lost but both Rostov and Zutter have been notified to stay away from designated locations and to protect all relevant material."

As to emphasize the travel difficulty, a gust of wind of tropical storm force slammed against the building. Even though they were in the basement of the concrete building, the building could be felt straining. Moments afterward, the lights flickered and went dark. It lasted only a second before they came back on.

Ray said, "Generators kicked in. We'll stay on them now until the storm is fully out of here. The hospital should be on backup power now as well. Hope Tillie and Sidney are okay."

An EMS truck could be heard heading away from the building.

Sam Cashman looked puzzled as he asked, "Tillie James and Sidney Lake? Are they at the hospital?"

Ray turned to Sam as he answered, "Yes, but they're fine. I'll tell you about it later." Then to Nora, "Where does this Rostov person fit into all of this?"

"He's the main player. Or rather I should describe him

and the conductor. It's the way these people operate. He doesn't personally make any music and he doesn't give any specific direction to anyone, but they all know what he wants. They know what each flick of the baton means and what they are expected to do. One of Rostov's people made the overtures to the leaker at Interior and another of his people made arrangements for the payments. A third was the actual recipient of the information. It may sound complicated, but it's a well-oiled composition played by very experienced professionals."

Georgia asked, "Do they have Rostov in custody?"

"No. He's not in New York. In fact, they believe he's here in South Carolina. He has a place on Crow Island here in Morgan and he often holds meetings at Magnolia Development's offices on Hilton Head."

Ray reached down and drew some papers from his briefcase, one of which was Sidney's list of questions. "I wonder if you could indulge me for a minute or two? In anticipation of this meeting, I've worked up a few questions about this case that have mystified Sidney and me."

"I don't see why not. I don't exactly have any place to go at the moment." She waved her hand toward the door, indicating outside and the storm. "How about you, Nora? Sam?"

Nora answered first. "I live up in Columbia. I'm certainly not going back up there tonight. The more we can analyze what Rostov has up his sleeve, the better."

They looked at Sam who said, "I agreed to work the emergency center tonight. Dede and the kids are upstairs helping to set up cots and a daycare center. This is our evacuation center along with the other people keeping the emergency center going. So, I'm already where I'm supposed to be for the night."

Georgia said, "The floor is yours, Ray."

"Okay. Sidney, from the beginning, has said that the land manipulation scheme and the theft of the Brontë novel were connected somehow. He sees the link as Larry Carter, the young man killed at the craft fair, and Howard Springwood, the attorney who was murdered in Charlotte a few weeks ago. We found out that Carter worked for Springwood at his Crow Island house. Springwood, we learned, is an expert in rare books, especially of the eighteenth and nineteenth centuries. The Brontë novel fits in there. Springwood was a customer of the rare book dealer on Skidaway Island, Sackville-Bedford, and represented clients who wished to remain anonymous. One of those clients, we believe, was David Rostov."

"Hold it right there, Ray," said Georgia. "I like Sidney. Have a lot of respect for him. He's been through a lot, but I have to believe he's reaching a bit here." She leaned back in her chair as she spoke and began to play with the pencil in front of her. "Just because two people show up at a common public event, doesn't mean they're connected or knew either one would be there."

"Just a minute, Georgia," Nora Sullivan had her FBI case folder open in front of her and started to shuffle through some of the pages. "What Ray said just triggered something. Ah, here it is." She pulled out two sheets of paper and read over them to herself. "Sidney keeps looking for a literary connection...I may have one. P. L. Zutter. Her profile indicates she's an art collector, but not just paintings. She's also into rare books."

"Wait," Ray interrupted this time. "You said *she*. Zutter is a woman?"

"Yes. Pavia Ludmila Zutter. Parents were Russian. Came to the US in 1991." Nora was reading from the profile in front of her. "Married Zutter in 2004. She took over the company after he died six years ago."

"But wait," interrupted Ray, "wasn't there a report the shooter at the craft fair was a woman named Lucy, or something like that?"

Nora looked up, "Yes, but we haven't been able to confirm that. The sheriff's office dismissed it as they were concentrating on gang members that Carter was affiliated with. No one, until now, has looked at Zutter for any connection to Springwood or Larry Carter, and certainly not the craft fair in Walterboro. She's in the FBI's sights for benefiting from the leak of information from the Interior Department and her connection to Rostov." She went back to flipping through the pages in front of her. "Eh...here it is." She found the paragraph she searched for. "She has an interest in seventeenth-century art and literature. Mainly German and Russian." She looked up. "Not English, Victorian."

"Don't think it matters. Rare books are rare books. The point is where was she the day of the craft fair?"

More flipping through the pages. "Not in South Carolina, as far as I can tell they've been watching her for a couple of weeks and she hasn't left Naples, Florida during that time. Although..." Nora paused. "They do have that office on Hilton Head."

Sam Cashman listened to most of the conversation with a growing smile on his face and finally said, "Don't discount what Tillie and Sidney come up with. I know from experience. Believe me."

Ray raised an eyebrow and shook his head. "Very good advice, Sam. Very good advice." Then, directly to Nora, "Those profile pages you have, what do they show for Rostov? Can you make a literary connection with him?"

Nora shuffled more papers and then took out one to

review. "Hmmm...yeeeeah...I think we can. It claims he's an avid collector of both fiction and non-fiction of the eighteenth and nineteenth centuries. But wait." She looked up again, "I know everyone keeps wanting to connect all the dots with rare books, but people like Rostov are always investors in art in one form or another. It's a competition for them. Everything is a competition. The biggest house, or houses, the fanciest car, the most money, the biggest private plane, the best connections money can buy. It's all about them and the conventional rules don't matter. If it's not art it will be horses, or yachts, or, yes, rare books."

Georgia joined the fray, "Sooo, Sidney Lake could be right. It may not be the primary motivation for everything, but it's definitely in the mix."

Silence.

Nora looked down at the papers in front of her and picked one up. "Well, we may be looking at more than we thought. It seems that Pavia Ludmila Zutter is known professionally as P L...and to friends...Lucy."

TWENTY-SIX

The evening wore on and the hurricane winds and rain continued. The good news for the Lowcountry came in the form of *Javier* taking another jog to the east and speeding up. The eye of the storm would not come onshore in South Carolina but would continue up the coast and make its landfall somewhere above Wilmington, North Carolina.

The flooding from Savannah, Georgia to Charleston, South Carolina was extensive. Because of the surprise nature of the storm, many of the people who would have normally evacuated to higher ground, didn't. Sidney, Hattie, and Mickey never had the opportunity to use the reservations in Columbia and canceled them, so the rooms could be used by someone else. Sidney stayed at the hospital and Hattie took Mickey home to her second-floor condominium. Ray went home to be with Marie, while Nora Sullivan stayed in the county building and spent the night on a sofa in the county administrator's reception area. Georgia Sawyer, made use of a sofa in the EMS director's office.

The wind and rain hammered the area all night, but the wheels of government and law enforcement continued to drone on. By morning, the storm was off Charleston and the sky, looking south toward Savannah, appeared promising. The worst was over. Now it was time to assess the damage and start to get everything up and running again.

The FBI had assembled people from the Columbia and Charlotte field offices as well as the resident agencies in Charleston, Beaufort, and Savannah. This would be their show as they were dealing with bribery of a government official at the Interior Dept. The problem was to quickly get to the target location on Hilton Head where the development offices of the Zutter International Alliance affiliate, Magnolia Development Projects, were located. The Crow Island home of David Rostov would be a more challenging problem due to its remote location. Given the storm disruption, the surprise element was lost as they were sure the Zutter office in Florida had contacted Magnolia. The logistics of navigating washed out and blocked roads impeded their planned swift and efficient arrival, but they couldn't wait any longer as the target locations in New York, Miami, and Washington D.C. had already been hit.

∽∾∽

David Rostov had been tipped off about the possibility of a raid on Magnolia Development's office. His informant had been stationed outside the Beaufort County Sheriff's office and easily spotted at least ten officers wearing jackets announcing either POLICE or FBI. Although he hadn't been sure of the exact timing, Rostov had put a number of contingencies in place. His company plane was at the Savannah airport and would certainly be watched, which played into his diversion plans. This was also true of his yacht, which was tied up at the Harbor Town Marina. Another place the police would have to divide their forces to cover. Rostov did not take the call directly, the informant notified Lucien Gruber, his personal bodyguard, the one person Rostov could always rely on to stand by him no matter what happened. Lucien put the escape plan into action on his own.

"*Héberger*." A single word showed up as a text on Rostov's phone. *Let them figure that one out*, Rostov thought as he left the strip mall office of Magnolia Development and tossed the phone into a nearby bush. He had no intention of being caught and needed to get to a safe place while his army of lawyers in New York worked out a deal on his behalf.

Rostov looked around but didn't see anyone, although he was sure someone was watching. His immediate destination was the townhouse development next to the strip mall. His car and chauffeur and Lucien Gruber were waiting there for him in the rear of the first building. It was parked behind a dumpster that concealed it.

The walk took no more than two minutes. His car immediately left for the exit, but Rostov wasn't in it. They assumed anyone watching would report they both left in the car. Being concealed by the dumpster, Rostov and Lucien walked slowly across the green area that separated one parking area on the complex from the other—about ten yards. They no sooner reached the area when an Uber car pulled right up next to them. The driver already had instructions to take them to a location near Hilton Head Airport, which had weathered many storms and was designed to be back in operation quickly. Because of flooding, it would not be able to support commercial aircraft yet, but small private planes and helicopters would be the first to use portions of the runways, especially for emergency purposes.

Lucien watched from the parking lot as Rostov's chauffer drove to the south toward Harbor Town and the Uber driver—with Rostov aboard—headed north to

Island-Life Boat charters on Mathews Drive. Two minutes later, another Uber car picked up Lucien and headed for the same destination. Waiting at Mathews Drive was a Lyft car.

Rostov had just entered the Lyft car when Lucien arrived and got in beside the driver. No one spoke. The driver had instructions to take them to Hilton Head Airport, a five-minute drive.

A turboprop Cessna Caravan waited for them, all warmed up and ready to go. Lucien wasted no time in dismissing the car and driver, who immediately took off for another customer, an appointment made by Lucien under another name. The intent being that he and Rostov would be long gone by the time anyone traced the ride. No one knew about the plane, as it was a charter also arranged for by Lucien. Due to the storm, commercial flights were not scheduled to begin coming in or out of the airport for the next three hours, as there was still flooding on the main runway, but with the storm gone and the sky clear,, the short take-off and landing capabilities of the Cessna would have no difficulty and had approval for the flight. The plan had them going to Augusta, Georgia. They were in the plane and going down the runway in five minutes.

Once in the air, Lucien instructed the pilot to fly low over the Broad River as he advised the pilot they wanted to take a look at some property from the air, an island they were planning to buy near Spring Island. The request was not unusual as the pilot had done similar maneuvers for people who wanted to see the condition of the property they were interested in after a flooding storm. Rostov then surprised the pilot by telling him to change course, stay low over the river and follow it inland to the Beaufort River, and then head for the Beaufort airport on

St. Helena Island. Lucien looked at Rostov in surprise.

"Don't worry, Lucien, I've arranged for us to change planes in Beaufort. I felt it was best if you didn't know."

Lucien merely smiled. He was not surprised by anything Rostov would do. He knew his boss very well. Personal survival was Rostov's first priority, and everything and everyone else came in second. Lucien knew this. Lucien was well paid. Lucien was loyal.

"I can't do this," the pilot objected. He feared they were too low and would track too close to the Parris Island Marine Recruit Depot - a no-fly zone.

TWENTY-SEVEN

Ray Morton stood at the curb in front of the Beaufort County government center and looked at the clearing sky. He and Nora Sullivan made the trip from Morgan in twenty minutes as there was no one else on the road. Nora's car had been damaged overnight by the storm and Ray volunteered to get her to Beaufort so she could join the task force. There were still some gusts around, but the storm had moved on and now harassed Myrtle Beach. The outer bands of heavy rain and high winds began to punish the outer banks of North Carolina. The clean-up in the Lowcountry had already started.

Turning to look back at the buildings behind him, Ray now focused on the contingent of Sheriff's deputies and FBI agents as they pulled out from behind the government center and headed down Ribaut Road toward Hilton Head. He would not be going with them as this was neighboring Beaufort County and he worked for the Coastal Rivers County Solicitor. He felt a sense of nostalgia for all the times he had once been a part of the group that was leaving him behind. It was time to call Sidney, who was still at the hospital in Morgan with Tillie. He described what was happening.

"I hope they don't think they're going to surprise this David Rostov person," Sidney said.

"Oh, I think they know that. From what I've been told, no one ever surprises Rostov." Ray looked around the streets of the county government complex. "I'll bet he's got someone watching us right now. I'm also sure we've got him under surveillance as well."

"Somehow I don't think we'll ever see those Brontë volumes again."

"Well," Ray agreed, "with all those people that have been killed because of them—well, maybe not entirely because of the books—I think your right, don't think they'll ever see the light of day again."

"That's a shame." Sidney looked wistful as he spoke. "I would have loved to get my hands on them."

"Yes, I'm sure, but they were forgeries."

"Possibly, but the volumes themselves weren't. Burke verified that and the mid-high five-figure amount for an original first edition of *The Tenant of Wildfell Hall.* Then again, it's possible some of the handwriting could have been original and T. J. Wise or someone else just enhanced it. It's been known to happen."

A siren sounded in the distance. Ray looked in the direction the sheriff's SUVs headed. Sidney could hear it over his phone. "That doesn't sound like a police vehicle."

"It's not. I know that sound. It's coming from Parris Island. A security breach of some type."

Ray stood and watched, as other people did. They knew what they heard and stopped what they were doing. Everyone looked south toward Parris Island. A small plane appeared in the far distance. It flew low and erratically. It rose and twisted before heading for the bridge across the Beaufort River just beyond Spanish Point. Another turn and then dropped out of sight and seemed to be headed back the way it came.

"Hang on Sidney, I'm going to drive over to the Bay Street Marina where I can have a better view." Ray's car was right in front of him at the curb. "I have a funny feeling about this."

Sidney, now becoming an expert with his cane, made it to the window in Tillie's room and looked to the south toward Beaufort. Tillie was still not back from the diagnostic center on the second floor.

"I'll be there in a couple of minutes down North Street," Ray said getting in.

❧❧❧

The pilot of the Cessna had decided to overrule Rostov and pulled the plane up and to the left to avoid the Parris Island air space. Lucien was not happy and grabbed the man's shoulder. "Turn back the other way or get out of that seat."

"No way." The pilot resisted.

"Get him out of there," Rostov yelled. "I've got to get to that to that plane in Beaufort."

The Cessna continued to rise and Rostov lost his footing and fell back away from Lucien and the pilot. Lucien tightened his grip on the pilot's shoulder and grabbed at the man's right hand with his own. The engine screamed in protest at the plane being jerked around. It made a turn to the right and dived.

Lucien held fast and his superior strength over the pilot began to show. His left arm was around the pilot's neck as he dragged him out of the seat. Lucien removed his gun from its shoulder holster and put it next to the pilot's temple.

"One time I say this. Shut up and sit down."

The pilot did as he was told and stopped his resistance as he yelled, "You can't blow up Parris Island. You can't."

Rostov took over as Lucien moved into the pilot's seat. "Blow up Parris Island? Who do you think we are?" He handed the gun to a now recovered Rostov.

"Terrorists."

Lucien laughed as he righted the plane. They were now over the middle of the Broad River heading away from Parris Island.

"Terrorists?" Rostov said. "Are you mad? What terrorists would purposely want to anger the Marine Corps? No. We're not terrorists. We are in the midst of a very dicey negotiation worth hundreds of millions of dollars, which you are jeopardizing." Rostov's voice modulated and became calm as he held Lucien's gun against the pilot's head.

"Are you planning to kill me?"

Lucien let out a laugh as he maneuvered the plane and gained altitude.

No. No." answered Rostov. "But I do hope you know how to swim."

ↂↃↂↃ

Ray pulled up behind the marina store, jumped out, and headed for the gangplank to the floating docks. He spoke with Sidney as he ran, "I don't see it anymore. The sirens are still going off though."

As Sidney listened intently, a policeman on a bicycle pulled up next to Ray. They spoke briefly and then the policeman leaned his bicycle against the stone marker for the sign indicating that only boat owners and their guests were permitted to go any further.

Sidney finally said, "Ray, what's going on?"

"Sick pilot."

"Sick pilot, what does that mean?" Sidney turned

away from the window.

"Local uniform said the passenger in the plane called Hilton Head and told them the pilot got sick and lost control of the plane. The guy's a pilot himself and said he would bring the plane down in Beaufort."

The sirens stopped and a small plane could now be seen in the distance.

"There he is," said Ray. "It's heading for St. Helena."

Sidney, leaning on the cane next to his right leg and began to rub his chin in deep thought.

Ray recognizing the silence said, "What's up, Sidney?"

Sidney didn't answer immediately. Just continued to look out the window imagining the plane as if in a trance. Finally, he said, "Interesting. I wonder if it is a coincidence that at the same time a raid is underway at Magnolia Development's office on Hilton Head and a warrant has been issued for Mr. Rostov, a plane takes off from the Hilton Head Airport, flies low over restricted air space, and is now making an emergency landing at Beaufort Airport. Meanwhile, the police are focused on going in the opposite direction at a distance of more than thirty land miles away."

"Wait a minute. You think…"

"Perhaps."

Ray took out his phone and dialed Nora Sullivan and began speaking the moment he had a connection. "Nora, do you have Rostov in your sights?"

"We're not there yet. Just got onto two-eighty-seven a few minutes ago."

"But do you have eyes on Rostov?"

Silence

"I believe so. Hold on."

Silence

"Last report we have is he's in his car heading for Harbor Town."

"You sure."

"Why, what's going on?"

"The plane. Did you see it?"

"Yeah. It's out of view now. Understand they have a sick pilot but it's all under control now. Hold on a minute."

Silence

"Ray, we lost Rostov. The car that went to Harbor Town was empty."

"Sidney thought so. Keep me posted. Sidney has a couple of ideas we're going to explore."

"What's he got up his sleeve, Ray? I need to know."

"Call you back in a couple of minutes."

Ray ended the call and redialed Sidney, "Rostov was supposed to be in a car heading for Harbor Town but when they got there it was empty."

Nora Sullivan remained silent for just a moment and then spoke to one of the agents in the back seat, "Sidney Lake believes there's a good possibility Rostov is on that plane over the Broad River. What do you think?"

"Damn. He could be right."

"Really?" She paused and spoke with someone else in the car. "Talk to me."

"Rostov may not have a reputation for being the brightest light around, but the report on him shows he surrounds himself with a lot of people who are. It looks like he's outwitted and outmaneuvered a lot of smart people over the years. He always finds a way to stay in the clear. Even if he doesn't, his lawyers have always found a way out for him. This time it's different though. He can't call for a *no-contest* deal and just pay a fine without having to admit guilt. He needs to get away. We

want him for bribing a public official. He needs to re-
group so his lawyers can come up with something. He
needs a plan. Why do you think he would head for
Beaufort?"

"Time and access. Only two land ways to get to the
airport. Both over the Beaufort River and one is a
drawbridge known for its traffic jams. Could have
arranged for a way out of the airport. Car, plane, boat—
they're all possibilities. The boat is my bet. The airport is
surrounded on three sides by creeks and rivers that have
deep water access. And they all feed into the Morgan
River. The area around Morgan must have fifty islands of
all sizes and shapes. Mostly uninhabited. It would take
forever to find him. By the time they get a good lead on
where he is, he'll be in the Caribbean or South America."

While waiting for Nora to get back to him, Ray made
his way back to his car.

His phone rang. It was Nora again, "Ray?"

"Still here."

"Look, they tell me we've only got one helicopter
available to us. The rest are doing rescue work. Even the
two that are normally at the Beaufort airport are out at
Fripp Island doing rescue work. The one we do have is
doing support work in Bluffton and moved some of our
people in from Savannah."

"Not to worry. I'm on my way. Can be there easy
from here. Know a good spot where I can see the whole
airport."

"Stay in touch. We're heading your way."

The call ended. Ray got into his car, made a quick turn
and headed for St. Helena Island. The airport was a five-
mile drive. He punched up Sidney again on his phone.
"Eh, Sidney, I'm going to take a ride over to the Beaufort
Airport? Do you think Tillie might have any contacts

over there?"

"I wouldn't be surprised."

❦

After Lucien advised Hilton Head of their problem, he headed directly for the Beaufort Airport and requested an emergency landing. However, when checking with the tower at Beaufort, they instructed him not to come directly in. They didn't want an inexperianced pilot attempting a landing over route twenty-one, as he would have to come in too low to hit the end of runway seven. Instead, he was instructed to make a wide circle around so he could come in the opposite end on runway twenty-five. Much safer for someone not familiar with the restricted approach to number seven. Rostov told Lucien to agree and hatched a plan to come in right over Dataw Island where he could catch the river, drop down and dump the pilot out of the plane, claiming he went hysterical and jumped out. That would divert the police and EMS people to a wide water area along the river that touched on Dataw and Warsaw Islands.

Lucien executed the maneuvers and then signaled for Rostov to come forward. Rostov passed the gun to Lucien and they changed places.

"Hold it as steady as you can as our friend here goes for a swim."

The pilot panicked. "We must be five hundred feet up. Nobody can survive that."

"Well you're going to try."

The pilot lunged at Lucien who neatly side-stepped the attack and hit the pilot on the side of his head with the pistol. Down in the aisle and dazed, the pilot didn't move. Lucien stepped over him, holstered the gun, and dragged him to the door. The plane was over the water with the Dataw Island marina in the distance behind them. Lucien opened the door and pushed the pilot out. Leaving the door open, he went back and changed places with Rostov and called the Beaufort tower and told them the pilot panicked, completely lost control, and jumped out. He couldn't stop him as he was alone in the plane and couldn't leave the controls. He told them where to find the pilot and they instructed him to continue to the airport.

ℰↄℰↄ

Ray had just crossed the draw bridge to Lady's Island when Nora called.

"Ray, where are you now?"

"A mile or so from Beaufort Airport."

"Okay, keep going. What we've learned so far was there was an Uber pick-up at the townhouse complex that took a passenger to the Island-life Charter Boat office on Mathews Drive. The people at Island-life said no one came into their office, but we're checking to see if any of the charter boats are missing. We have another report of two people being picked up by a charter flight out of Hilton Head Airport. That's the same plane that's in trouble and heading for Beaufort with, reportedly, only one passenger and a disabled pilot. Ray, when you get to Beaufort Airport do not engage. Let airport security handle the situation as best they can until we get there. The Sheriff is sending back-up—what little there is now. I do want to know who comes off that plane. I repeat, do not engage."

"Understand."

"Good, we're a little thin at the moment. We're

checking Rostov's yacht and the security cameras at Hilton Head Airport should give us a look at who got on that flight."

"Agreed. We're not far away now." Ray ended the call and called Sidney, "Got any ideas?"

"There is something I'd like you to do. When you get to that spot on twenty-one where the planes come in low over the highway to hit the end of the runway, stop. See if you can spot someone waiting for that plane. I know they'll be emergency vehicles near where they expect the plane to touch down, but I want to know if anyone else is there."

"You still believe this is Rostov and it's all pre-planned?"

"Yes."

"Okay, you're probably right. Rostov may have a reputation for being impulsive, but he's also known for being calculating and he has the money to make things happen very quickly. He also isn't known to get his hands dirty, so whatever he's planned, he has lots of help."

The ride was a short one and Ray pulled off to the right side of the road where a make-shift parking area had been created by people stopping their cars to watch the small planes take off and land. He pulled in behind a blue pick-up with three beach chairs set up in the back.

A long and wide clearing had been created that ran from the chain-link fence border of the Airport back across the highway and then fifty yards into the marshland before some houses could be seen. Along the highway, there were telephone poles with large red balls to indicate where the wires were.

Ray looked at the wires and spoke with Sidney again. "Not a lot of margin for error is there? But I'm sure it's not a problem if you know what you're doing."

Ray got out of the car and looked across the roadway and the fence while holding his phone.

"Where are the emergency vehicles?" Sidney asked.

Ray went over to the truck and addressed the man sitting in the back of it, "Can you see any emergency vehicles out there?"

The man stood up. "There was one down here a few minutes ago but it went away. Is there something wrong?"

"Could be. Understand there's a plane in trouble that could be coming in."

"Ah, that explains it." He had binoculars on a strap around his neck and moved them to his eyes as he spoke. "I can see some emergency lights at the other end of the runway. If there is any trouble they'll try to bring him in over the water. They usually do. Here take a look." He removed the glasses and passed them to Ray, who stood up on the trailer hitch of the truck.

"Yeah, I see them. A couple of firetrucks spaced out along the runway." Ray also spotted a small private aircraft on the taxiway midway down the runway. It had its engine running waiting to take off. He handed the glasses back to the man and dropped to the ground. "Thanks."

Ray addressed Sidney, "I know what's going on. I need to get to the terminal building."

"There it is." The man in the truck said pointing to the sky above the far end of the runway."

Ray turned and looked. "Yeah, he's coming in. I've got to hurry." He jumped into his car and hit the accelerator.

"What did you see?" Sidney said.

"There's a plane warming up on the taxiway halfway down the runway. If Rostov's on the plane coming in, I'll bet the other one is his connection."

As Ray turned onto Airport Circle headed for the terminal, Sidney looked out the window in Morgan with a questioningly look on his face. He didn't believe Rostov was planning to use two planes to make his escape. Switching cars was one thing but it made no sense to switch planes, other than to cause confusion, although that was something Rostov had proved he knew how to do very well.

As Ray entered the airport parking lot, he had a clear view as the plane came down. A perfect, smooth landing. But the pilot made no attempt to stop, or even slow down. The taxiway sat between the terminal and the runway. On the far side of the runway was a deep-water creek that made its way out toward the Morgan River. The Cessna made a turn toward the creek, cutting across twenty yards of grass, and stopped. The waiting plane moved across the runway toward the Cessna and positioned itself at its side. Sidney then saw an EMS vehicle pull out from behind the terminal building and make a left onto Airport Circle. It headed away from them toward the river, away from the airport. Ray described to Sidney what was happening.

At the hospital, Tillie was wheeled into the room—she had been downstairs taking a series of tests—and saw Sidney by the window talking on the phone.

"That's curious," Sidney muttered just loud enough for Ray to hear him.

"Not anymore. I think that's Rostov's next ride."

"Not the plane. Based on the turn you said it took, that EMS truck is heading away from the airport and not going to the planes."

"What?" Ray looked up and saw the flashing lights circle off to the right and out of sight. "They must have another call."

"But airport emergency wouldn't answer a local call, the county EMS would."

Ray turned back to the two planes as he pulled up to the chain-link fence of the parking lot. The two planes were side by side with the Hilton Head Cessna being closer to the water. "Can't see what's going on. Wait. It looks like the second plane is moving. It is. It's heading for the runway. Can't see anything else."

Ray ended the call to Sidney and called Nora. "Nora, Ray. They're on the ground and there's a second plane. Looks like whoever was on the Cessna transferred to the other one. Can't see anything. Where are you?"

"Just passed the entrance road to Parris Island. We're sure Rostov was on that Cessna. We're checking with the Beaufort Tower, which doesn't have enough height to see what's with the two planes. Understand the charter pilot of the Cessna jumped the plane over by Dataw someplace."

"Jumped or was pushed."

"Right. We're pretty sure the Cessna had two passengers even though the passenger pilot claimed he was alone. Where are you?"

"Parking lot of the terminal. Emergency vehicles are heading for the two planes. The Beaufort plane now on the runway about to take off. Small plane. Won't need more than seventy-five yards to get up. It'll come off the runway heading your way. Right over twenty-one."

"Hold it for a moment, Ray."

As Ray remained quiet, he could again hear Nora in conversation with at least two other people. One seemed to be in a back-and-forth conversation on a phone while the other issued instructions over another phone.

"Ray, Beaufort tower just spotted a boat moving along

a tidal marsh channel near the other plane. Said it was almost completely obscured by the marsh grass. It's heading away from the plane. They can't see it clearly enough to identify it as yet. It's just creeping along."

Sidney said, "It would. Tide can't be more than a third of the way in so they're in very shallow water despite the storm."

"Right," Nora said. "Let me call you back."

The call no sooner ended when Ray's phone rang. "Sidney, I was just about to call you." Ray gave him the latest news.

"I'll bet Rostov's on that boat," Sidney said.

"Why? Why not the plane?"

"Switching planes never made any sense. He's a lot easier to track in the air than on the ground. Once the alarms were set off at Parris Island he had to assume they would add the plane to their search pattern. From what you've told me about the background information the FBI has developed, I have to believe Mr. Rostov is not one who can easily be caught off guard. He has lots of resources at his disposal. After all, he lives and breathes hedging his bets. It's what he does for a living and he's, apparently, very good at it. I'm sure he's already established a good reason for leaving Hilton Head by plane to begin with."

"Any ideas as to where he would be headed?"

Sidney walked from the window over to the chair where Tillie now sat "Let me put your question to the expert." He pulled the phone away from his ear and held it in a careful position so Ray would be able to hear his conversation with Tillie. "Tillie, it looks like Mr. Rostov may have transferred from the plane he was on to a powerboat. Given what we've learned about him, where would he head for in a boat to escape the law?"

"You kiddin'? Go where all the bad people have been goin' for more than 400 years. They don't call um the Pirate Islands for nothin'. Pirates, revolution peoples, Confederates, bootleggers, convicts, you name it, they've all hid out there. People said durin' the war Nazi subs used to hang around out there. Must be a hundred island sandbars. All sizes and shapes. Some of them disappearin' lately as the waters risin'. Besides, from talkin' to people out there someone bought up at least five of them since last year. One of them has a guest house hidden somewhere in the center of it. The big island is where Miss Ester lives. Others are mostly empty. Don't know. The government took over some back in the fifties. Doin' funny stuff. Experiments. All abandoned now. Yeah, if Mr. Rostov needs to hide for a while, that's where he's goin'."

Sidney pulled the phone back. "What do you think, Ray?"

"I think we've got a problem if Rostov makes it to those islands. Let me call Nora back."

Sidney turned to Tillie and asked, "Could someone hide out there for a long time?"

"Sure could. Slaves did it all the time. If you could get to the islands no one would find you. Especially a White man. Deep mud, quicksand, bugs, snakes, they ain't goin' after you. Figure you'd die on your own."

"But with all the modern technology around today, I don't see how anyone could hide out like they used to. Should be able to spot them from the air."

"Maybe, maybe not."

"Luckily it's still early in the day and the storm has completely cleared the sky so we should be able to track the boat when it gets to open water. Especially if we can get something up in the air."

When Nora Sullivan answered Ray's call she had the car's speaker on, "Ray do you still have that boat in sight?"

"We haven't seen it yet. Too well hidden by the marsh grass. Tower's got the best view and that seems to be hit and miss. We know they're heading for the Morgan River, as that's where all the creeks around here drain. The Morgan is open water and we'll be able to see it once it gets out there. The sheriff has a couple of boats, where are they?"

"That's what we were just discussing. In anticipation of the raid, the sheriff's watercraft have been deployed to the Broad River and Daufuskie Island. No way to get them to where you are in less than twenty to thirty minutes. Have a call into the Morgan County Sheriff, as he's probably our best bet at this point. You used to work there didn't you?"

Nora and the agents in her car listened as Ray gave them a rundown on what Tillie had said.

While Ray and Nora continued their discussion, Rostov, and Lucien hunkered down in the cabin of the large powerboat. Originally there were three people on the boat when it arrived but two of them made themselves visible as they climbed into the small plane. Lucien hoped they would be mistaken for him and Rostov and further confuse their pursuers. The plane was owned by one of Rostov's LLCs and piloted by a Rostov employee.

The plan was to slowly move toward the Morgan River and the deep water that would allow them to open the throttle, as they made for a group of islands within the Pirate Island group. These were nicknamed the ghost islands, as many of them were just barely above water and heavy with thick mangroves. Many of them often completely disappeared during high tides and storms.

Lucien planned for them to hide out on a figure-eight shaped island that had been a favorite of Stede Bonnet, the so called "Gentleman Pirate" of the early eighteenth century. It seemed most appropriate as Bonnet was considered a "gentleman" pirate and had outfitted his cabin on *The Revenge* as a library. The only water traffic that maneuvered in the island group were some sightseers and a Charleston tour company that ran boat tours in a replica pirate ship.

Rostov became angry with the slow movement of the boat. "Get this damn boat moving. They already know we're here. Why are you moving so slow?"

"Have to, Mr. Rostov, This channel's not that deep yet. Easy to get caught in the mud."

Turning to his bodyguard he growled, "Lucien, get up there and help him to understand our needs and get us the hell out of here."

Lucien moved up next to the man at the controls. One look at Lucien's face and the man's hand reached for the throttle.

Ray's car remained idling in the parking lot as he said to Nora, "There's no way we can get to them is there?"

"Not by land. If Rostov is headed for the islands off Morgan he can be there in fifteen minutes by water. For us, we'd have to drive a big horseshoe. Back across the Beaufort drawbridge and then all the way up to route seventeen—maybe between five and ten miles. Then another five miles to the north until you get to the Morgan highway and you're still ten miles from the Old Fort Marina. No, for us, he'd be long gone by then."

"Forget us, if air is the only option, what about an air-sea rescue helicopter from the Marine Corps Air Station? They wouldn't have to do anything, all we need is for them to keep track of where they're going."

Nora gave a look to the agent sitting behind the driver and he immediately began to dial.

But that was not the only option Sidney thought about as he and Tillie spoke.

While Ray was talking to Nora, Sidney and Tillie huddled together by her bed. Tillie looked at him with a smile of satisfaction, "Don't you worry Professor, I got me an idea. Yeah, I do. That Mister. Rostov, he ain't goin' nowhere."

As Sidney put his phone away he said to Ray, "Any luck with Agent Sullivan?"

He shook his head, "No, they already thought of MCAS Air-Sea Rescue but it's a no-go. I forgot that the Marine pilots do tandem runs between Beaufort and Savannah every morning to keep their skills up. With the storm over, they're back on schedule and Air-Sea Rescue has them as their first and only priority at this time. Nora said she's been in touch with Chief Hornig in Morgan and he's got some assets at the Morgan airfield he's looking into. Nothing we can do. I'm going over to the control tower and find out what's going on."

Tillie lost no time in hatching her plan. She made three quick phone calls and then a fourth to Sam Cashman, who immediately left the Morgan County building. His destination was Coffin Landing and the shrimp boats tied up there, a five-minute drive.

During that same five minutes, Rostov's boat finally broke free of the channel and raced into the Morgan River headed for the Pirate Islands. No one followed them. The dropping of the pilot overboard near Dataw Island had diverted the one airport rescue boat that could have tracked them. The sheriff's boats were too far away and the Morgan City police boat was tied up trying to unravel the collision between a kayak and a sailboat someplace off Deer Island. Rostov knew he was in the clear. By late afternoon he expected to be off the Georgia coast and in the Bahamas by nightfall.

After about fifteen minutes of full-throttle travel, Lucien said to the boat operator, "What's that up ahead?"

"Can't tell." He lifted the binoculars that hung around his neck, put them to his eyes and scanned the water ahead of him. "Looks like a shrimp boat. Maybe two of them. Probably going out on the tide. Wait there's a third. And I think there's another one behind it. What the hell are they doin'?"

The boat raced toward them as they all seemed to be heading toward the Pirate Islands. Lucien called to Rostov, who now sat in the cabin below smoking a cigar as he spoke on the phone. "Mister Rostov, I think we have a problem."

Rostov took the phone down from his ear and gave Lucien an exasperated look, "Well...what do I pay you for. Handle it as you usually do." He went back to his conversation.

The forty-four-foot powerboat had two sets of controls, one on the deck and one on the flybridge. Lucien called to the pilot, "Jackson, get up top so you can see better." Lucien grabbed the binoculars resting on the seat near him and looked toward the shrimp boats.

No more than a mile away the captain of the *Rear-View Mirror* looked through his own binoculars at Rostov's boat, one hand on the wheel and the other the hand-set for the short wave radio. "Bubba, let's line up offa your starboard side. See if we can get him to try to cut in front of us and head toward Teach channel. Nice an wide in the mouth but drops quick a hundred yards in. Looks good but don't stay that way for long. If he ain't never been in there, he's got a surprise commin'.

"Yeah, he sure does. That boat he's drivin' looks like it's gonna need 'bout four feet to keep movin'. This time o' day he sure gonna be surprised, 'Specially if he tries to keep that speed."

A voice came on, "Hey, Cap'n Clyde, this is Danny on the *Sally Two*. I got the *Polite* an the *Castaway* with me. If you tryin' to get him into Teach, we can sneak up from his starboard side, while you push his port."

"Amen, Danny. Come on in the waters fine."

From the flying bridge of Rostov's boat, Jackson could see four shrimp boats coming up ahead of him to his port side. If he tried to turn around both Rostov and Gruber would have his head. He knew they wanted to get to Cutlass Cove where he would drop them off and then head up toward Edisto. He was supposed to be going to the left, around the island ahead of him, but there were now four shrimp boats in the channel he expected to use. He knew there had to be another way but he left the charts below. He moved his binoculars, which were around his neck, up to his eyes and scanned the water ahead of him. Straight ahead he could see a wide channel that was beginning to appear slightly off to his right as he got closer to the island in front. It would be a little out of the way, but he was sure all the channels and estuaries were interconnected. In trying to visualize the carts below, he could not remember any of them coming to a dead end. He changed direction.

Lucien, felt the change and called to Jackson, "Why are you turning?"

"Going to go around the starboard side of the island up ahead. Some shrimp boats filling up the channel I was going to use."

"We're on a tight schedule. No delays."

"Understand. We'll be okay."

Rostov sat at a large table and puffed on his cigar as he looked at some papers in front of him, his cell phone in his hand. He called to the deck above, "Everything okay up there?"

Lucien answered, "Yeah, just some minor maneuvers. We're good."

"Better be. Got to get out of this damn state."

Captain Clyde saw the Rostov boat's course correction. "Hang on everybody. Easy now. He's got the bait. Let him run with it a bit. Danny, as soon as he passes you, drop your booms and come in behind him. We'll do the same."

Jackson kept his eyes fixed on Teach channel. It was even wider than it first looked.

Lucien called to him, "An awful lot of shrimp boats around here. Some more off to your right."

Jackson took a quick look to starboard. "Where'd they come from? Didn't see them before. Must be some sort of training or something going on. That makes seven of them around here. Maybe it's not unusual. Anyway, looks like we're good to go up ahead."

As Jackson refocused on the water ahead, Captain Danny's boat and the two others dropped their booms and moved to be side by side but keeping a safe distance among them. Once Rostov's boat entered the Teach channel, Captain Clyde's four boats did the same and started to head in the same direction.

Jackson kept moving but began to slow his speed as he got deeper into the channel. It suddenly narrowed and the marsh grass became taller. There was another turn up ahead and he began to get worried. He looked behind him and exclaimed, "Whoa!"

Lucien heard him and said, "What's the matter?"

"Problem, take a look." Jackson pointed behind him at

the entrance to the Teach channel.

Both men looked in surprise as they saw seven shrimp boats, all with their booms lowered sitting side by side across the entrance of the channel.

"Holy shit," said Lucien.

Then they heard a familiar sound up in front of them. They both turned and could see the Marine Corp Air Sea Rescue helicopter coming toward them.

"Step on it, Jackson. Get us out of here."

Jackson did as he was told and headed down the narrowed channel. He heard the bottom of the boat hit something, but he dared not slow down. Another hit and another. He knew what was happening. The boat tilted to the side as the muddy bottom of the channel rose up beneath him. Ahead, the channel widened again. But it didn't deepen. The boat tilted to its side as it skidded to a jolting stop. Jackson fell from the flying bridge. Rostov was knocked from his chair and first hit the floor and then the wall. Lucien Gruber was not to be seen, as the bull horn distorted voice from above ordered them to remain in place.

TWENTY-EIGHT

The storm was now a memory and the sun shone brightly on the rear patio of the City Hall Café. A week and a half had passed. "All right, Tillie," Sidney said, "explain to all those present who don't know you very well—and maybe a few of us who do—just how you managed to assemble a shrimp boat armada in fifteen minutes time?" They all sat at two large tables with market umbrellas fully extended: Sidney, Tillie, Ray Morton, Nora Sullivan, Hattie Ryan, Burke Masterson (in a wheelchair), Georgia Sawyer, and Mickey.

"Weren't no problem. Nobody liked that Mr. Rostov. Even though they didn't know who he was. Always someone trying to steal the land out from under us. Nothin' new. But this time it was different. Especially when people found out he was behind some of those tax sales in the County. Most times nobody bids on 'um so the people livin there can keep their land and home till they can get the money together to make a payment. Mr. Rostov, he's a sneaky one. Buyin' peoples places for a few hundred dollars an hidin' behind a bunch a lawyers an phony companies. Usually it's just some local real estate person but Rostov was big-time slick. Miss Ester's been livin' on that piece of land of hers since she was born. An her mother and grandmother before her. Well, nobody knew who it was trying to take her property, and a bunch of others on the islands. Hidin' behind a bunch of lawyers. Stole 'um. We didn't know it was one person doin' most of it. Professor Lake figured that out when they was tracein' some of those books that went missing.

"We spread the word when we found out Mister Rostov was doin' all the buyin'. Although there were some others. There's always someone tryin' to steal land from Gullah people. This wasn't the first time. Probably won't be the last. All remember the last time someone tried to make a resort out there. That was a local fella. He used the courts to steal the land back then some thirty years ago. We didn't have much help from the police that time. Had to rely on God to help us out. An help He did. Sent us that hurricane, Carrie, and wiped out the whole development.'

"But what about the shrimp boats, Tillie," Ray interrupted.

"I'm getting there. Hold your horses, Mister Morton. I gotta set the stage." At this point, she did an impression of Sidney Lake looking over his glasses at a college student. Everyone saw what she did and burst out laughing, especially Sidney. Georgia Sawyer, who sat next to Ray, gave him a playful punch in the arm.

"Okay," Ray said, "I'll keep quiet. Note for the record, I have been properly chastised and dutifully reprimanded."

Tillie with a straight face reached over and gave Mickey a rub behind the ear, as the Lab placed her head in Tillie's lap, showing whose side she was on. "To continue, made a call to the phone at Coffin Landing after Professor Lake an I had a talk and he told me what was happening and Mister Rostov was getting away.

"Well, George Ba-cote answered. His aunt was one of the ladies that lost her land to somebody like Mr. Rostov. Wasn't him. Some lawyer from Atlanta." She stopped and looked as though a light bulb went off in her head.

"Unless it was him. Don't think we ever found out. Her place was just torn down. Nobody built on it." She got back on track. "Anyway, I explained what was happenin' an all, and they finally got the goods on Mr. Rostov for orderin' Mr. Springwood's killin' and that Carter fella too."

Sidney interrupted, "To be fair Tillie, as Ms. Sullivan will confirm," he gave Nora Sullivan a quick look, "Mr. Rostov has been arrested for bribing a federal official and not for murder."

"That's correct, Sidney, we're working on the murder part, but we're still trying to find Lucien Gruber. We know he was on the boat with the Rostov and the operator but managed to disappear over the side before the shrimp boats trapped them."

"Yeah, but you'll get um. FBI always does. That Lucy-an fella ain't gonna last out there for long on those islands by himself." Tillie looked up and saw Detective Sam Cashman come out onto the patio. "Ain't that right Mr. Sam?"

Sam made his way to the table and grabbed the chair that was left for him. "All depends on Gruber. Has everyone ordered?" He saw the iced teas, sodas, and coffee already in front of everyone.

Ray answered, "No, just had some drinks delivered. You haven't missed anything. Tillie was just telling us how she arranged for the Gullah navy to go after Rostov."

Sam smiled and addressed Tillie, "Well, keep going. I want to hear this myself."

"Okay. Well as I said, Georgie Ba-cote answered the phone an I explained everything that was goin' on. 'Well, what you want me to do?' he asked. An I said, 'You got to stop Mister Rostov from getting' to Pirate Land.' Well,

Georgie's a good boy an' a smart one too. After he thought for a moment he said, 'I got it. Don't you worry Miss Tillie, The Rostov man, he ain't goin nowhere.'

"Well, it seems there were four shrimp boats sittin at the dock at Coffin Landing. The crews all doing clean-up and repair stuff and another three boats sittin' out in the channel doing testing of one kind and another. All it took was a couple of phone calls from Georgie an they set up a trap.

"That area around Pirate Islands is full of narrow marsh channels. If you don't know what you're doin' you get hung up real quick. That's why the pirate people liked it there. Shrimp boats just blocked off the channels the Rostov boat needed to get to. They was hung up in no time. I told the professor what they was doin' an he called the FBI, Miss Sullivan." She looked at Nora who took over.

"At the time I heard from Professor Lake, the Marine Corp Air Station in Beaufort had freed up one of their Air Sea Rescue helicopters for us and they were on the scene in less than ten minutes."

Sam Cashman spoke up, "Yeah, the Sheriff's still got some people combing those islands for Gruber along with the FBI. No sign of him yet. They'll keep trying. Lot of territory to cover."

Tillie nodded in agreement, "Yeah, lotta places to hide."

"Nice work, Tillie, you did a great job," said Ray. "He's going to need lots of survival skills out there. Between the alligators and the snakes, they may not find all of him." He looked at Sam Cashman who just smiled in agreement. Then turning to Sidney, "You know Sidney, I never understood what turned you on to Rostov in the first place? He just didn't seem to be on anyone's radar. Everyone just kept looking for the murderer of Springwood in Charlotte and you immediately went in another direction."

Sidney looked surprised, as though he couldn't believe Ray didn't understand. "I thought it would be obvious. Springwood's murder wasn't about money. It was the books. Remember, he was the attorney for General Brewster's uncle. Anne Brontë's *The Tenant of Wildfell Hall* wasn't the only stolen book he palmed off on people. From the beginning, the book held more interest for me than the murder. Burke, here, made the connection for me when he mentioned that Springwood was a customer of Sackville-Bedford and a good friend of Ryan Bedford the owner. It was Mr. Bedford who put me onto the fact that Springwood represented his neighbor David Rostov when buying rare books for him at auctions."

Hattie spoke up. "Sidney, what was the motive for the murder of Howard Springwood?"

"Ah, let me answer this way. Miss Sullivan, who was the intermediary between the person leaking information from the Interior Department and David Rostov?"

Nora Sullivan looked surprised and, at first, hesitated but then said. "I suppose it doesn't matter now. It was Howard Springwood. It's the way Rostov worked. He was very careful to distance himself from anything that could be traced back to him. At first, Springwood's dealings with Rostov dealt with rare books. He collected them. It's how he became associated with P. L. Zutter, the planned developer of the Pirate Island. She was also a collector, but a legitimate one."

Hattie looked surprised and said, "Legitimate? I don't understand."

"Her background is Russian. The P L stands for Pavia Ludmila. She and her parents were Russian immigrants.

Went to the University of Florida and studied European literature. Has an extensive collection of books from the eighteenth and nineteenth centuries. Well known as a scholar dealing with the period. Rostov, on the other hand, has no interest in the content of the books he collected for investment and vanity purposes. Liked to put down intellectuals by detailing his extensive rare book collection."

Georgia Sawyer asked, "Ludmila? I had a classmate in college by that name and we referred to her as 'Lucy.' Is there a connection here to Larry Carter?"

"Yes and no. Yes to her being referred to as Lucy and no to a connection to Larry Carter. At the time Carter was murdered at the craft fair Ms. Zutter was confirmed as being in Florida. Yes, we thought of that."

Ray now asked, "So who killed Springwood and why?"

"Our main suspect is Lucien Gruber, Rostov's bodyguard. Our information indicates that Springwood became nervous about his involvement in being the middleman between Rostov and the Interior Department leaker. It was one thing to play around with forging or 'enhancing' author signatures in a book, and another to be involved with bribing a government official. Gruber has a past history of violent behavior."

Georgia Sawyer said, "We've run into him in South Carolina before. The county solicitor tried to put him away on a manslaughter charge for killing a man in a fight in Columbia a few years ago but he managed to get off on self-defense. Had two lawyers from out of state defending him."

"Ah," exclaimed Ray, "that's why I recognized the name."

Sidney Lake had been quietly listening to the analysis

and finally decided to step in. "If you're wondering how Mr. Carter fits into all of this and the rare edition of *The Tenant of Wildfell Hall,* there is a connection. I think Detective Cashman has the answer for us."

"As usual, Professor Lake, you and Tillie were right on the mark." Sam shifted in his chair as he began to address the table. "But why don't you tell us about the connections you uncovered. It's only fair, since you and Tillie put us onto it all."

"Well, yes, I suppose it is somewhat convoluted. All right. Well, this all goes back to the theft of the three-volume first edition of Anne Brontë's *The Tenant of Wildfell Hall* a few years ago. It was stolen from the back seat of a police car by Howard Springwood. They were part of a group of rare books that were stolen from the home of General Lawrence Brewster in Morgan and recovered by the police to be used as evidence. The original connection to Mr. Springwood comes as the books in question were inherited by General Brewster from his uncle in Charlotte North Carolina, a client of Howard Springwood. It was Springwood who originally hid the volumes in the library of a client, something he apparently did from time to time.

"What confirmed this for me was the existence of two inventory lists of the books that came from Charlotte, as part of the inheritance. One of the lists omitted the books Mr. Springwood hid in his client's library and the other was Mr. Springwood's personal list."

"But why was he hiding them?" asked Hattie.

"There may be a couple of reasons. One has to do with a report from INTERPOL that had him as a person of interest in the acquisition of stolen rare books from Europe. Nothing was ever proven. The other could be that some of the notations appearing in the books—

supposedly made by the authors—were forgeries. I personally feel that the latter may be the case with the notations attributed to Anne Brontë. However, until we find the books we will never know." Sidney spotted a questioning look on Ray's face across the table from him. "Ray, you seem puzzled."

"I am. At first, I thought you were off the mark in tying the Pirate Island land grab to the missing rare books. But you kept finding links. And then you came to the conclusion that Larry Carter was a major link to everything. I still haven't figured that out. Sure, he started everything with the *National Arts and Crafts Show* appearance but I'll be dam...er darned if I can put together his murder by Lucien Gruber, as being part of everything else."

Sidney had a slight smile on his face as he listened. Tillie did as well. Ray looked at them both, shook his head, and said, "Wait, what do you two know, that no one else does?"

"Well, first of all, Mr. Gruber had nothing to do with the death of Mr. Carter. I don't believe they even knew one another."

"Wait, isn't Lucien Gruber the 'Lucy' Carter referred to before he was killed?"

Sidney looked at Nora Sullivan. "Ms. Sullivan, are you aware of anyone ever referring to Lucien Gruber as Lucy?"

"No. In fact I would seriously doubt it. My understanding of his background is that if you ever tried to call him, Lucy, you took your life in your hands. No Lucien Gruber is not Lucy."

Ray, now frustrated, blurted out, "Well who the hell is Lucy?"

Sidney now looked at Detective Sam Cashman. Their

eyes locked momentarily and Sam gave Sidney a 'go-ahead' nod.

Sidney turned and spoke to Burke Mansfield, "Tell us again, as best you can remember, what you heard Mr. Larry Carter say to the person who shot him."

Burke, looked around the table at the people now focused on him. "Well," he gave a second look at Harriet Ryan sitting next to him. "I've gone over this many times and I'm convinced he said, 'You little shit. What did you do with them?' To which the response was, 'Nuthin. I ain't got 'um. Lucy, don't hurt me. Don't hurt me!' Which elicited a response of expletives and the statement and question, 'You stole them from the island house. I know you did. What did you do with them? Tell me. Now!' To which he replied, 'I put them back, Lucy. I put them back.' The Lucy person responded with more very angry expletives and called him a liar...," Burke's hand began to shake and his face went white as he remembered the trauma. Hattie saw the change and put her hand on his to calm him "...and...and that's when I heard the popping sounds and, obviously mistakenly, asked the question, 'What's goin on out there?' After that I recall falling backward and, apparently, out of the portable toilet. I remember nothing..." He started to regain his composure. "I remember nothing else until awakening in the hospital." He looked over at Hattie and said, "Thank you."

Sidney very apologetically said, "Burke, I'm so sorry to put you through this again and I appreciate your being here, but I needed everyone to hear the statement by Mr. Carter that 'I put them back,' in response to the statement by Lucy 'You stole them from the island house.' In hearing that and knowing about the missing rare books, especially the Anne Brontë ones, you might assume that what he referred to was the three-volume original edition of *The Tenant of Wildfell Hall*. However, you would only be partially correct.

"You see, what we had been unaware of was there have been reports of minor thefts of items from a variety of homes on Crow Island, despite all of their security. Those thefts were made by Mr. Larry Carter. Also, not only did Mr. Carter occasionally work for Howard Springwood, he also did odd jobs for a Real Estate company that managed a number of the houses of part-time residents of the island. The owner of the company sometimes went by the name of 'Lucy.'"

Hattie reacted with, "Lucy, I don't know a Lucy. I have many female friends who work for real estate companies and I can't think of a Lucy. Are you sure?"

"Hattie, I said," a look over his glasses accompanied the comment, "*he* sometimes went by the name of Lucy."

Nora Sullivan reacted this time with, "He? Lucy is a man?"

"Quite so. A man in a trusted position. Not only as the owner of a real estate company but also as a 'special policeman' in the Morgan auxiliary police force. Lucy had been asked to, quietly, investigate the thefts. A case of the fox guarding the henhouse. Lucy had hired Mr. Carter to take certain items from target houses. He was very specific and careful about what was to be taken, as he had pre-arranged their sale with an antique dealer in Walterboro. However, Mr. Carter decided to free-lance and began taking extra pieces on his own. It is most likely *The Tenant of Wildfell Hall* was something Mr. Carter decided to take for himself."

Ray gave a quick look at Sidney and said, "Wait a minute. Are you talking about Casey Yarborough? He's Lucy?"

"L. Casey Yarbrough. Yes. His actual full name is Lamar Unruh Casey Yarborough. Owner of the Morgan Real Estate Company. Southern names can be very misleading at times."

Ray could see the smile on Sam Cashman's face. "You knew about this?"

Sidney answered. "Sam and I spent some time together at the hospital during the storm. His wife Dede came to see Tillie and Sam and I put a number of things together. Being in school in Columbia, he had a broader overview of what was going on around Morgan and had a number of run-ins with Casey Yarborough over the years. After the storm, he did some checking on his own and came to visit me on Howard St. Mr. Yarborough, although with the auxiliary police, was known to be somewhat impulsive."

Ray interrupted, "He was a hothead, Sidney. We all knew it, but he liked to play cop and Chief Hornig could use him on simple stuff like traffic for a funeral or special events such as a concert in the park, that would free up his people to concentrate on real police matters. Hornig must have twenty people signed up for the auxiliary now. No politician wants to raise taxes, so the chief has to find some way to do his job. Anyway, I guess I was so focused on the Pirate Island land side of things, I just wasn't aware of what you were doing with the missing book. Which reminds me, where is it?"

Burke chimed in, "Yes, Sidney, did you ever find it?"

"On that score, I'm afraid there's good news and bad news. On the bad side, as a result of the storm, a large oak tree came down on Howard Springwood's home on Crow Island right over the library and broke all the windows. Rain and wind coming through both openings went on for almost twelve hours before someone reported it. There was extensive damage. Ms. Sullivan's FBI team went through everything after the storm and cataloged everything, which is how they found out about some of the other stolen rare books in Mr. Springwood's possession. They were in a separate locked area on an inner wall. Something Tillie identified the day of the storm. The good news is that none of the books in those cabinets were damaged. However, *The Tenant of Wildfell Hall* was not among them." Seeing Burke Mansfield's reaction, Sidney asked, "Burke, you have a comment?"

"Well, yes. I clearly remember the Larry Carter said, 'I put them back.' Was he lying?"

"I think the problem we have is we don't actually know what 'them' refers to. We're making the assumption that it refers to Anne Brontë's novel, when it could very well relate to other things that were stolen from some of the houses that were under Mr. Yarborough's care. Remember, Mr. Carter had a least a month or more from the time the books were on the *National Arts and Crafts Show* to sell them to someone. So, I think they're still out there. Let's just hope it's someone who truly realizes what they have.

"I think it's time for the FBI to handle it from here on. Once they found some other books in Springwood's damaged library I would imagine your..." he looked at Nora Sullivan, "friends in the art fraud area of the FBI would be very interested. I'm only sorry Burke here had to get mixed up in all of this. How are you doing?"

"Oh, quite well, I'm staying with my niece in Beaufort. She's a nurse at the hospital over there and insisted I stay with her. She drove me over. Hattie, here, has very kindly volunteered to drive me back later."

"I'm sorry you became the prime suspect for the FBI and the Sheriff for a while. Although I must admit you were also on my list as well—but not for long."

"Understandable," Burke said with a smile. "I was kind of uncooperative at first. Just trying to protect customer's privacy."

Ray said, "So where do we go from here?"

"Well, I know where I'm going," said Nora. "We never did catch up with that bodyguard of Rostov's, Lucien. He's a slippery one and very dangerous. I'm not sure how he got away. He was supposed to be on the boat with Rostov."

"He was by all accounts. Ray and I are sure we saw him at the Beaufort Airport when they transferred to the boat and the operator, Jackson, confirmed it." Sidney grabbed hold of his cane and used it to shift his position. He had something on his mind and said, "I wonder…"

Tillie, with eyebrows down and squinting, said, "Never you mind, Professor. You let the lady here," she pointed at Nora, "do the wonderin'. It's her job to do it. Time you got back to writin' books instead of chasin' em."

"Amen to that," Hattie said, "Amen to that."

END

About the Author

Tim Holland is the author of the Sidney Lake Lowcountry Mystery Series as well as the novel *What the Mirror Doesn't See*. He recently received a Keating award for his fiction.

Over the years, he has written for a wide variety of magazines and newspapers, on a contributing basis, and wrote book reviews and literary criticism for *Recorder Publishing* in New Jersey. He also wrote a monthly column for *The Beaufort Gazette,* Beaufort, SC when he served as Chairman of the Learning Exchange of the University of South Carolina Beaufort. During his time with a major financial institutional in New York, he specialized in global finance and product management and wrote numerous articles on international trade and product management for financial trade publications.

His writing career began while at St. Bonaventure University where he studied English Literature and was the editor of the literary magazine, *The Laurel*.

He is currently on the Board of Directors of the Williamsburg Book Festival, is a member of Mystery Writers of America, The Brontë Society of Haworth, Yorkshire, England, and is a frequent speaker at writing events both large and small.

CPSIA information can be obtained
at www.ICGtesting.com
Printed in the USA
JSHW062249070822
28923JS00001B/3

9 781953 434784